1 6 FEB 2011

KU-264-877

THE CRUELLEST MONTH

THE CRUELLEST MONTH

Janet Mary Tomson

20037356

MORAY COUNCIL
LIBRARIES &
INFORMATION SERVICES

CHIVERS

British Library Cataloguing in Publication Data available

This Large Print edition published by BBC Audiobooks Ltd, Bath, 2010.
Published by arrangement with Robert Hale Limited.

U.K. Hardcover ISBN 978 1 408 49259 8
U.K. Softcover ISBN 978 1 408 49260 4

Copyright © Janet Mary Tomson 2010

The right of Janet Mary Tomson to be identified as author of this work
has been asserted by her in accordance with the Copyright, Designs and
Patents Act 1988

All rights reserved.

20037386

MORAY COUNCIL
LIBRARIES &
INFORMATION SERVICES
F

Printed and bound in Great Britain by
CPI Antony Rowe, Chippenham and Eastbourne

For Suliman, Syreta and Ayeisha—my claims
to immortality.
With love.

CHAPTER ONE

'For as much as it hath pleased Almighty God to take unto himself our dear departed sister . . .'

A few people sat uncomfortably in the body of the church, like the last crumbs at the bottom of the biscuit barrel.

You took your time, thought Grace Harrison, addressing her silent accusation to the Lord, lurking somewhere among the heavenly beams of the parish church. She alone sat in the front pew, the sole official mourner of a mother who, in twenty-four months and nine days would have reached her century. You took your bloody time.

Her mother, Edna Harrison, had somehow taken root on life and with amazing tenacity refused to let go.

'Your mother is marvellous,' they said. 'So many problems but she keeps on fighting.'

Those unwelcome, shameful thoughts came back to her daughter: Give up, Mother, when will you give up? What had she been hanging on for anyway? What did she have to look forward to? What pleasure was there in a life that took forty minutes to dress, an eternity to chew on a mushy piece of bread, permanently smelly knickers and a hearing aid that screeched its signal to everyone except the

1

wearer?

Grace reached for the hymn book. She had chosen 'Morning is Broken'—if chose was the right word. The funeral was the last hypocrisy, and after that? She turned her thoughts back to the present. Let's get through this, somehow.

The vicar spoke of Edna's early life, how she was one of seven children, long since dead (unlike their sister they had paid attention to the rules about three score years and ten, not overstaying their welcome by a quarter of a century). He talked of her marriage to Gordon (who had smoked himself into an early grave) and of her devotion to her needlework that she had donated regularly to church sales until her sight became too poor to see the stitches. He acknowledged the value of knowing your community, of staying where you belonged, not being greedy for adventure but content with the small things of life.

Grace silently argued with the sentiments. At what cost to her had Edna clung so resolutely to her small life?

'We give thanks for the devotion of her daughter,' the minister announced and the hypocrisy crushed Grace. Tears gathered in the corners of her eyes but they were tears of rage, not bereavement. Above all, she hated herself for feeling as she did, this lack of generosity of spirit. When her own time came, would she give up easily, or was there

2

something she didn't yet know that made people fight against impossible odds just to remain in this unfathomable world? There was one thing, though, there would be no daughter to grudgingly fetch and carry for her until the end.

After the funeral the coffin was making another journey to the crematorium, piling on the agony. At Grace's insistence she alone would accompany it. The others who were present were invited to go ahead to the Star where a melee of sandwiches and pastries would be laid out. Tea and coffee was available for those who took exception to alcohol before midday. This solitary journey would give her the chance to steel herself for the social bit, the awkward, empty words, the universal pretence that Edna's passing was a reason for regret.

With a sigh they sang a last hymn, the good old 'Lord is my Shepherd'. How was that for originality? Grace made a mental note to get that exercise book and write down exactly what she wanted when her time came—no church, no platitudes, a rendering of Jimi Hendrix's 'Purple Haze' perhaps?

The vicar intoned a last prayer asking for God's comfort to those left behind? Fat chance. The only comfort was that it was time to go.

Alone in the black saloon car, Grace and the chauffeur followed Edna and the four pallbearers to the crematorium. The chauffeur had the decency not to speak to her. She gazed out of the window at life going on in the main street, a pushchair parked too near to the kerb as an impatient mother waited to cross, the random zig-zag of human passages along the narrow pavement. People glanced at the hearse and then away, not wishing to associate their thoughts with death.

A quarter of a mile further on and they were out in the country, narrow lanes, hedges heavy with white blossom. A curious cow raised her head from the serious business of grazing to watch their progress. Grace wondered how long before the poor animal began her own journey to the slaughterhouse but then she realized that she looked pregnant. She took comfort from the thought that sentence of death was postponed for the time being.

The prospect of the empty cottage began to impinge on her, the knowledge that she, the only daughter, was now the owner. Perhaps it was fortuitous that her role as carer should end just before her sixtieth birthday. At least she now had a pension to look forward to. Only yesterday she had received confirmation that her state pension would be paid directly into her bank account.

'You should collect it from the Post Office, help to keep it open'—this advice from Molly who lived three doors away along with her second husband, Reg.

Molly had agonized over the unfortunate circumstance that she and Reg were booked on a coach tour to Scotland and now Edna had died.

'If you want me to, I'll stay behind,' Molly offered.

'Of course you won't. You go and have a good time. There's nothing you can do.'

Edna had seen to it that her affairs were in order at least two decades earlier. The remaining formalities were minimal.

At the crematorium the coffin was carried inside and placed on a mechanical device surrounded by burgundy-coloured, plush curtains. A moment's silence then it was trundled away to the inferno below.

Grace felt paralyzed inside as if her thoughts could not be accessed. She wanted to say goodbye to her mother but there were no words, no way out of the empty cavern inside her head. Aware that the chauffeur was hovering at the back of the chapel, she walked out. He opened the door for her, a tall, willowy figure in black.

On the ride back she viewed the route from the other side of the road. She could not identify the cow that had watched her earlier progress. They were all black and white but they did not look alike. Only familiarity with them would make recognition possible. Good mothers were cows—that was their downfall.

Grace thought about how compassion was her favourite word. If ever anybody were to ask her, that was what she would say. It told of wisdom and tolerance, not taking things at face value, trying to understand. She had managed very little compassion for Edna though. Oh, she had gone through the motions—what would you like to eat, Mother? Can I get you anything? Are you ready for bed? But the other things, the affection and sharing, the common humanity had been missing. Where had it gone? It had been there once, when she was a little girl, mummy's girl. What had happened? She closed her mind to the pain of the past.

The private room in the pub seemed strange in daylight, a muted yellow intrusion from outside through the stained glass of the window. Was it stained or was that yellow a build-up of decades of nicotine? Whichever, it did not hide the faded, scuffed, beer-stained interior. As she stepped inside, the vicar was about to leave.

'So sorry to dash off. Another funeral, I'm afraid.'

Grace thought that he had been born to be a vicar. His smooth, pink cheeks were plump and comfortable. His body was soft and lacking muscle. Above all, nature had endowed him with a voice surely designed to fill every cranny in the lofty, emptiness of the church.

Grace shook his hand and thanked him for the sermon. She wondered if she should pay him but then the undertaker would have taken care of all that.

A waitress came over with a tray of wine and sherry. 'There's tea or coffee if you prefer it,' she offered. Grace grabbed a sherry, knocking it back with indecent haste. Steady on, don't end up saying something you'd regret.

Her cousin Joan waved at her across the room. They rarely met and the family resemblance startled her. For a shocking moment she thought that a younger version of Edna had found her way into the room. Beside Joan stood her only daughter Louisa. The last Grace had heard, Louisa was off to university to study history. She felt her own pang of regret at lost opportunities. Louisa did not favour her mother's side of the family. She must take after her long-forgotten father.

Neighbours and friends of her mother drifted over to pay their condolences. Grace played her part admirably, stoic regret, brave in the face of adversity. If Molly had been here she would have lightened the proceedings. She had a facility for finding the bizarre, the amusing in anything. Grace missed her.

'It will be strange for you after all this time.' She turned to find John Smedwick the chemist standing next to her. Over the years he had dispensed lorry loads of medication for Edna.

7

Single-handedly she had kept him in work. Grace nodded and smiled.

'What are you going to do?' he asked.

The question she dreaded. What was she going to do? She had now reached some Shangri La, some distant shore that had occupied her thoughts for an eternity and now that she was there, there was the terrifying possibility that none of her daydreams were accessible.

'I'm not sure yet.' She looked round, hoping that the drinks tray would be within reach.

'Take yourself away, indulge yourself.' John smiled paternally. 'You've had a long innings.'

A long innings, yes. She nodded, relieved that the Charltons from the bungalow opposite were waiting to say their piece. John obligingly faded into the background.

'What are your plans now?' Mrs Charlton asked after they had expressed the obligatory regret.

'I . . . I haven't quite decided.'

'It's a good job you didn't get another cat. That leaves you free now to do whatever you want.'

Perversely Grace wished that she had acquired a pet, something to anchor her, to fend off the necessity to do something.

'I might go away,' she offered.

Where? All those pipe dreams flickered past her—lounging in the Caribbean, trekking up Annapurna, trailing around the Uffizi, dancing on the deck of a liner. The list was endless, everything from whale watching to illicit sex at the Ritz.

With relief she realized that people were beginning to drift away. She longed to go home and soothe herself, be bathed in the calm silence of their empty house, and yet she felt uneasy, as if the accusing presence of Edna might be there, expressing her disappointment at having such an unfeeling daughter.

Joan and Louisa were the last to leave. 'We must keep in touch more,' said Joan knowing they wouldn't. 'I shall be lonely when Lou goes away.'

Louisa smiled at Grace. Such a pretty smile, lighting up a face whose owner was full of hope for the future.

'When do you go away?' she asked.

'Not until October. I'm going to find a summer job so that I can save up, then I'll be off.' She glanced apprehensively at Joan and Grace remembered that look, that feeling of trying to escape from a cloying mother.

'Well, just make sure that you do go, and have a great time.' She kissed the girl goodbye and awkwardly embraced her cousin. Such a pity that blood ties didn't make you soulmates.

On the way home she stopped twice, at the library and the off licence. A good book, more sherry, between them they should get her through the evening.

As she walked along the narrow lane behind

the church she felt the first spits of rain. Earlier it had been warm and sunny. Sheltered in the lea of the stone wall, tufts of grass formed a narrow verge strewn with cherry blossom, crushed and abandoned by yesterday's wind. April was a treacherous month. She regretted not having her coat. Perhaps she would light a fire, a focal point for warmth and comfort.

Two white envelopes were on the doormat, more sympathy cards. As she picked them up she imagined the writers struggling to find something appropriate to say. What would they think if she wrote what she really felt? Thanks for the condolences but I'm over the moon at being free at last. Was she though? Or was that old enemy, conscience, going to spoil her last, belated fling? Time would tell.

She opened the sherry and poured it into a wineglass. Steady on, girl, you know this stuff can be lethal. She took a large mouthful, savouring the taste, wondering if it was already being absorbed even before she swallowed. She opened the cards, one from a distant cousin up in Renfrew, the other from her mother's old friend Charlotte Everett. Charlotte sounded genuinely sad. It must be hard to see all your contemporaries slip away. Once you got into your eighties, or even worse, your nineties, it would be even more devastating for there would be nobody left to share your early memories. Resolutely she

10

pushed the incipient sadness away.

It was probably time to eat but she wasn't really hungry. There was a piece of cold flan in the fridge. She took it out, placed it on a baking tray and popped it into the oven on a low heat for about ten minutes. That would do There was a packet of shortbread too. In spite of all those self-promises to eat sensibly she knew that the shortbread would follow. Anyway, for a sixty-year-old she wasn't in bad shape. At least she hadn't been stretched in all directions by childbirth, had her belly distended so that it looked like crêpe paper, seen her boobs balloon until they sagged like deflated paper bags, or suffered the disfigurement of varicose veins from too much weight inflicted by a bouncing baby. Her hair was grey but it was a nice grey, thick and silver, surely soon to be that alpine white? She still had good legs, a waist, a face sufficiently full not to sag or wrinkle.

She lit the fire, ate the flan, sat for a while and read the first pages of the book but the sherry had blurred the edges of her concentration. Putting it aside she tried to think of the practical things that still needed to be done. Anything to put off the moment when she was face to face with herself and would have to make a decision.

There were still people she hadn't notified about her mother's death. She fetched address book from the desk. Mostly it only

11

came out in December ready for the dreary routine of sending Christmas cards. Starting with A, she flicked through the entries, thinking it better to write now rather than wait until the next flurry of Christmas cards arrived addressed to Edna. Picking up a biro she crossed out one or two names, knowing that, like her mother, they had died. Foolishly she imagined Edna meeting up with them for a chat. There were a few others she hadn't heard from for at least two winters. Perhaps they too had snuffed it but she'd wait and see what happened one more time—if she was still here at Christmas.

She stopped at the Ws, the third entry down. She studied the entry, the careful way she had written the address—Margaret and Joe Weston, Wollambula, Ararat, 3377, Victoria, Australia. She marvelled at how she had taken such care to write down his marital status, to put his wife first—Margaret Weston, a woman she had never met, a woman who had known Joe even longer than Grace had—and married him. Her heart notched up another beat per second. Perhaps she should write to him now? Re-phrase that—perhaps she should write to *them*. Her movements suddenly felt uncoordinated as she pulled open the desk drawer and extracted a packet of note cards with suitably sombre pictures on the front. Sitting down heavily she grabbed her pen and wrote:

Dear Margaret and Joe,
Just a line to tell you that mother passed away last week, April 7th. She had been ill for a long time. The house seems very empty without her. I don't quite know what I am going to do. Stay here probably, although I will no doubt take a holiday. Anyway, I thought that you would want to know. I hope that this finds you both well.
Best wishes as always,
Grace.

CHAPTER TWO

In spite of the sherry, Grace had trouble sleeping. As she was on the point of dropping off, some tormenting device in her brain popped into action and, just as she was gliding towards oblivion, applied the handbrake. Try as she might, she could not bypass the obstacle.

Difficulty in sleeping was not new and she had various strategies for dealing with it that usually involved making mental lists. One was of breeds of dogs beginning with each letter of the alphabet—Alsatian, Beagle, Cairn Terrier, Doberman. Some, of course, were impossible unless there was a South American hound with a name like Xavier. She also had a fight with

13

herself as to whether she could allow both Alsatian and German Shepherd, seeing that they were really the same thing.

Similar distractions followed, names of English towns, remembering every child who had been with her in the infants' class at school, visualizing the High Street as it had been when she was a child—Eastman's the butchers, Macfisheries, Doris Kingswell's wool shop, the Co-op, the Coffee Pot.

She had been to the Coffee Pot only once as a child and that was with Edna. There had been an uneasy feeling of straying into unfamiliar territory. Coffee at home was a pale, milky liquid made with a teaspoon of Camp Coffee from a bottle with a soldier on the label. She was used to the slightly sweet taste and a generous dollop of chicory. At the Coffee Pot they were presented with an alien drink, darker, aggressively biting, the whole served on a tray with a lacy cloth. The sugar came in cubes and had to be picked up with tongs. In retrospect, it was really such a small adventure but throughout her childhood there had been few enough.

As far as the stand of shops went, perhaps they had not all been there at the same time. Her youth seemed set in stone when nothing changed. Later on, the El Caballa coffee bar arrived, a very different place from the Coffee Pot. El Caballa had darkened windows and imitation palms where young people gathered to drink frothy coffee dispensed from a spitting, fizzing machine, and there was a real edge of danger to the place. She had gone there with Joe.

Savagely she tried to stamp on the memory. Now was not the time for masochistic reminiscences. Anyway, El Cabana had been replaced aeons ago by the gas showroom.

The muffled darkness closed her off from the present. She punched her pillow and turned over but try as she might, the memories had to be reborn. Like childbirth, it might be painful but they were coming nevertheless.

A Thursday morning, the school holidays, just before Easter.

'I want you to pop down to the corner shop and get some bread,' said Edna. At that time Edna was perfectly capable of going herself but she rarely strayed from home.

Grace probably grumbled, showed resentment at being forced away from her own daydreams, but she went anyway.

To get to the Co-op, you turned left at the front gate, followed the road to its end, left again, then first right. The Co-op was the third on the right-hand side. Exams were looming and as she walked she recited to herself the chronology of events during the French Revolution, Jacobins, sans-culottes, Robespierre, Danton, storming the Bastille, the new calendar. The details were long since forgotten but one of the months had something to do with lobsters—Thermidor, that was it.

'G'day. Can you tell me where's the post office?' Her revision was interrupted by a very unfamiliar voice. For a moment she was taken by the sound of it rather than the words and the speaker added, 'Y'know? Where I can buy some stamps?' He pronounced it as 'stemps'.

Grace looked at him. He was young, several inches taller than her with questioning blue eyes and short, blond hair. Of its own volition her face suffused humiliatingly with blood. Her answer, when it came, was inhibited by a sudden dryness in her mouth, a throat that felt strangely constricted.

'It's just up there.'

'Thenks.' That strange pronunciation again.

She wasn't sure whether to just walk away, but the young man said, 'D'you live near here?'

By way of answer she nodded, trying to think of something intelligent to say.

'It's a beaut place.'

'Do you live here?' she asked, knowing very well that he almost certainly didn't.

'No, I'm just visiting my grandparents.'

Everything he said seemed to be in the form of a question. He continued: 'They're Mr and Mrs Solomons at Peach Cottage. Do you know them?'

'In Church Lane?'

'Yes.'

'That's where I live.' The coincidence took

16

away her shyness.

'Small world,' he replied, then, 'What's your name?'

She told him.

'I'm Joe, Joe Weston.'

All the time they were walking and Grace slowed down opposite the post office.

'That's the post office over there.' She was aware of stating the obvious, as there was a large sign outside.

'Gee, thanks, Grace. I'll just get some stamps. Must write home to the old folks, y'know?'

She nodded, not knowing at all, uncertain as to whether she should just walk away. He resolved her difficulty by asking, 'Are you going home now?'

She nodded.

'Then shall we walk back together? Seeing that we're neighbours.' He grinned, showing very white, regular teeth. 'You'll wait for me?'

And so she did. On the way home Joe told her about his home in a little town called Ararat that was half way between Melbourne and Adelaide. She tried to visualize it but had no idea where to begin.

'Have you heard of the Barossa Valley?' he asked.

She shook her head.

'It's the wine-producing area. We run a winery. Have you ever had Australian wine?'

Again she shook her head. She had never

17

tasted wine from anywhere. It was as alien as frogs' legs and caviar.

To avoid the question, she asked: 'How long are you here for?' Then she could have kicked herself because it sounded forward, but he replied chattily enough.

'A couple of weeks, then I'm going home. I'll be back by October, though. I've got a place over here at uni, to study rural affairs, y'know?'

Rural affairs, it sounded exotic. Her knowledge of colleges was limited to subjects like Latin and history or teacher training and engineering. It was her own dream to go to university but she knew that it wasn't going to happen.

'What do you want to do that for?' Her Dad, puzzled, unused to such pretensions, couldn't begin to comprehend his daughter's new fangled ambitions. He and Edna had met when he was a gardener and she was in service at the Big House.

Grace longed to travel. She had been thrown a small lifeline by being entered for a Civil Service exam. That way she might get to London. She stopped the incipient panic at the thought of failure by asking Joe, 'Do you like it here?'

'Too right. There's not a lot to do in the evenings though. Do you ever go to the cinema? There's one in town, isn't there?'

Was he asking her out or was he simply

18

making conversation?

It was all going too fast and she had strayed way too far from the safety of the shallows, barely treading water.

'Sometimes,' she admitted.

'Do you know what's on at the moment?'

So he wasn't asking her to go with him, just enquiring about the film. Her breath escaped in what could have been a sigh of disappointment.

By now they had arrived outside the Solomons' gate and she slowed down.

'Well, I'd better be going.'

'Yes. Great to meet you, Grace. Perhaps we'll bump into each other?'

She nodded, feeling an opportunity slip through her fingers and yet having no idea what to do with it. She turned away and began to trudge up the road. Behind her, she heard the Solomons's gate open and then shut and the sound of Joe's footsteps as he reached their front door.

On auto pilot, she walked home, absorbed by the thought of him. Something profound had just happened. As she lifted the latch of the back door she knew that she had just discovered a new world.

'Where's the bread?' Edna's voice cut into her self-examination.

'I—' Again her face flooded, this time with guilty failure.

'Honestly, Grace, I don't know what's got

into you. You walk around in a dream these days. I'll be glad when those exams are over.'

'I'll go and get it now.'

'No you won't. I want to get some more wool. I'll go myself.'

So Edna went, leaving Grace alone with her staggering thoughts.

*　　　*　　　*

The morning after meeting Joe, Grace awoke and was immediately engulfed again by those strange feelings of discovery. The sun came through the skylight, preventing her from going back to sleep, so she lay on her back and gave her mind free rein. A year or two before, she had begun to ask herself: *Where do I come from and why am I here?* The answer must surely lie in that neglected book, the Bible, and before long she was Grace Harrison, believer, missionary and handmaiden to the lord. Her family had never been churchgoers, which seemed perverse seeing that their garden rubbed shoulders with the churchyard. She was aware of the Sunday comings and goings, the smart hats and crunching gravel, then the grim days of funerals, the happier celebration of weddings. Watching over the church wall, she studied the brides, frothy in white, envied or pitied them according to the appearance of the bridegroom. Mr and Mrs Solomons, *the* Mr and Mrs Solomons who lived at Peach Cottage, seemed to run everything to do with the church except for the sermons, when Mr Graham the vicar took over.

Since she had seen the light, Grace attended church services, prayer meetings, social gatherings, played games of Beetle and went on occasional outings. Her religious fervour left little time for anything else. Sometimes she worried because her parents were not churchgoers and there seemed little likelihood of them being saved. She had tried to talk to her mother about it but Edna just said, 'You don't need to go to church to be a Christian.' End of conversation.

With a sense that there were endless wonders she had never even thought about, Grace cast the memories aside and climbed out of bed. As the morning progressed she thought of dozens of reasons to go out.

'Where are you off to now?' asked Edna, irritated by her restless daughter.

'Just to the library.'

'But you went yesterday.'

'There's a book I need. For my homework.'

Edna sighed and shook her head, grasping the teapot with unusual vigour.

Grace bowed silently out of the kitchen and hurried up the path, a greyhound released from the traps. Instead of turning right towards the library she turned left, making a detour past the Solomons' house. Her

21

breathing began to come unusually fast, distorting her hearing with its unnatural thumping. She needed all her wits about her but although she strained to pick up the slightest suggestion that there was anyone about, the house seemed to be empty. An already familiar disappointment claimed her. Perhaps they had all gone out for the day. As she dragged herself reluctantly on around the detour to the library, she wondered what she would have done if Joe had been in the garden or about to come out of the gate. The very possibility sent her senses haywire.

For the rest of that day she paced restlessly around the house until Edna said, 'For goodness sake, go and do something. Why don't you go and see your Auntie Rose? You haven't seen her for weeks and if you don't go soon, something will be said about it.'

Edna gave her familiar disapproving sniff. Rose was her sister-in-law and they didn't get on. Dad was fond of his sister, a widow, victim of the slaughter of the First World War. She had no children and liked to spend time with Grace, her only niece. Sometimes she gave her money, took her shopping, much to Edna's chagrin.

Grace seized the opportunity to escape and followed the familiar trail past the Solomons' front door but there was still no sign of anyone. When she got to Auntie Rose's, she was out. A whole day had been wasted.

On Sunday morning she got ready for church and, for the first time, what to wear took on monumental proportions. Her usual frock and spring coat suddenly seemed childish. What could she get away with that wouldn't cause her beady-eyed mother to question her motives? With a valiant attempt to look fashionable she put on her pencil skirt and a frilly blouse that Aunt Rose had given her for her birthday, *'When an earth are you likely to wear that?'* She remembered Edna's acid comment.

It was a short walk across the graveyard to the church, short enough to wear her new stiletto-heeled shoes, although she stumbled once or twice on the gravel. Others were arriving and she looked round hopefully for a glimpse of Mr or Mrs Solomons, and in particular their new and exotic grandson, but she was disappointed. As she went inside and made her way down the aisle, her heels produced an accusing clatter.

She slipped into a pew quite near the front, for congregations were never large and tended to 'congregate' together. As she sat down and assumed an attitude of prayer, the sun lanced through the stained glass of the window, creating kaleidoscopic patterns on her hands. She studied them, wondering about the science that produced such images, then she tried to clear her mind of any impure thoughts. Concentrate on the Lord now, that's all that matters.

As she opened her eyes she saw Mr Solomons come in on his own. Clearly the Lord wasn't listening as her first prayer had specifically asked for Joe to be there.

The organ stopped playing. Mr Graham, the vicar, made his way to the pulpit and after the first prayer and a hymn he called upon Mr Solomons to make the announcements.

'Next Sunday will be a special service to celebrate the raising of Jesus from the cross,' he boomed.

'On Thursday evening there will be a special meeting here for prayer and worship.'

'Miss Henderson's coffee morning for the missionary fund raised three pounds eleven and sixpence.'

Miss Henderson played the organ, a grey, sweet faced but glaringly plain spinster whom Grace guiltily despised.

'This morning we welcome a special guest from the other side of the world to our service.'

Mr Solomons's words took a moment to penetrate and with a jolt Grace twisted her neck to see. Sitting across the aisle and back a few rows next to Mrs Solomon, his hair a glow of reflected blond light, his cheeks hot with discomfort at the unwelcome attention, was Joe! When he glanced up, she caught again the brilliant blue of his eyes, his fleeting, embarrassed smile. She looked away as if she

24

had been blinded by sunlight. Thank you, God, thank you!

'Let us all say a word of welcome to Joseph,' said Mr Solomons. 'Joseph will be staying with us for a few weeks, so let's make his stay a happy one.'

The rest of the service passed in a blur and finally everyone was standing up and heading for the door. She remained in the pew, unable to decide what to do. Without looking up, her antenna registered that Joseph Weston was coming towards her.

'I said we'd bump into each other,' he started, 'but I didn't expect it to be here.'

She nodded, afraid to look at him because then he would read her foolish thoughts.

'Coming outside?' He stood back and she had no choice but to follow him. They stood in the sunshine, other members of the congregation chatting, making their farewells.

'You at college?' Joe was seemingly unphased by her catatonic state.

She shook her head and managed to say, 'I'm taking my A levels this summer.'

'What are you taking?'

She listed them and he grinned. 'Clever girl!'

His praise was like cream spooned over sponge pudding.

Now she found her tongue. 'You said you grow wine?'

'We grow grapes and make wine,' he

corrected, his grin showing a healthy pink mouth and those devastatingly regular teeth.

Grace blushed. Never before had she felt so inadequate. From somewhere, the Holman Hunt portrait of Christ as the Light of the World and the vision of Joseph Weston standing with sunlight lancing through the chapel window merged into one.

'Are you religious, then?' Joe asked.

She shrugged, not sure how to reply. Any stock answer about being saved seemed inappropriate.

'I'm not. To be honest, I think it's all hokum, but it only seemed polite to come this morning.'

Grace felt a momentary stab of unease then in a flash, Jesus the Light of the World took second place to Joseph, the epitome of flesh made human.

When the Solomons came out, as she had hoped they would, they offered her a lift. By taking the shortcut across the churchyard she could have been home in seconds, but Mrs Solomons had bad feet and was always driven everywhere she went. Soon Grace found herself sitting beside Joe in the back of their Ford Popular. The car suddenly seemed very small and Joe's presence exerted an invisible pull. She was afraid that their arms might accidentally touch, for if they did, she might spontaneously combust.

In the front passenger seat, Mrs Solomons

chatted so that there was no need to make conversation. Grace tried to soak up every second of the journey so that it could be analyzed over and over again. Too soon they pulled up outside their gate at the bottom of the lane.

'Are you all right to walk up the road?' Mr Solomons asked.

It seemed a silly question, as she made the same journey several times in any day, but she said, 'Yes thank you and thank you for the ride.'

As Joe emerged lithely from the car she sent up a silent prayer that he might offer to escort her but it went unanswered. Perhaps Jesus was sulking at having his nose put out of joint. Perhaps he took exception to being relegated to second place. With something approaching panic she wondered whether the Lord, a jealous god, might not punish her for her infidelity.

Joe raised a hand in farewell and said, 'See you around?'

Leadenly she turned away. Something very disturbing was happening to her. Now that she knew of the existence of Joe Weston, a new sense of urgency and longing seemed to engulf her at every turn. She was horribly aware for the first time in her life that everything, but everything, was outside her control.

Cautiously she turned to look back down the road and it was to see Joe watching her.

He waved his hand and, although it was too far away to be sure, she thought that she saw him wink. In this small gesture, remained hope.

*   *   *

The morning after Edna's funeral Grace came to slowly, her mind wading through a pea-souper that was reluctant to clear. For several minutes she lay still, trying to assemble her thoughts. She couldn't remember actually coming to bed. Outside, the light was bright enough to tell her that it was late. Sparrows squabbled in the birch tree outside her window.

With an intake of breath she cursed herself for last night's sherry and reluctantly stumbled from bed in urgent need of rehydration. As she imbibed rhythmic gulps of water she was dimly aware of wisps of a dream that was already past recapturing, but it left her with a hint of the sensual, a heaviness inside that told of unfulfilled desire. It was rare these days, that feeling of lust and sexual drive. It was hardly surprising. Nature had intended it for the procreation of the species. That was by now something far in the past, so it had nearly petered out. Nearly. She knew what had revived it.

As she gulped down a second glass of water she thought that desire didn't necessarily relate to anyone in particular, it was just there,

28

as indiscriminate as drawing breath or the beating of her heart. That other thing, love, was something else entirely.

She felt brittle, burdened by a remembered sense of anguish, faced with what might have been and now wasn't. This wouldn't do. It would be easy to sink into a cycle of alcohol and regret. She filled the glass from the tap for a third time, drained the contents then returned for her dressing gown and went downstairs.

Passing her mother's room, she was aware of a contradictory sense of Edna's absence yet presence, silent, accusing, waiting to be lifted on to the commode, to be patiently fed with sips of tea. Grace shuddered.

The day spread ahead vast as the Sahara. What should she do? Be practical, empty the cupboards, pack up Edna's clothes to go to the charity shop? Perhaps if she worked hard enough she could load them into the car and drive into town before lunch, take herself out, have a meal, look around the shops? Above all, she must keep busy.

Her mother's *People's Friend* was on the doormat. Another job, remember to cancel it at the newsagents. She took it to the breakfast table and thumbed through it while she ate her toast. Perversely, its positive style depressed her. Why could she not be like the women who formed its readership? She was a misfit. She didn't belong here in the village where the WI

29

and the church reined supreme. Perhaps she should sell up and go somewhere—but where? First things first. Sort out the clothing.

Later that morning she loaded three cardboard boxes and five carrier bags into the back of the car. There would be more but for the present this felt like progress. She drove into town, parked precariously outside the Oxfam shop and stumbled in with her contribution. The ladies behind the counter reminded her of her mother, local, well meaning. There was a notice pinned on the counter asking for volunteers. For a microsecond she considered it but even as the thought came to her she knew that this wasn't her role. Accepting their thanks, she hurried back out to the car just as a traffic warden stopped to inspect it.

'I've been unloading things for Oxfam,' she started.

'You still shouldn't park here. It's dangerous. I could give you a ticket.'

She bit back all the retorts, saying 'I'm going now.'

He did not comment and she drove away to the car park. She was half tempted to go straight home but to do so would be return to the empty, haunting presence of the house. Instead, she walked back to the High Street and wandered aimlessly along its length.

She spent twenty minutes in the bookshop, eyed the rails in Marks and Spencer, lunched in the Black Cat—chosen because it didn't serve alcohol and she wouldn't be tempted to have wine with her meal. Afterwards, she browsed the shelves of the travel agent, selecting several brochures she knew she would never follow up. It was as she passed the post office that she remembered Joe's letter and purchased the necessary stamps. Australia. Was it coincidence that one of the brochures now in her bag was for trips to the Southern Hemisphere?

*   *   *

For the next few days Grace managed to keep busy. In her dream time she planned holidays. While something organized would be easier, she balked at the thought of being a lone spinster, pitied by the other travellers. The alternative was to do something independent but she was aware of her own limitations. She knew that there were singles holidays and those eighteen-to-thirties where everyone shagged each other senseless. A fleeting vision of herself surrounded by copulating humanity made her shake her head to dislodge the image. Perhaps she should settle for a few days in London. The thought of the galleries and theatres lifted her spirits but in parallel was the knowledge that there would be no one to enjoy it with. Part of the pleasure was in sharing the experience, or at least recounting the adventures afterwards. In spite of the aridity of their relationship, she realized that over the years she had used Edna as a sort of listening device. Edna might have been deaf and out of touch but that hadn't stopped Grace relating the trivia of a morning's shopping in town or passing on the local gossip. Now there was no one.

She took comfort from knowing that Molly would be back in a couple of days. At least she would have someone to talk to. She dutifully put a jacket potato in the oven—*you must eat properly*.

So where had her life gone? All that promise—or had it all been an illusion? Had she always been destined to stay at home, a village girl, a peasant, clever enough, but lacking that inbred confidence and culture or whatever it was to launch her into the wider world?

Grace stopped the memories, returning instead to the prospect of Molly's arrival. At least she and Molly would have a laugh together, but already she knew that this would not be enough. She wanted more than the commonplace. Something must be made to happen in her life, the last, dying flame before the embers cooled forever. Anyway, Molly wasn't a free agent. She was married to Reg who was elderly, beginning to fail and demanding. Grace made a mental note: don't get tangled up with an older man, not that she intended to enmesh herself in any relationship. Too late for that now, definitely too late.

CHAPTER THREE

The clocks had gone forward and, as if taking its cue from the amended time, the weather began to make huge leaps ahead. Sun now stretched right into the evening, birds had got the message and were rehearsing their love songs. In the garden, things had popped up where a few weeks ago there had been only bare soil. Grace began to work hard, digging in the compost, wondering whether to risk planting the new potatoes, eyeing the broad beans for signs of life. She loved their long, eager leaves that sprouted so trustingly, oblivious to early frosts. There must be a name for that particular green, pale and creamy, highlighting the darker growths around it.

Growing vegetables was a duty she had inherited from her father, something ageless that had been passed on from parent to child since men had stopped being hunter-gatherers. These days, everything was available at any time of the year in the local Co-op but Edna had enjoyed the advent of the seasons and so, in her turn, Grace had grown to appreciate it. The flavours, the freshness of home-grown fare was so much better. Anything surplus to requirements she would either give to Molly or leave by her gate for people to help themselves.

As dusk began to set in, she came into the kitchen and washed her hands under the cold tap. She was healthily tired. Perhaps tonight she would sleep easily. She began to make plans for the next day, go to the garden centre, mow the grass for the first time this year. At that moment the telephone jarred her back.

As she went to answer it she glanced at the clock. Ten to eight. It was probably Molly, due back from her holiday that afternoon. It would be good to catch up.

'Hello?'

'Grace?'

She felt for the edge of table, lowered herself into the chair.

'Hello?'

'It's me, Joe. We just got your card this morning. I'm just ringing to say how sorry I am.'

'What time is it?' The question rescued her, gave her a chance to swallow down the shock and emotion.

'Nearly nine—in the morning. How are you?'

'It . . . it feels a bit strange. I haven't quite got used to it yet.' She scrabbled round for what she should say, searching for anything she wanted to ask. She wasn't prepared. At any moment he would ring off and she would be left with emptiness. Nothing came. She tried to imagine what he must look like but couldn't. She hadn't seen him for thirty-nine years.

'What are you planning to do?' That question she dreaded from everyone, but most of all from him.

'How's Margaret?' she asked, cutting across him.

'Not bad. Well, not too good really.'

'I'm sorry.'

He did not enlighten her.

Aloud, she asked, 'How's the winery?'

'Frenetic.'

It was that time of the year again, spring in Europe, autumn out there.

He said, 'That's partly what I'm ringing about. We're rushed off our feet because Alex is away. He's over in Europe.'

Alex, their son. Please don't suggest I come out, she thought. I'm not ready for that. She waited.

'The fact is, he and his wife have split. He's taken it badly. Meg and I thought it best to pack him off for a while, so he's visiting some of the French vineyards.'

Meg. That was what he called her. Margaret Abbot, alias Margaret Weston, aka Meg Weston. Grace was aware that she made her sound like a criminal but that was what she was, stealing him, tricking him. That was how Alex Weston had come into being, through a stupid, conniving girl getting herself pregnant.

35

'Are you there?'

She cleared her throat. 'Yes.'

'Well, please say no if you'd rather not, but I wondered if you might like to meet him? He'll be in England next week. He hasn't really got any plans and I've told him about where you live. If you could manage it, he could pop over, just for the day, just to say hello.'

'I . . .'

She couldn't think fast enough. What the hell was she supposed to do with some heartbroken stranger?

'Sorry, it's a crap idea.'

'No. No, really. Of course I would like to see him. I've got plenty of room, he could come and stay.'

'I wouldn't want to impose him on you.'

'You wouldn't be.'

'Well, if you're sure . . . ' She sensed that he was worried about the boy, or perhaps it was his mother who was worried.

'Give him my number,' she said. 'I'd be pleased to see him.'

'Goodonya,' She saw his face, probably fuller now, or perhaps craggy. Would she even recognize him if she saw him in a crowd?

'How are you?' she asked to break the tension.

'Good. I'm good.' His voice was not entirely convincing but she did not pursue it. 'Well, I'll be in touch then.'

'Fine.'

'Sorry again to hear about your mum.'
'Don't be. She was nearly a hundred.'
'Right. New pastures and all that.'

New pastures. As she allowed the call to end she wondered where on earth it was going to take her.

* * *

Of course sleep wouldn't come. His voice had been within touching distance and yet in every way he was beyond reach. She got up again, angry with herself because for years she had managed without him, without anybody, and now she was adrift and in danger of doing something crazy.

Her anger notched up several points. What had possessed her to say that his son could come and stay? How could he be so insensitive as to suggest it? Didn't he realize that seeing his son, his reincarnation, would be rubbing salt into a very deep wound?

She poured herself a glass of milk and found a digestive biscuit, comforting food for the middle of the night.

Sitting at the kitchen table she tried to work out how old he was, this Alex. With shock she realized that he must be heading on for forty. That was what it was hardest to get used to, the passage of time. As far as she knew, Alex didn't have any children. So Joe wasn't a grandfather—Joe, her Joe with his lean, boyish face and agile body.

She wondered why the marriage had foundered. If Alex was that upset, it sounded as if his wife had left him. What was she called—Sally was it? Grace, of course, had never met her. Oh God, what was she going to do with him mooning around the place? What would he be interested in? Could she take him to the local heritage sites or would he be bored silly? The local beach hardly compared with Bondi. She couldn't think of anyone who might take him off to a football match either or to some other sporting activity. The cricket season was about to begin. Aussies liked cricket but she didn't know anyone who played.

The practicalities of entertaining him actually calmed her and, going to bed, she dug out her book. As her eyes grew heavy she closed it again and tried to think of a flower beginning with every letter of the alphabet just to keep her mind occupied. She stumbled when she got to the letter 'E' but the effort of thinking was enough to send her into a dreamless sleep.

The next morning she had an alarming sense that the whole business of Alex Weston and a visit was just a dream. For a moment she wondered how to find out if it was true, and then she saw her empty glass on the table and knew that it was going to happen.

She showered, dressed, made toast and

coffee, put out the litter for the dustman, washed up. It dawned on her that if she was out when he rang, he might change his mind. She even considered turning off the answer phone, just in case. The trouble was, this train of possibilities now had her in its grip. If he didn't contact her, didn't turn up, she would be forever wondering what he was like. Another thought occurred to her. If he was that depressed, supposing he rang and she wasn't there and he did something crazy like jump off a high building or under a train? When they discovered at the inquest that she hadn't even bothered to take him in, his father would never forgive her. She shrugged away the foolish thought. Hopefully, Joe wouldn't say anything about her inviting him to stay. Perhaps the boy would just come over for a few hours or the day. The boy—she laughed at her description. She could cope with a few hours—just.

*   *   *

Although Grace had diverted all her journeys so that she passed the Solomons' house, there was neither sight nor sound of Joe. Then, just when everything seemed lost, her new, extraordinary life was turned upside down. She was upstairs making her bed when she heard a knock at the front door. This was a rare occasion, as everyone they knew always came to the back. Stopping to listen, she heard Edna open it and a low murmur of voices. Seconds later her mother called up the stairs 'Grace? There's some boy to see you.'

Mystified, hardly daring to hope, Grace stumbled down the stairs and into the hall. There, a vision in shorts and shirt, stood Joe.

'G'day, I . . . I was wondering if you'd like to come to the cinema tonight?' He glanced uneasily towards Edna who was hovering like a bat in the shadow by the kitchen door. She sniffed audibly and returned to her work, pointedly leaving the door open.

Grace was too overwhelmed to think straight. Her mother's presence was like some shackle, holding her back. Joe was part of her private world not to be exposed to her other life at home. For the first time, the modesty of their cottage impinged upon her. In the intervening days she had conjured up an idea of his home, something approaching a wild-west ranch. What must he think of this tiny cottage, her mum in her apron?

'They're showing something called *The Defiant Ones*.'

He was waiting for an answer and, being cornered, Grace said 'All right.'

'Tonight?'

'All right.' From the corner of her eye she saw Edna retreat now that she had heard the conversation.

'I'll call for you at 6.30?'

'All right.' Grace thought that the needle had stuck but couldn't find anything else to say.

With a bow of his head Joe stepped back and set off up the path. Grace took a deep breath before closing the door and facing the inevitable inquisition.

Edna was putting on a show of polishing her brass. 'Who was that?'

'He's staying with Mr and Mrs Solomons. He's their grandson.'

'What's he want with you then?'

'He . . . I don't think he knows anyone else around here.'

'Foreign, isn't he?'

'He's from Australia.'

That familiar sniff. 'I suppose he's Edie's son.'

'Edie?' Grace was surprised by her mother's words.

'Edie Solomons. She ran off with some foreigner, went to the other side of the world, broke her mother's heart.'

Grace had no idea that Edna might know about him. So Joe's mother had eloped with a stranger! She realized that here was a whole history about which she knew nothing. She wanted to ask Edna about Joe's mum, what she knew about it, but decided that it was safer to say nothing.

'Have you got any money then?' Edna cut into her thoughts.

41

'Money?'

'To go to the pictures with.'

'I've got my pocket money.'

Sniff. In the silence Grace guessed that Edna was trying to think of a reason to ban the outing but clearly nothing occurred to her. There were now seven hours and twenty-one minutes to endure before the magical time arrived.

The Regal was a cinema of some status, situated in the High Street, slightly elevated from the road and reached by wide steps. Austere geometrical designs decorated the façade and the outer doors while photographs of the film currently showing were posted up outside behind glass. Once Grace had seen a film with Dirk Bogarde and fallen in love for the first time. His photograph gazed out from the frame and Grace had agonized about whether she could ask for the picture once the film moved on. She must only have been about eight, and needless to say she hadn't done so.

Pretending that she had some revision to do, she retired to her bedroom and set to wondering what on earth to wear. Her wardrobe was hardly bulging with dresses. She did, however, have a green skirt with a wide hem and a fairly new sweater that pulled pleasingly across her bust. Bust was the word you used to refer to your chest. The idea of uttering breasts aloud was unthinkable.

The day inched forward. Dad came home

from work and went through his routine of washing off the day's dirt. Grace liked the way the pink soap left a lather on the black hairs of his arm, the way the hair waved and shone as the water coursed over it, swilling the day's grime away. Mum boiled the kettle for tea while Grace went to lay the table. Everything was unbelievably normal except that in one hour and forty-seven minutes a new life was to begin.

Joe was exactly on time and to avoid any discussion Grace hovered by the front door, ready to slip out as soon as she heard the gate click.

'Good evening, Grace, you ready?'

She nodded, that old enemy shyness capturing her tongue.

As they walked along, Joe told her how he had taken the bus into Newport and bought two records. 'You like Bill Halley?' He asked. Again she nodded. It was the sort of music that Mr and Mrs Solomons would certainly not approve of, smacking of sin. Apart from their religious beliefs, they were both old, although she had to concede that they were sprightly for their age. Thinking of the records, she wondered if he had played them yet.

'What was the other one?'

'Fats Domino. "Blueberry Hill". You know it?'

Once again she nodded. If you keep nodding like that your head will fall off, she

43

imagined Edna's warning.

He asked: 'Have you got a record player?'

Already Grace was leaping ahead, wondering however she could invite him home to play records. It was so out of character it would be as unthinkable as—well, something she couldn't even begin to imagine. Knowing it wouldn't play the new records she said, 'We've only got an old gramophone.'

'Well, perhaps you can come down to my place and we'll play them.'

His place. She wondered if the Solomons ever went out and if she would dare to trespass in their absence. A hazy, romantic scene captured her thoughts and she fell into silence.

At the box office she insisted on buying her own ticket although Joe offered to do so. Stepping into the familiar gloom she followed him down the gently sloping aisle. He stopped quite near the back.

'Here OK for you?'

She nodded behind his back but he seemed to know her answer because he stepped back for her to take one of the red plush seats. Someone just in front of them had already lit up a cigarette and a wisp of smoke curled its way towards the ceiling.

The lights dimmed and the film started. Grace had never been to the cinema with a boy before but she knew that it was here that some of the girls in her class came to kiss and cuddle. At the prospect her insides began to

44

sink away. Would Joe kiss her? Would she know what to do?

However, he sat back to watch the film and made no attempt to take her hand. After a moment's disappointment—or was it relief—she quickly found herself absorbed by the story. Two convicts escaped from a prison van, one black and one white. They were chained together. They hated each other but had no choice but to cooperate if they were not to be caught. The situation enthralled her, the unfairness of the treatment of the black man, the fact that he was very handsome.

There was an intermission and Grace found herself flung back into the present with Joe at her side.

'Enjoying it?'

'I think it's sad. I'm glad we don't put people in chains over here.' As she spoke she remembered history lessons about transporting convicts to Australia. Surely, Joe's people hadn't been convicts? To deflect that line of thought, she asked, 'What about the black people where you live?'

'There aren't any.'

'Yes there are, the Aborigines.'

'I mean there aren't any where we are.'

'Where are they then?'

He shrugged. 'Various places.'

'Have you ever met one?'

'There's a guy works with my uncle on their sheep station. I went up there to work last summer.'

At that moment the lights dimmed again and they were both drawn back into the film.

When it finally ended they beat a hasty retreat, by mutual unspoken agreement not staying for the National Anthem. Grace was still absorbed in the story and the feel-good factor it ultimately produced.

They walked up the street in silence. When they reached the junction that led to Church Lane, Joe said, 'Do you have to go straight home?'

She should do. Mum would be keeping an eye on the clock, but the thought of parting from Joe a moment sooner than she needed to stirred up her rebellion.

'Not really.'

'Let's go for a walk then.'

They continued on up the street and down towards the main village, quaint and thatched and not quite real. Near the top of the slope was a road leading off to a small, leafy public garden. Grace was surprised that Joe seemed to know where he was going. 'I walked up here the other day,' he said by way of explanation. A stab of alarm as she wondered who with.

He took her hand and she absorbed the feel of his skin, dry and warm against hers. In silence they wandered along the shadowy paths.

For something to say she informed him 'There used to be a house here once. I remember it. It was fenced off and was going to fall into the chine.' The gardens were on the southern edge of a natural fissure, green and chaotic, the local beauty spot.

'What happened to it?'

'They pulled it down.' She glanced in the direction in which it had once stood in case it had magically reappeared. In the increasing gloom the shrubs darkened and seemed to lurk along the winding paths. There was a faint, musty smell of rhododendrons.

The gardens were provided with benches and, on reaching one, Joe sat down, taking Grace with him. This is it, she thought. He's going to kiss me. A maid taking her first communion could not have felt more overawed. Her mind, however, had other ideas.

'I think it's wrong, the way they treat the Aborigines,' she announced to her own surprise.

Joe did not answer immediately and she wondered if he was going to disagree with her, to reveal himself as a racist. At last he said, 'The trouble with the Abos is that they see the world differently. I'm not saying they're wrong and we're right but the way they see things has made life doubly difficult for them.'

'How?'

'Well, for starters they have never believed that they owned the land. Rather the reverse, in fact, they were part of the land. Their gods

47

and spirits lived in things like rocks and trees so when they were moved away they had to leave all their beliefs behind. Sad, really.'

As she absorbed this he continued. 'If they had thought the land was theirs then it would have been harder to take it from them, if you see what I mean?'

She thought that she did. 'Where are they now?' she asked.

'Well, there are areas where they mostly live. Some are in the towns but they don't work, not like we do. Their idea of work is hunting and travelling and well, being in tune with where they live. The idea of factories and offices and suchlike they just don't buy.'

'What can anyone do about it?'

Joe shrugged. 'Sometimes it's too late to make a bad job good. The kiddies go to school. Perhaps they'll adapt better than their parents.'

For a second Grace had a vision of herself going to teach them about Western ways and about God until she remembered that Joe had said it was hokum. While she was pondering this future he turned towards her.

'Anyway, that's enough of that. How about you?'

'What about me?'

'What are you going to do, once you've taken your exams?'

'I don't know. I'd like to go to university.' Why did she mention it when she knew that it wasn't going to happen?

'Then why don't you?'

She didn't know how to explain to him that people of her sort just didn't do that. The girls at the school who had university careers carved out for them were the daughters of doctors and teachers and bank managers. Her parents were not only from lowly stock, they were also of a much earlier generation where education meant leaving school at fourteen.

Edna and Gordon had married late, when Edna was thirty-eight and Gordon forty-one. They had not expected to have children. Once Grace had passed puberty and knew the facts of life, Edna often said to her, 'When my monthlies stopped I thought it was the change but I didn't feel too good so I went to the doctor. He told me I was expecting.'

These thoughts were interrupted by the feel of Joe's fingers smoothing back a strand of hair that had strayed from her ponytail.

'Penny for them?'

She must have looked startled, for he added, 'Your thoughts.'

She shook her head, afraid to look at him.

'Hey, don't look so worried.'

The cool breeze fanned her burning cheeks and she kept her eyes averted. Then, the miracle of miracles happened. His face came close to hers. 'I think you're a really nice girl, Grace.' As she continued to look at the ground he tilted his head and his lips rested lightly

49

against her mouth.

She closed her eyes and knew that this was it. Her fate was sealed. Her future belonged to him. No matter what happened next, she was the luckiest girl in the world.

For quite how long they remained on the bench she had no idea but suddenly she realized that it was dark. No one had walked by to disturb them, so it must be very late Pulling back she said, 'I must go home.'

To her relief he didn't argue. 'OK, let's go.' He pulled her up and put his arm around her shoulders. The magnet of his body drew her closer and closer to him.

Once out of the gardens and back in the street they separated, but even as they walked she felt herself edging towards him. The next day was Saturday and she wondered how she could find some way of spending the day with him.

As if tuning into her thoughts, he said, 'Gerry Hawkins—you know him? He's taking me to Portsmouth tomorrow to see a football match.' She cursed Gerry Hawkins for his interference. He was a solid, squat sort of boy who lived next door but one to the Solomons. Trust him to poke his nose in when there was something so much more important to do.

Sensing her disappointment, Joe said, 'If I'm back in time we could go for a walk?' She nodded, her mind already trying to plan out a reason for going out.

'I could call up when I get back?'

'No. I . . . I'll meet you somewhere.' She scrabbled around for a suitable place to suggest, settling on a path that ran next to the brook, fronting what was once the village forge. 'I . . . I'll probably go and see my friend Mavis then I can look out for you on the way back.'

'Shall we say eight o'clock then? I should be back by then. If I'm not though, don't hang about for me.'

She shook her head. By now they had reached Church Lane and as they approached her gate they slowed down. He turned towards her.

'Well, thanks for coming to the pictures, Grace. Glad you enjoyed it.' Slowly, magically he leaned towards her and kissed her again. She wanted to put her arms around him and capture him forever, but all the time she was aware that a few yards away her mother would be watching out, wondering where she was. Reluctantly pulling away, she said, 'I'll see you tomorrow then.'

'Right. Tomorrow.' He raised a hand in farewell and began to walk on down the road, hands in pockets, hips gyrating with a gentle swing, hair touched by moonlight.

In a dream she floated down the path, opened the door and stepped into the kitchen. Her parents were in the living-room, Dad dozing and Mum furiously knitting.

51

'What time do you call this?'

She glanced guiltily at the clock. It was just before eleven.

'I . . . we met some of the girls from school. We went to have a coffee.'

'And where was there anywhere open at this time of night?'

'The El Caballa,' she offered, not sure what time it closed.

'Well, next time you go to the pictures, you just come straight home.'

Next time!

Dad jerked awake and the newspaper on his knee tumbled to the ground.

He blinked and looked around. 'Had a nice time?' he asked.

'Yes thanks, Dad.'

A nice time—this was the understatement of Grace's life.

CHAPTER FOUR

'How did the funeral go?'

Molly, back from her trip, had called round to deliver a box of fudge.

'Sorry? What did you say?'

Grace wasn't listening. She had hardly slept.

'The funeral.' Molly frowned. 'Are you all right?'

'Yes, really. The funeral was fine. How was

your holiday?'

'It was OK.' Molly's mouth pursed with discontent. 'Reg gets tired very easily.' She sighed and Grace detected a younger woman, trapped, trying to get out.

'Did you manage to do much sightseeing?' she asked.

'We did a couple of coach trips.'

They both fell silent until Molly said, 'When I met Reg I thought he was the strong, silent type. He seemed so self-contained. Now I realize he was always the weak silent type. He leaves everything up to me. I used to think it was because he was easy going and wanted to please me but now I think it's just that he doesn't have any confidence in himself.' She shrugged. 'I have to do everything.'

Like having an aged parent then, Grace thought. Aloud, she said, 'Well, he is a lot older than you.'

Molly nodded. 'I guess I should have known.' She drained her cup and sat back. 'And what about you, then? You're fancy free now. What are you going to do?'

Grace shook her head. 'I haven't got any plans.'

'Then you should make some. You're still young. You should get out there and find a new life for yourself, have a bit of an adventure.'

Grace laughed. 'Find a toy boy, you mean?'

'Time you got that Aussie out of your

53

system.'

Was it so obvious, the direction in which Grace's thoughts lay? Joe's name had come up in the past, in those rare occasions where Grace had needed to let off steam or, in unguarded moments, when she and Molly had shared the odd bottle and drifted into reminiscence mode.

Molly, biased, thought he couldn't have been up to much, not if he had let Grace go. Grace didn't know how to explain. He had been just a boy. Circumstances had overtaken him as much as they had her. She looked at Molly, a few years older than her but somehow light years away in outlook. It was easier not to talk about it.

She wished that Molly would go so that she could get back to her own thoughts but it was another half an hour before she managed to say, 'Won't Reg be waiting for his dinner?'

Molly sighed. 'If I'm gone too long he starts to panic. I'm afraid he'll do something stupid like turn the gas on.' The look in her friend's eyes was bleak, and when she said, 'Why don't you come round for a bite tomorrow?' Grace couldn't say no.

Once she was on her own again she went to fill the kettle but she and Molly had already drunk two mugs of coffee and she was swimming with liquid. She cast her eyes in the direction of the sherry bottle but the warning signs were loud enough to make her turn away.

She felt cheated, expecting that Molly's return would bring an opportunity to get her life back into perspective. Now she felt that Molly had no idea of who she was. Instead of offering encouragement and understanding she had become another obstacle to get over, someone she needed to justify herself to before she could find her way forward.

She went out into the garden to survey her earlier work. Plenty of weeding still to do. The forecast was for a frost that night. The weather was a bit like life really, totally unpredictable.

*　　　*　　　*

Perhaps it was something to do with Molly's predicament, but by the next day, Grace was aware that a fog of desperation was threatening to envelop her. She knew with her mind that it was perfectly normal, a reaction to a bereavement, however much one had been expecting it. It was more than that though, a sudden paralysis, admitting that all those foolish dreams that had kept her going for so many years were really pie in the sky.

As she got ready for lunch with Reg and Molly she thought for the umpteenth time about her visitor. Saying yes was such a mistake. Yesterday she hadn't mentioned it to Molly but today she would have to.

Reaching for her jacket she let herself out of the house, stopping for a few moments to inspect the flowerbeds. The lily of the valley was growing increasingly prolific, in the tight cocoon of leaves the delicate white buds were already showing. Cheered a little by the wonder of nature, she walked the few yards to Molly's house.

A delicious smell of cooking greeted her, a rich aroma of garlic, fried onions, toasted cheese, something else she couldn't identify. Molly was a good cook. She felt gratifyingly hungry.

She was hardly through the door when Molly pushed a very full wine glass into her hand. 'Here, take this. I need one.' She nodded meaningfully towards the living-room where Grace assumed Reg must be. Lowering her voice, Molly said, 'He had an accident this morning, messed his pants—I suppose this is the way things are going to be from now on.'

'You should talk to the doctor.'

Grace was profoundly grateful for her own, as yet unfamiliar, freedom. She sat in the kitchen while Molly prepared things on the stove. The wine slipped down easily. From habit she glanced at the bottle to see its country of origin. It was Chilean.

Calmed by her wine, Molly asked, 'Well, what have you planned to do then?'

'Nothing for the moment. I've got a visitor in a few days.'

'Oh yes?' Molly strained what looked like spinach into a colander.

'It's . . . a friend's son.'

'That seems a bit inconsiderate, doesn't it? The last thing you want is playing host to somebody at the moment.'

'I really don't mind. He's only here for a short while.'

'Where does he live?'

'Australia.'

The word acted like touch paper. 'Not that fellow who—?'

'His son's over here visiting. His father rang the other night and wondered if he might—'

Molly's expression was familiar, lips like prunes, brow creased and oozing disapproval.

'You just be careful. Don't forget that you will look like a good prospect now, a woman of property, especially one with no ties.'

Grace shook her head and smiled. 'Hardly. They've got a successful winery, hundreds of acres. They're not likely to come gold digging.'

'Well, you be careful,' she repeated.

'Yes, Mum.' The words came out as a joke but Molly remained serious.

'You think I'm being silly but you are in a very vulnerable state at the moment. Don't let that boy persuade you into going to visit to Australia . . . his mother's still alive, isn't she?'

Grace nodded, trying to hide her amusement at the idea that Joe was sending his son to lure her to Australia and somehow claim her millions—or in this case, thousands.

'With the price of property these days that

house is worth a fair bit.' Molly was in full flow now. Grace reached out and filled their glasses, letting the diatribe slide over her. Moments later they were carrying the food into the other room where Reg sat vacantly at the table, his body at an angle as if he had been dumped there like a Guy Fawkes. He looked uncannily like Grace's father.

'Hello, Reg, had a good holiday?' She took a seat and waited while Molly dished out vegetables. A very tasty lasagne steamed its way on to their plates.

Reg mumbled and Grace suspected that he had already forgotten he had been anywhere. Her own dilemmas were forgotten as her sympathy for Molly grew.

After the meal and the wine she felt sleepy. Reg was already snoring gently and, having helped to wash up, Grace made her excuses to leave.

'Don't go spending too much time on your own.'

Grace suspected that it was Molly who wanted company but just at the moment she wanted some solitude. She said, 'I won't. I'll probably see you tomorrow.'

*   *   *

Using revision as an excuse, Grace managed to escape on Saturday evening to visit Mavis. Mavis had not been born in the village and that alone set her apart as someone sophisticated and exciting who understood the ways of the world. Grace was amazed that Mavis had chosen to be her friend. She was small, with amber-gold hair and corn-coloured eyes flecked with green. Her cheeks had a peachy sheen with no hint of teenage spots and her teeth were small and perfect. In her presence, Grace felt clumsy and gauche and in awe of the wisdom that Mavis had gleaned from her life on the mainland.

As soon as she was in the door Grace poured out her new discovery, breathless with the wonder of it.

'He's terrific. He's going home at the end of the month, though. I don't know what I'll do then.'

Mavis smiled that wise smile and said 'Be true to yourself, that's all that any of us can do.' It felt like a blessing, permission to pursue her love to the ends of the earth if necessary.

Mavis had just ended a serious romance with her cousin Sean.

'We've both agreed. I'm going to university and he's going back to Ireland.' Her expression was sad but sage. 'Who knows. Perhaps in some future time we'll meet again.'

Grace felt sad for her friend, being able for the first time to imagine what parting from a loved one would mean. She closed her mind against that particular possibility.

She stayed until just before eight and then

59

set out for her meeting. Mavis untied her hair and brushed it into a shimmering sheet of brown.

'There, that looks better.'

Grace had nice hair, she knew that. It was thick and long and perhaps one of her best features.

Her heart fluttering with expectation, she walked to their meeting place. In a panicky moment she wondered if he knew exactly where she meant. How terrible if she was waiting in one place and he in another. It wasn't exactly isolated. People passed by on their way to the British Legion. The odd cyclist took a short cut. After heavy rain the stream in the brook was noisy and frenetic.

It was nearly dark and getting chilly so Grace walked up and down between the end of the lane and the point where it bent so that their meeting place would be out of sight. Minute after agonizing minute ticked by. Her heart lurched each time she heard footsteps approaching and lurched again when she saw that it was not he. She looked at her watch, quarter past, half past, quarter to nine. He wasn't coming. She hung on for another agonizing fifteen minutes before turning towards home and the sanctuary of her bedroom where she could have a subdued but heart-felt cry.

* * *

'What's the matter with you?' Edna eyed her suspiciously when she came down to breakfast the next morning.

'Nothing.'

'You look peaky. Are you unwell?' It was Edna's euphemism for having a period. Grace nodded, relieved to have an excuse for her misery.

'You'd better have a quiet day then.'

This was not what she planned. 'I must go to church,' she said, panicking at the thought of being housebound. It was Easter Sunday. Surely Joe would accompany the Solomons this morning and then they could arrange another meeting.

'No. You just stay home for once. If you want a hot water bottle I'll bring you up one.'

Against Edna's steely determination Grace was defeated. Unable to bear to stay in the kitchen, she retreated to her room and climbed back into bed, hiding her misery under the covers. With rare maternal cosseting, Edna brought her a tray of cereal and tea and a hot water bottle.

'Just you stay there now. I used to be like you, have trouble every month. By the time I was your age, though, I was out working so I had to get on with it.'

Grace rarely wondered about her mother's early life but thinking of her with a stomach ache, dragging herself into some cold kitchen

61

to light the fires and lug in buckets of coal, she felt pampered and guilty.

All the time as she lay in bed she thought about the progress of the church service, what hymns they might be singing, the vicar's sermon, the announcements and then the return home. Joe should be back at about 12.30. Would he come straight away to find out what had happened to her? What would he say to her mother? Her Dad had gone to his allotment but he would be back in time for Sunday dinner at one. Supposing he bumped into Joe coming up their path? She could imagine the rich, rural burr of her father's voice saying something that Joe might not even understand. What would he think of her lowly background? The agonies went round and round in her head and, perhaps in defence, she fell asleep until her dinner arrived on a tray.

So, Sunday inched along and Grace was unable to leave the house. Never had a prisoner felt so trapped, or so desperate, not even those people in the Tower of London waiting to be beheaded.

*   *   *

By next morning she put on a brave face and came down to breakfast early.

'You look better.'

What a relief, now she could regain her

freedom. 'I . . . I've just got to go to the library to take some books back,' she started.

'It's Easter Monday, everything is closed.' Edna glared at her suspiciously as if she might be losing her grip.

'Of course it is. Well, I think I'll just stretch my legs after being cooped up all day yesterday.'

To her relief, her mother didn't object. With the prospect of escape, Grace ate her breakfast and wondered how best to play it. She would walk past the house and see if Joe was there. If he wasn't, she would wander around and then on the way back, if he still didn't appear, she'd just knock at the door. If Mr or Mrs Solomons should answer then she would use the excuse of apologizing for not coming to church the morning before. Now that her strategy was planned she relaxed.

In fact, she had to put her last option into action, having found no signs of life on her outward journey. As she opened the Solomons's gate she felt like a burglar, entering with ill intent. Knowing that she might have already been spotted, she fought back the desire to run away and instead knocked at the door with trembling knuckles, awaiting her fate.

Joe answered the door. Confused by his sudden appearance, Grace looked away, ashamed of her daring in coming to see him. Keeping her eyes lowered the first thing she noticed was that he was wearing slippers. This cosy detail made her feel unaccountably tender.

'G'day. Have you come to see Mrs Solomons?' he asked.

Of course she hadn't but she had to go through the charade. 'I wasn't able to go to church yesterday so I thought I'd just explain,' she started.

She wanted to know if he had gone, if he had been disappointed not to find her there, but she simply waited.

'I think Mrs Solomons is in town,' he said. 'D'you want to come in?'

Delighted with the way things were turning out she followed him into the house. She had been inside before but now it took on a special significance. It was fast turning into a shrine, a place that would forever be associated with him.

They went into the sitting-room and she perched sedately on an armchair.

'Did you enjoy the match?' she asked, hoping to elicit some information from him.

'Match? Oh, the football. Too right. It was fair dinkum. We didn't get back until late.'

This was some small consolation, that he hadn't simply not bothered to turn up.

'Did you go to church yesterday?' she ventured.

'No. It's really not my scene.'

Treacherously, she regretted now having

hinted that her reason for calling was to apologize for her own absence. Was she denying the Lord? Was Joe doomed to hell? She didn't want to think of any of that right now.

He plonked himself down in another chair, leaned back and studied her.

'Well, what are you doing today, Grace Harrison?'

'Nothing.'

'Nor am I. Shall we go out somewhere?'

'Where?' She couldn't believe her luck.

'Anywhere. I don't care. This is your island. You tell me.'

Her mind went blank. She had no idea what he might like. 'We could go to Carisbrooke Castle,' she started.

'History?' He pulled a face.

'Take the bus to Sandown?'

'What's there?'

'Nothing.' She grew increasingly anxious.

'Tell you what, let's just go for a walk, shall we? You can show me the local landmarks.'

Could she? Were there any? She thought of Sunday afternoon walks with her parents. An idea came to her. 'We could walk to Bonchurch through the Landslip and catch the bus back.'

'If you say so.'

It was settled. The only thing to do now was to go home and break the news of her outing to Edna.

'There's just a few of the girls,' she lied. 'We thought we'd go for a good walk.'

'Who are you going with?' Edna looked suspicious.

'Just Jill and Mavis.'

Sniff. 'Better take your raincoat, it doesn't look too settled. What time will you be back?'

'That depends on how far we go.'

CHAPTER FIVE

Grace was delighted to find that Joe was impressed by the route that their walk took them. The Landslip, as its name implied, was a rocky area of coastline where periodically the land slid unannounced into the sea, leaving a wild, chaotic tumble of rocks. In some places trees leaned at odd angles, trying to keep a grip on life. Here and there they passed the foundations of a house, its back broken by a fall, seeming to cry forlornly to be remembered. Now and then the path drew ominously close to a ravine, steep and bottomless, threatening to draw them over the edge like some sprite from folklore.

'This is seriously wild,' Joe announced. 'We've got nothing like this where I live. Everything is so green here. Around Ararat the countryside is red and arid, although there are the Grampians.'

66

'Aren't those mountains in Scotland?' They had reached a place where the path had tumbled away and Joe took her hand to help her over the gap.

'It was probably Scottish settlers that named our mountains, thinking that they reminded them of home.'

The path grew increasingly uneven. Around them, the occasional squawk of a startled bird burst across the distant hiss of the sea.

'Can we get down to the beach?' he asked.

'There is a way down but it's very steep. It might have fallen away over the winter.'

This did not deter them. Scrambling along, they eventually came to some rickety steps and descended on to a sparse plateau. Joe turned to gaze out across the water.

'I wouldn't mind living here,' he announced. 'It's so remote. Do you think if I staked a claim like the old prospectors I could make it mine?'

'People used to live here once.' Grace was pleased with her knowledge. 'There used to be about eight fishermen's cottages but it all fell away.' Her Dad had told her that an old cousin had once lived here. She smiled, adding, 'If somebody died they had to take the coffin to the church by boat.'

She could tell that he was listening although he was still gazing across the restless haze of the water.

After a while he turned towards her. She couldn't read his expression but it was serious.

'We could make this place ours,' he said.

He took her hand and, choosing a flat spot, sank to the ground, taking her with him. He seemed to have trouble speaking. 'Grace, I've never felt about anyone like I do about you. I know it's mad and all that. We hardly know each other but . . .

She smiled to show him that she understood and he began to kiss her, first slowly and then with increasing insistence. When his hand came to rest on her breast she stopped him.

'You mustn't. It's wrong.'

He pulled away. 'How can it be wrong if you love me? You do love me, don't you?'

'Of course I do.' Troubled by the Ten Commandments, she was equally troubled by the fear of losing him.

'It's up to you,' he said. 'I've never felt like this about anyone before. I wouldn't want you to do anything you don't want to do but . . .'

His mouth strayed from her lips to her temples, her eyelids, as if he was bestowing a blessing on her.

She knew that this moment might never come again. Here they were, alone in a magical place. She loved him. Soon he would be gone. How could it be wrong to give herself to him?

His hands massaged her shoulders, pulled her closer, finally cradled her breasts. This time she did not object. All those rules about not doing things with a man surely didn't apply

68

when you were in love? None of Edna's warnings to keep herself nice or boys would not respect her applied. From now on, forever more, they belonged to each other.

At the last moment she panicked but she knew that it was too late to go back. Made tense by ignorance, he hurt her. It was not as she expected and all she felt was bruising and pain. Most of all was regret for her failure to please him. He lay on his side, head supported by one hand, teasing her damp hair away from her cheek.

'I'm sorry,' he said. 'I didn't even ask if you were a virgin.'

A different shame filled her now. It had not occurred to her that he would think otherwise. Her own suspicions loomed. Did that mean that he had had other girlfriends? Jealousy, corrosive, burned in her for every girl he had so much as looked at. To her shame, she began to cry.

'Hey, there's no need for that.' He shook his head as if at a loss. 'I'm sorry. I really am.'

Unable to look at him, Grace accepted his hanky and blew her nose, wiped her eyes, felt the enormity of her failure.

'You won't want to see me again,' she blurted out.

'What a crazy thing to say. Of course I want to see you.' He planted a paternal kiss on her forehead. As she gazed down she saw his tumescent manhood begin to stir. He was the first naked man that she had ever seen. The mystery transfixed her.

Following the direction of her gaze, he said, 'I'll be really gentle this time, make it right for you. You just lay back and let me make you feel happy. We're right for each other, you and I. Just you wait and see.'

She longed to block out her failure. All these new sensations were crying out to be felt properly. Leaning back she closed her eyes and gave herself up to her new destiny.

Afterwards, they walked to Bonchurch, wandered the length of the village pond, bought ice creams in the teashop and she told him about all the famous writers who had come here. 'Even Charles Dickens,' she finished.

'It's a bonzer place.' He gazed round at the untamed woodland creeping into every crevice. It was getting late, they were tired and agreed to take the bus back home.

On the way back she told him about the Civil Service exam and how she planned to go to London.

'It's a pity that you can't work in Warwick,' he said. 'That's where I'll be for the next two years.'

'Perhaps I could.' She knew that the Civil Service had offices all over the country. If she passed the exam she would ask if they had a vacancy there. Her mind thrilled with the thought of being near to him, being independent, with her own job and her own flat. Everything was possible. The fantasy kept her busy for the rest of the journey.

'That,' said Joe as they walked from the bus stop, 'was one good day.'

'That,' thought Grace, 'was the happiest day of my life.'

*　　　*　　　*

Walking back to the cottage from Molly's after lunch, Grace took time again to admire the front garden. The recent high wind and angry rain had filled the bed with the last of the leaves that had until now resisted winter's worst and were finally being pushed out like milk teeth by new growth. In their place buds of a delicate green began to ornament the branches. Spring, a time of hope.

As she opened the front door the phone was ringing. From habit she rushed to its command and immediately wished that she hadn't.

'G'day. You don't know me but my father is an old friend of yours? You used to know him years ago?' She recognized that habit of Australians to turn everything into a question.

'Alex,' she said. 'Your father said you might phone.' Now was the time to make it clear that she would be pleased to meet him but only for a drink, or maybe a meal. He was still talking.

'It's real kind of you, Grace, to say that you'll put me up. To be honest I've been

71

wondering what I was going to do until the flight home.'

With sinking heart she wondered how long before then. 'When do you fly back?' she asked.

'The seventeenth.'

More than a week! She almost groaned.

'I won't get in your way,' he was saying, 'But I've always wanted to see your island. Dad always said he wished he could go back.'

The memory of her time with Joe approached like a tsunami, devastating in its aftermath. Somehow she turned the tide.

'Where are you now?' she asked, hoping that he wasn't already within walking distance.

'I'm still in France but I'm booked on the Eurostar tomorrow. I'll be staying in London tomorrow evening but if I could come down on Friday?'

'Of course. Let me know the time of the train and I'll pick you up.'

'That's real kind you, Grace. Dad's talked a lot about you. I really look forward to meeting you.'

As she replaced the receiver she wished that she could say the same.

For a while she simply stood by the telephone, gazing at nothing. She wondered what on earth Joe would have said to him. Their time together all those years ago, surely he hadn't told him about that!

Grace was due back at school on Monday so there was no chance to see Joe during the daytime. As she sat in the history class she carefully wrote his name in the margin of her book, embellished it with hearts and kisses, counted the number of letters in his name to see if it came to her lucky number. Her lucky number was eight. Joseph Weston added up to twelve letters, while Joe Weston came to nine. Not getting the answer she wanted, she dismissed the exercise as silly.

'Are you with us, Grace?' Mr Sheldon, her teacher, interrupted her daydreams. She blushed and put her pen away, trying to work up some interest in the Factory Acts.

After school she slowed down outside the Solomons house and Joe must have been looking out for her because after a moment he came out. The late April sunshine had begun to tan his skin, enhancing the blue of his eyes, bleaching his hair. She thought that he looked godlike, someone so beautiful that she could have cried for the joy of looking at him.

After an initial greeting, he asked 'Are you free tonight? Or have you got too much revision to do?'

Two more days and then he would be leaving. How could she have anything more important to do than spend her time with him? She shook her head.

'Shall we go to the cinema, then?'

'All right.' She wanted to go somewhere lonely where they would be free to make love, but there was a problem. She immediately thought of Tower Gardens but in the early evening it would still be light and too many people would be about. By the time it was dark it would be too late for them to walk to somewhere remote and get back in good time. Besides, Edna wasn't keen on her going out on school evenings. She would have to be careful. The cinema it would have to be.

She took her leave with the promise to meet him outside the Regal at 6.30. The film showing that evening was called *Separate Tables*. Joe was a few minutes late and as she loitered outside a too familiar fear mocked her, warning that he wasn't coming. When she finally saw him turn the corner and start across the road tears of relief prickled in the corners of her eyes.

'Sorry I'm a bit late.'

In silence they went in and bought their tickets, slipping into the cinema as the adverts came to a halt.

As soon as they were seated she tentatively slid her arm through his. He took her hand and she leaned against him, longing for him to kiss her but she was aware that other people sat behind them. He guided her hand to his lap and she could feel the hard bulge in his trousers. The realization both excited and

74

shocked her. Carefully, suddenly embarrassed, she withdrew her hand and rested it on the arm of the seat. Joe crossed his legs and turned his shoulders away from her, tense, rejected.

Slowly the film unfolded and the story went straight to her heart, watching the heroine part from her true love, returning to her duty. As they came out she felt transported by the agony of love.

'Do you think they were right to part?' she asked him.

'I don't know.' He seemed distant and she touched his arm for reassurance.

'If she loved him and not her husband then surely it couldn't be wrong to be with him?'

'It's just a film.' She heard the irritation in his voice and a sort of terror began to claim her. She couldn't think of anything to say to put things right. She had no clear idea what was wrong except that for some reason Joe was angry with her.

As they reached the point where the road branched he asked, 'Are you going straight home?'

She knew that she should do so but she couldn't, she simply couldn't leave him. For a terrible moment she wondered if he wanted her to go and she heard herself say, 'I mustn't be long.'

'Long enough to go to Tower Gardens?'

'All right.'

She felt him relax, he took her hand and her spirits lifted, knowing that for this evening they would be lovers.

Cruelly, as they passed through the gates into the dark seclusion of the grounds, fine drizzle began to descend. Joe slipped his jacket over her shoulders and they cut across the grass, finding a shelter of sorts in a hollow formed by the rhododendron. Around them the earth was damp but beneath the shrub it was still dry. Joe placed his jacket lining down on the ground and they sank down together.

'I don't want you to go.' Grace broke her promise to herself to be brave now that their parting was so near.

'I have to. I'll be back before you know it, and you've got your exams to keep you busy.'

Her head nestled against his shoulder and she absorbed the rise and fall of his chest. Again he took her hand and guided it towards his trousers.

'Are you afraid to touch me?' he asked.

He must have sensed her hesitation in the near darkness and he said, 'Do you want me to touch you?'

She couldn't answer. It wasn't something that she could say out loud. By way of answer he undid his own trousers, guided her hand inside and reached out to slip his fingers inside her knickers. The sensation sent her reeling with raw feeling. After a while he pushed her flat and climbed above her, pushing himself

76

into her. She held him tight, trying to swallow him up so that their bodies merged into one, indivisible, united forever.

'Oh, Grace.' He came with a shuddering gasp inside her and she cuddled him close, overwhelmed by the bitter sweetness of it all. This was what it was about, the mystery of love. No one could have felt such profound ecstasy as she did at that moment.

'You will write to me?'

'Of course I will.'

He kissed her, calm now his early frustration had been banished.

She privately considered the possibility that she might be pregnant, hoping that she was, for then their love would be evident for everyone to see. Grace nestled closer to him.

The rain began to come down faster, driving them from their refuge. Already she knew that she was far too late. Edna would be waiting for her, watching out, ready to exact some awful punishment for staying out. As they reached her gate, she said, 'I must go in. Now.' She wanted him to kiss her again but she was too afraid that Edna would see. Supposing she came out and started shouting at him. She couldn't bear that.

Quickly she said, 'I'll see you on the way home from school tomorrow,' and before he could respond she opened the gate and hurried down the pathway. Opening the back door, she hoped that she didn't look too bedraggled.

'Hello, all right?' she issued the usual greeting.

By way of answer Edna pursed her lips in a particularly disapproving way, confirming her daughter's worst fears.

'It was a good film,' she ventured, hoping that she was wrong about her mother's mood.

'And just where have you been to, young lady?'

'To the pictures,' Grace floundered.

Edna said, 'Young Jill Perkins came round to see you. You told me you were going to the pictures with her. Where have you been?'

The game was up. Grace gazed at her feet, waiting for the axe to fall.

'I have been to the pictures,' she started.

'It's that boy, isn't it?' She could see that Edna was building up a head of steam. 'I knew it just by the way you looked at him. What on earth do you think you're playing at?'

'I'm not playing at anything.'

Edna was off again. 'Well, it's got to stop. You've got your exams to think about. We don't know him from Adam. If you've got any plans to sneak off out again you can just forget them.'

'But—'

'Don't but me, young lady. I don't know what your father would say. Fortunately, he doesn't know.' Grace guessed that he had already gone to bed. She had no idea what he

78

would say if he knew, but suspected that he wouldn't be nearly as angry as her mother. It occurred to her in that moment that nearly all her contact with her father was through her mother, a sort of go between—Daddy will be pleased, I don't think Daddy would like that, and so on. They rarely had a conversation face to face.

Edna suddenly asked, 'You haven't been doing anything silly, have you? Tell me you haven't been . . .' She could not bring herself to put her worst fears into words.

'Of course I haven't.'

'Well, that's something.' Edna's sharp eyes looked her over.

'What's that on the back of your skirt? It looks like mud. Just what have you been up to?'

'I slipped, it's raining. Nothing!'

'If I find out that you—'

Grace began to cry then. 'It doesn't matter anyway,' she shouted. 'He's going away tomorrow.'

The news seemed to mollify her mother.

'Come on now, stop that snivelling.'

The agony of it all was too much. Now that she had started to cry, Grace couldn't stop. She was in love. Her sweetheart was leaving. Life had suddenly become unbearable.

Edna pushed a hankie at her. 'Here, blow your nose. You think you're in love now, but you'll get over it, you'll see.'

I won't! Grace thought. How could I ever get over this. Besides, I don't need to get over it because one day soon, I'll be away from here and then Joe and I will be together forever!

She slept badly, agonising about how to escape the next evening—Joe's last night. She had to see him. If necessary, she would climb out of her bedroom window and meet him when they were all in bed—except that she would have to explain it all to him, how her mother disapproved, forbade her to see him. How could she say such a thing?

As she walked to the bus stop to go to school the following morning the Solomon's house was silent. Somehow she would have to get through the day until she came home, and meet him then.

The day dragged. She was inattentive, anxious. Mavis lent a learned ear as she poured out her troubles at lunchtime. Mavis's mother would impose no such restrictions. She recognized that her daughter was an adult and should make her own choices. Mavis's father was dead. She wished that they could swap parents.

Before leaving school she paid a hasty visit to the cloakroom and tried to repair the damage to her face caused by too much crying and too little sleep. She felt heavy eyed and pallid. She didn't want Joe to see her like this but there was little that she could do.

By the time she reached the Solomons's

house, the familiar increase in her heart rate, the thundering of her pulse and tightness in her chest had all claimed her. Awkwardly, she loitered at the gate and to her relief the front door opened and Joe came out.

'Had a good day?' he asked.

She shrugged, hoping that he would come up with some miraculous suggestion for the evening. Instead, he said, 'I'm afraid Mr and Mrs Solomons are taking me over to see Aunt Moira this evening. She is cooking me a farewell meal.'

The disappointment was staggering. 'But it's your last evening,' she wailed.

'I know, but I can't very well get out of it. Aunt Moira has invited some other friends over to say goodbye to me.'

The sense of loss and jealousy was so great that she could find no words. As the silence lengthened, Joe said, 'Perhaps it's as well. Saying goodbye is never easy.' With an attempt at lightening the situation he added, 'Anyway, it isn't goodbye. It is just a temporary separation.'

Made desperate by the thought of losing him, she said, 'I needn't go to school tomorrow. I could come with you to the station.'

He shook his head. 'No. We'd both be upset. Just think of it as a short break. Before you know it, I'll be back.'

Symbolically, angry spots of rain began to

assail them. Silenced by her misery, she let him take her hand, the future as uncertain as the weather. Where would he go when he came back to England? Would he return first to the Solomons or go straight to Warwick? Where was she to see him? When? It was all too painful for words.

The rain grew heavier. Glancing up at the lowering clouds, Joe said, 'Look, I've got a little present for you.' He reached into his pocket and brought out a small object wrapped in tissue paper.

For a marvellous moment she thought that it might be an engagement ring. That would show them! That would show everyone that he was hers.

She held out her hand and accepted the package half hoping that he would open it himself and slip it on to her finger. Made clumsy by her emotion, she unwrapped it to reveal a small brooch of a kangaroo.

'Thank you.' She hoped he wouldn't detect the degree of her disappointment. It must have been something that he had bought in Australia, just in case he needed to give a gift to someone—anyone. Perhaps he was only giving it to her because he didn't want to have to take it home again. In spite of her disappointment, she knew that she would wear it always, knowing that it was a symbol of their love.

Joe said, 'Give me a kiss now and I promise

I'll write when I get to London, before I catch the plane. I'll write often. Truly I will.'

'I haven't got your address.'

'Don't worry, I'll put it on my letter. Our telephone number too.'

Grace's parents didn't have a telephone. She had no idea how you made a phone call to Australia in a public call box. By the second, he seemed to be slipping further and further away.

'I'll walk up the road with you,' he offered but the thought of Edna spying on them, spoiling their last moments together, made her shake her head.

'Well, we'd better say goodbye then—not goodbye, *au revoir* as they say in French—until we see each other again.'

He leaned over and gave her a fraternal kiss on the cheek. 'You take care now. Look out for my letters and be sure you write back.'

There was nothing she could do but walk away. Clutching the kangaroo brooch, she was soothed by this material link with him. The rain was now coming down in a deluge.

CHAPTER SIX

Grace couldn't decide which bedroom to put Alex Weston in. The cottage had three bedrooms, her own, her mother's and what was little more than a box room. She looked round Edna's room but her death was too recent. Her presence was still in the room, the faint scent of Yardley Roses she had always favoured, ornaments, photographs, the physical remains of her life. Grace could not oust her so quickly. In the end, she decided that she would take the box room herself and put him in her own, except that it would be inconvenient as all her clothes were in the wardrobe and she would be forever forgetting to fetch something vital. Still, it was for less than a week. She would manage, somehow.

She had baked a pie, lentils, leeks and mushrooms in a creamy sauce. Vegetables were peeled, ready to cook. She hadn't looked forward to catering for him but the act of making the pastry had been soothing. Edna's diet had reduced over the years so that meals had become formulaic. She found an unexpected pleasure in extending her range of dishes.

A bottle of red wine stood on the side and a bottle of white chilled in the fridge. The red was French and the white German. Jacob's Creek, Nottage Hill, she hadn't quite had the courage to risk the more popular Australian wines in case he disapproved.

There was nearly an hour to go before she set out for the ferry. Quickly, she checked the house over, bathroom all neat and tidy, bedroom. She had forgotten to put out any towels and she fetched some, placing them at the foot of his bed. In the lounge she tidied away the local paper she had been avidly scanning to see if there were any new tourist attractions, or anything that might appeal to an adult, male Australian. There was nothing and she panicked at the thought of keeping him entertained.

She wandered outside, wondered whether to tidy up one of the flower beds, but then realized that as it had been raining earlier she would probably get mud on her clothes, grime beneath her fingernails. The sun was now shining so she sank on to the garden bench and surveyed her surroundings.

This was the cottage where she had been born, indeed spent nearly all of her life. It was old, at least three hundred years, built of what was called island stone, mellowed blocks in grey and yellow, some permeated with iron giving them a rich, rusty look. It was the sort of place that visitors stopped to admire, still thatched, tiny windows looking out from beneath straw eyebrows. She had always taken it for granted. As far as she knew, generations of her ancestors might have lived and died here, their footsteps echoing along the path that led round to the back door. She couldn't remember ever using the front entrance. The graveyard next door hosted lines of headstones bearing witness to her ancestors' all too brief presence on earth.

In the yard the old pump remained, still in working order. In dry summers Gordon had used the water for his garden. Her father had loved his garden. Dahlias, asters, golden rod, michaelmas daisies then the rota of vegetables, sprouts, spring greens, parsnips, potatoes, tomatoes, so it went on. Dad, dear, easy-going Dad. Suddenly she longed for this silent communication with her past to continue, not to be disrupted by the arrival of a man from hall way round the world. Resolutely she closed her eyes, raising her face to be bathed by the tepid sun.

Strange to think that Joe had left all those years ago and now, for the first time, a part of him was coming back. The morning after his departure for London, a post card had arrived with a picture of Trafalgar Square. Fortunately, the postman arrived before Grace left for school so she was able to get to the door before Edna did. In future, though, it was going to be impossible to retrieve all Joe's letters before Edna spotted them, and having an Australian post mark they would be hard to disguise. Anyway, there was no harm in writing to him, was there?

The post card did not say as much as she had hoped but there again, anyone could read it so of course he couldn't write anything personal. She read it for the third time before glancing around to make sure that no one was watching then she kissed it and stored it inside her history textbook.

Glancing back at the doormat she noticed that there was a second letter for her and before she even picked it up she knew that it was about the Civil Service appointment. Its significance hit her as she thought of the importance of getting a job away from home. Holding her breath she opened the envelope and extracted the contents. She was being asked to go to London for an interview. The details passed her by. All that mattered was that by the time Joe arrived back, she would be free to see him.

Moments later, Edna appeared from outside where she had been feeding the chickens.

'Was that the postman?'

Grace handed over the Vernon's football coupon that her Dad religiously filled in every week. He had once won seven pounds on the Three Draws and was determined to repeat the achievement.

'I've got a letter about the job.' She held it out for Edna to see. Her mother went very quiet.

'You seem far too young to me to be gallivanting off to London. It isn't like the island, you know, all kinds of things happen up there.'

'Mother, I am eighteen!' Grace bit back her irritation. She wanted to say *I'm going and that's that*, but she needed her mother's support with the complexities of moving. The only thing she knew for certain was that she had to go.

As it happened, for once Edna pulled out all the stops. A week later she accompanied her daughter to the interview in London. Neither of them knew their way around but in a moment of sheer extravagance Edna took a taxi from the station. The interview was held in a towering stone building, each room as lofty as the village church. Cornices and picture rails sat cheek by jowl with filing cabinets and utilitarian desks. Grace felt paralyzed with nerves. She and Edna sat in a corridor waiting for the summons.

'I'll come in with you,' said Edna. 'You will make sure that you hold your head up, and speak properly, won't you?' There was an edge of anxiety in her voice.

As it was, when Grace was called it was made clear that her mother was not expected to accompany her. The interview room was rectangular with a beige-coloured carpet and a very large desk beneath the tall window. A chandelier converted to electricity hung over the middle of the room.

Three people sat behind the desk, one woman and two men. They made a point of putting her at her ease. Soon she was telling them about her expected exam results and why she wanted a career in the Civil Service.

At the end of the interview they implied

that subject to a medical she would be appointed to Her Majesty's Income and Revenue, the exact location still to be agreed. The idea of the tax office held little appeal but she struggled to smile her pleasure. The thought of being in London was all that mattered. Who knows, before long perhaps she could get a transfer to Warwick?

As they left the building, the doorman pointed out a bus that went directly to Waterloo. The bus stop was just across the road. Within minutes the red double-decker came along and together they boarded it.

They made the journey in silence each preoccupied with her own thoughts. The bus trundled along a wide street, round a square where to her delight Grace recognized Nelson's column then past prestigious stone buildings complete with porticoes and wide stairways. Grace took it all in with gathering excitement. Soon she would be here every day, exploring, earning her own money, planning to meet up with Joe!

Once they were back at home Edna went even further. Declaring that she needed to know exactly where her daughter was going to be living, she found out that the vicar had a married cousin on the outskirts of London who would be willing to take in a well-behaved lodger. They lived near a station that had a direct service into town. Miraculously, within a couple of weeks, it was all settled.

'I don't know what you're getting so excited about,' Edna observed. 'You won't be going until September.'

She didn't need reminding that it was a lifetime away. There were still her exams to take, a summer to get through and then the pot of gold at the end of the rainbow—Joe's return.

Every day now depended on the arrival of the postman. He usually reached their cottage about twenty minutes before she left for school and she hovered near to the front door in an agony of hope and fear.

'Grace, if you've got nothing better to do, go upstairs and fetch that washing I left by the bedroom door. I clean forgot to bring it down.'

She flew up the stairs, straining to hear the postman's footsteps, stumbling in her hurry to get back to her vigil. So far, in two weeks, she had received two letters. It was disappointingly few but, like some vivid poster, they announced what she wanted to hear—I Love You. He loved her. That was all that mattered.

That same week she had her period. At the first signs she felt a bittersweet mixture of disappointment and relief. It would have been wonderful to have Joe's baby but that would mean that she couldn't go to work in London and would perhaps be separated from him for longer than ever—and whatever would her parents say?

When the third letter finally arrived, nearly

a week later than she had hoped, she opened it hoping for some confirmation of his travel plans, some reassurance that before she left the island, he would be back. All she could think of was the moment when they met in person to plan their future, to kiss and make love. The anguish of wanting him melted her insides.

She slipped the letter into her school bag and hurried for the bus, determined to find a seat where she could read it in peace. She was lucky. There was a seat next to a woman she did not know so she sat down and took out the treasured words. Her eyes began to glaze as she skimmed down it, looking for those special references to their love. As she reached the end she returned to the top and began to read more slowly.

My dear Grace,
Something has happened here that has thrown all my plans into chaos. I don't know what to say. Of all the rotten things, I never expected this. I'm so very sorry. It doesn't look as if I'll be back in October and even if I am, things have changed here so that anything we might have wanted is no longer possible. I can only ask you to forgive me and to believe me when I say that I still love you. I wish you a happy life.
Yours, Joe

She passed the rest of that journey, the hours at school, as if she were under water, separated from everyone around her. Even the everyday sounds were muted by a film of misery. When she got home she wrote him a long letter saying that no matter what it was—and she had no idea what it could possibly be—she would wait for him, that she loved him and always would and to be brave because she would never desert him. As she lay in bed she wondered how she might travel to Australia, how much it would cost. It distracted her from the black hole of terror that hovered around her.

Week after painful week drifted by. Her exams came. She took them in a state of numbness. A few days after the final exam, she came home from school as usual and Edna was in her accustomed place, making a cup of tea ready for her return.

As she poured it out, she said 'I saw Mrs Solomons today. She said that that grandson of hers has got some girl in trouble. Her daughter is that upset. The girl's parents are insisting that they get married.'

The last earthquake, the last terrible tumbling descent into betrayal, Joe, her Joe, had made another girl pregnant. He had done with someone else what they had shared. Edna was still talking. 'He's hardly more than a boy. You wouldn't have thought he was old enough to get up to something like that.'

That night Grace sent him a letter.

Dear Joe,
Your Grannie told my mum that you are
getting married. Congratulations. I hope
you will be very happy.
Grace

In these few lines she packed in all her pent up emotion, all the hurt and betrayal. Thinking of the shame he would feel when he read it sustained her for a few days but within a week an answer came back.

. . . it isn't what you think. Before I came to England Mum and Dad had invited some business friends to stay. They are thinking of going into partnership with the wine distribution. Their daughter Margaret came with them and it was left to me to entertain her. I didn't really even fancy her, honestly I didn't, but she liked me and—well you can guess what happened. It was only twice. After I came to England and met you I knew that I wanted to be with you but when I got back they dropped the bombshell. I know this won't make you think any better of me but what happened was before I met you. Please try to forgive me. I am the one who is losing because I am losing you. Never forget that I truly loved you.
Joe

Grace's head jerked forward and she awoke with a start. For a second she couldn't remember where she was or what she was doing, and then she realized that she was supposed to be meeting Alex Weston. She glanced at her watch. Damn, she was going to be late for the boat. Casting all her pointless memories aside, she made for the gate.

CHAPTER SEVEN

Alex caught the 3.15 ferry and arrived at 3.45. At this time of the year most of the passengers were Friday afternoon commuters, returning from work, some from just across the water, others who spent their weeks in London and fled to the solitude of the island each weekend. Their sense of purpose marked them out as regulars, not a lone traveller looking out for a woman he did not know.

A brown-haired man with a large case and a rucksack jostled among them. Something about his uncertainty made Grace decide that this was probably him. He was the right age although he certainly did not look like Joe. He must favour his mother she thought, suppressing any negative conclusions.

Grace stood by the car like a chauffeur, waiting until he emerged on to the pavement where he glanced around, hoping to identify her. She strode forward then. 'Alex?'

'Grace! Good to meet you.'

He half held out a hand, then dropping the case, awkwardly hugged her. He smelt of soap and warmth and his brief proximity was pleasurable.

'I can't tell you how much I appreciate this,' he said.

'Had a good journey?'

'Great. It's a lovely sea crossing. This is a beaut place to live.' He had corn-coloured eyes flecked with brown. They gleamed with pleasure.

As she turned towards the car he picked up the case again. 'Sorry about all this luggage. I was going to leave it in London but the left luggage places are all closed; some security alert.'

She nodded. 'No worries,' the phrase came back to her, adopted from Joe. She hadn't used it in years.

They drove the fifteen minutes from the port, Alex commenting on the scenery as they passed.

'You like the countryside?' she asked.

'Love it. Ours is nothing like this, though. The colours are different. Ours is all red and gold. Here, it's green and—more green. Yours looks overindulged. Ours is always parched, struggling for every sip of water.'

They made small talk until the car slowed to

a halt in her driveway.

'Wow! You live here?' He stood on the gravel taking in the detail, the small windows, thatch, hedges, rustic stone.

She said, 'My family has lived on the island forever. Not very adventurous, we Harrisons.'

'You were, though, when you were younger? You went travelling?' It must have been something that his father had told him.

'I . . . I went to work in London. It was all organized, a job and digs and everything. I wouldn't have had the nerve just to take off.' She cut him short, not wanting to remember that period.

'Amazing.' He ducked beneath the lintel, and she had forgotten how low the ceilings were. For a moment she saw the cottage through his eyes, quaint, ancient, historic. Although she had made a few interior innovations, most of the furnishing dated from a past age, from Aunt Rose and from Edna and, in turn, from grandparents. They were in keeping with the place and Grace felt an unexpected twinge of pleasure.

After she had shown him the bedroom they went outside to explore the garden. Everything was in full shoot, hungry buds chasing the lengthening daylight. The sun shone through the old apple trees making yellowing lace on the lawn.

'Wow, you're right next to the graveyard.'

She looked over the low stone wall at the

headstones leaning higgledy-piggledy. They in turn rested in the shadow of the church, its massive, squat tower having taken root centuries ago when it was a fortress as much as a religious house, laying claim to the entire village.

'What a place. Can we go next door and have a look?'

She nodded. 'You're religious?' she asked, hoping that he wasn't.

'No. Just interested in history.' As an afterthought he asked: 'Is that where my great-grandparents are buried?'

It was a second before she remembered that the Solomons, Joe's grandparents were of course related to this Alex. She nodded her head, remembering that it was when they had died that her family had got back in touch with his. Edna had taken it upon herself to write to the Solomons's daughter, Janet Weston, nee Solomons, who had long ago gone to live in Australia with Joe's father. Funny, she thought. If it hadn't have been for the unforeseen pregnancy that produced this Alex, I might have followed the same route.

Aloud she said, 'We'll go after tea.'

Alex had a good appetite. He ate appreciatively, appearing to approve of the wine, and Grace began to relax.

'Tell me about your time in Europe,' she started.

He had been to Italy, Germany and France,

all in pursuit of the grape. She listened as he talked, warmed by his accent, amused by his descriptions of people and places. He had a habit of raising his hands and throwing them apart to emphasise some point. That was Joe. He had done the same thing. Something about his mouth, too, shared that generous, humorous breadth.

'Are you looking forward to going home?' she asked, then remembering that his wife had left him, wished she hadn't.

'Not really. It's bloody hard grind, you know? I guess I'm kind of trapped by tradition. It was my great-grandfather started the winery, then grandfather, then Dad and now me. Being an only child puts demands on you.'

It does indeed, thought Grace, filling his glass.

He made no mention of the absent wife and to keep him away from the subject, Grace asked, 'Are your parents well?'

'That's the problem really. Dad has angina. Mum . . . well, she's had several cancer scares. They're finding the winery hard work. I think they should move away but—'

'Could you run the place on your own?' She wondered for the millionth time what his being an only child implied—a parental choice, a failure in their relationship? Anyway, what difference did it make?

'I could run it. We've got good staff, been there for years, some of them.'

It was beginning to get dark. They hadn't found their way next door to the churchyard but she felt sleepy, settled. She wouldn't remind him tonight. They could always go another time and she would point out the family graves, both his and hers.

'What would you like to do tomorrow?' she asked.

'I don't want to trouble you. I could get up early and catch a bus. You wouldn't even know that I was here.'

'Nonsense. I'd like to show you around— that is, if you wouldn't rather be on your own?'

'That's really kind, Grace. I'd like to make myself useful, though. I could mow your lawn or do some digging, something like that?'

'Then that's kind of you.' She hesitated. 'Actually, there is one thing you could do for me. That old plum tree over there by the wall is rotten. It's going to fall down one day and I don't want it toppling into the churchyard. Perhaps you could give me a hand to uproot it?'

'Consider it done.'

'This isn't a working visit, though. Is there anything you'd like to see?'

He thought for a moment. 'Your Carisbrooke Castle looks good.'

'Then that's where we'll go.'

* * *

Grace slept well and, in spite of the wine consumed the evening before, awoke feeling fresh and rested. By seven, the determined sun was invading her room. The birds were shouting to her to get up.

With a sense of well-being she made coffee and knocked on Alex's door.

'C'min.' He sounded sleepy and she immediately regretted waking him but when she walked in he was sitting up, his hair tousled. He looked strangely childlike.

'Gee, thanks Grace. This is four star.'

She smiled and left him to dress.

After breakfast they drove to Carisbrooke to explore the castle. Alex was surprisingly well informed about the English civil war, about King Charles's misjudged flight from Hampton Court into the arms of a reluctant but dutiful governor who invited him in first as guest and later as prisoner. He related the tale as they drove along the narrow twisty lane that Grace insisted was a main road.

Grace had little sympathy for King Charles. So many people had died as this arrogant, haughty figure tried every trick he could think of first to retain and then regain his crown. The little chapel in the castle grounds held an annual remembrance ceremony on the anniversary of his death. She thought there were better things to remember.

'Is that it?' There was boyish excitement as Alex got his first glimpse of the fort, perched on a rocky mound nearly in the centre of the island. It was the perfect location. Before the Normans came the Romans had chosen the same spot to build a villa.

'How old is it?' Alex asked, shaking his head in disbelief that the curtain wall and surrounding ditch had survived for hundreds of years. At the entrance, romantic twin drum towers guarded the way where once a drawbridge would have barred enemy access.

It always took Grace by surprise that as far as Colonial history went back; it was only about three hundred years since Europeans had stamped their mark on much of the world. Ignoring the far older history of the indigenous peoples, most Westerners seemed to think that history only started with their arrival. Grace couldn't resist pointing this out to her visitor.

When they had explored the grounds and the museum Grace insisted that Alex should watch the spectacle of a donkey turning a wheel to raise water from the well. The castle water supply had at one time suffered the fatal flaw of running dry in summer, the problem finally being solved by the sinking of a spectacular well. As they queued patiently, Grace thought that for visitors the highlight was the sight of a bored, long-suffering donkey waiting to be asked to perform his not too onerous task. At the signal, he entered the huge, creaking wheel and began to walk until he knew by instinct exactly where to stop as a bucket emerged from the depths. For Grace, the magic moment was when the custodian took a jug of the water and poured it back into the well. There was a long, stomach-clenching silence before it hit the water table at the bottom with a resounding splash.

She was telling Alex about this when the door to the well house opened and they were invited inside. To her surprise, the custodian was her cousin Louisa.

'What are you doing here?' She smiled at the girl neatly kitted out in a uniform.

'My summer job. Aren't I lucky?'

The visitors crowded in and Louisa began to recount the history of the well, depth of water, diameter of the wheel. As she talked, Grace watched her, thinking that she could not see a family resemblance. Louisa was dark, dark skin, brown eyes and wavy deep-brown hair. Her face was animated as she spoke, her mouth curved in a permanent smile. Grace fleetingly thought how preferable this job would have been to incarceration in the tax office. This was only a stopgap, however, filling in time until Louisa went off to study history. Grace felt the too familiar regret and resentment at chances long since denied to her.

When the talk was over and the visitors filed out, Grace introduced her cousin to her visitor. She watched as they chatted, at first politely and then with increasing enthusiasm as they talked about the castle, about England and their respective futures. They both seemed animated and Grace wondered if she might invite Joan and Louisa over to distract Alex and keep him entertained. Too soon she realized that the next group of visitors were outside the door waiting for admittance and they said their goodbyes.

Before leaving, they walked the length of the ramparts then completed the perimeter outside, marvelling at views, the cowslips, the feat of engineering. Alex bought post cards to send home. The act brought Grace that little shiver of danger, the knowledge that the man standing next to her was in constant touch with the man who had shaped her past. As they lunched in the village pub, she asked, 'Do you have any plans when you get home?' She wanted to know about his wife now. He didn't seem that upset but perhaps distance had helped, or he was just a good actor.

He thought for a while, sipping cold lager. 'You know I'm . . . I was married?'

'Your father said something about it.'

'Well, I guess that's in the past now. Susie, my wife has left me—run away with another man.' He grunted. 'It sounds dramatic, doesn't it? I was upset at first but to be honest, Grace, I don't think we had much going for us. She was damned pretty and I fancied her like mad but after a while, that isn't enough. You want something back from a person, don't you? You want to trust them and—well, like them. I guess it was the sex that I mistook for something more important. We didn't really share anything. I don't think we thought alike about anything.'

He sighed and gave himself over to his own thoughts. Grace in her turn wondered what she had really known about Joe. She didn't even know how he voted, what were his views on homosexuality, on animal welfare? In short, she really had no idea who he was. Unlike Susie and Alex, they had never been together long enough for her to see beyond the passion. What Alex had called fancying someone was the sum of it, really. It was a revelatory moment.

In the afternoon she took him for a drive around the island, travelling the length of the south coast with its chain of chalk and sandy bays, across the ridge of Arreton Down where the valley below spread out like some beautiful patchwork counterpane.

'Can I take you out to dinner?' he offered as they drove home.

'No need. I've got something organized.'

'You're a star, Grace.'

She smiled, thinking that this was the last evening she had planned for. From now on things would come off the supermarket shelves.

'Is there a winery around here?' he asked as they drove back 'I'll see if I can find anything

Australian you might enjoy.'

'There's an off licence.'

'Strange name.'

'There was a time when you could only sell wine and spirits at certain times of the day. I'm not sure if it still applies. The laws are more relaxed now.'

They stopped in the village and he spent a long time perusing the stock. Eventually he came out clutching a carrier bag. 'A bit of luck. They have a few decent vintages. Have you heard of the Barossa Valley?'

She nodded her head, again remembering the conversation of so long ago. 'That's where we grow most of our grapes. We've the perfect climate, plenty of sunshine, mostly just enough rain. We'll see what you think of these.'

Helped along by the wine tasting, the evening passed comfortably. They watched the ten o'clock news, viewed a half-hour comedy, both declared themselves tired and prepared for bed.

'What shall we do tomorrow?' she asked as they made ready to retire.

'First of all I'll get that tree dug up. Then I'll leave it to you.'

On impulse she kissed him on the cheek. 'Sleep well, Alex.'

'Sleep well, Grace. And thanks for being such a friend.'

*   *   *

The next morning dawned with all the optimism of spring. Alex was up early and, true to his word, disappeared into the garden to start work. As Grace pottered in the kitchen she kept glancing out of the tiny window as he worked by the boundary wall. This was a novel experience, having someone male labouring away for her benefit. He was driving into the tree with force, sawing, digging, dragging the wood into a pile. An ugly wound appeared where the plum tree had lived for so long and she felt a sort of sadness at its loss, but everything has a lifespan and the old tree was virtually dead. While the ground was exposed, it would be a good opportunity to plant something else. Perhaps they could take in a garden centre that afternoon.

Grace made coffee and called Alex in. He padded in barefooted, his face and hair moist from the exertion. He smelt of fresh sweat and it was dangerously heady.

'You're doing a good job,' she said, handing him a mug and pushing a tin of biscuits towards him.

'I'm unfit. I need to exercise more.'

She suggested the afternoon outing and he quickly acquiesced. 'Then this evening we could walk over the Warren, look at the Needles lighthouse. It is a pretty spectacular view.' She thought of the hills to the west, now verdant with new growth. By the end of

106

summer they would turn into a purple haze as the heather metamorphozed into a regal carpet. 'Afterwards, I thought I'd take you to a pub.'

'Sounds good to me.'

He went to shower while she prepared a lunchtime snack. She told him that it was called a ploughman's lunch, bread, cheese, pickled onions and chutney.

'Very rural,' he observed, tucking in with gusto. He was pleasingly enthusiastic about everything placed in front of him.

At the garden centre she bought a maple tree. Its remarkable feature was the snakelike bark. For a moment it crossed her mind that she could scatter Edna's ashes around it. They were still at the undertakers and soon she must collect them. She shied away from the thought of her mother's remains in a pot. It raised too many questions as to where the essential Edna had gone. The mystery of that spark of life niggled at her but she had no answers.

When I go, you can put me on top of Dad's grave, Edna had suggested. Grace's father was across the wall in the cemetery. His was a double plot but Edna had a fear of being buried alive and insisted on cremation. Sometimes Grace took flowers to place on the spot but although, unlike Edna, he was there beneath the soil in his entirety, she had no sense of his presence. The visits grew increasingly infrequent.

When they got back Alex unloaded the tree and stood it in a bucket filled with water. 'I'll get the rest of the roots out tomorrow,' he said 'then plant this little beaut.'

Grace nodded. They stopped long enough for a cup of tea and then set out for their walk and the pub.

The Warren had, as its name suggested, in the distant past been enclosed for the breeding of rabbits. Rising sharply on a headland, over the years, paths had been scooped out through sandy hollows, where straggly hazels overhung, offering welcome shade. The banks were pocked with rabbit holes, descendants of those original imports. Occasional, bigger earth workings had been constructed by badgers. There was a scurry in front of them as a sand lizard scuttled for shelter.

'God, I haven't seen one of those in ages.' Grace followed its path but it was nowhere to be seen.

'We've got lizards coming out of our ears.' Alex stopped to get his breath. 'Well, not literally, of course, but there are plenty of them.'

Grace wondered what it would be like to see a kangaroo in its natural habitat, a koala. She remained silent, not wishing to give him the impression that she had any wish to go to Australia.

They walked for a mile, coming out of the hollow on to the chalk where the short springy turf was nibbled down by the rabbits. The view was spectacular, diamond sea, a natural bay, the remains of a once busy pier reaching out into the water. At the headland the path descended again until they reached the cliff at the edge called Heatherwood Point. From the foundations of the old Victorian fort there was a striking view of the famous Needles rocks threading out to sea.

They remained for some time, simply taking in the view. Where they stood, the fort had been erected to guard the narrow strait between the island and neighbouring Hurst Point. Any enemy ship daring to pass between the two had risked being blown out of the water. Now both fortifications were ghosts of what they might once have been. It occurred to her that one day they might take a boat across to Hurst and view the old castle. She felt relieved at having another project to amuse her guest with. Meanwhile he skipped up and down the broken steps, poked his head into empty gun emplacements and she stood back to watch, enchanted by his lithe movement. In truth, he was a rather beautiful man.

Afterwards, they made their way to the nearby pub that had once been frequented by writers and painters who came to soak up the atmosphere of the landscape. The surrounding land had belonged to no less a person than Alfred Lord Tennyson. Today, only a couple of locals were in the bar drinking beer. Alex ordered a pint of the local brew and Grace tentatively asked for a glass of red wine. She wondered if his expertise might make him turn his nose up in disgust at the mass-produced liquid but he set it in front of her without comment.

For a while they were both silent but gradually the drinks relaxed them and Alex began to tell her about his hopes for the future. They were tentative, wondering if he might persuade his father to sell up and move to France.

'It feels good there,' he finished. 'If he needs to be surrounded by grapes, there's plenty of scope.' In spite of herself Grace felt a quickening of her pulse at the thought that Joe might suddenly be so much nearer. To ward it off, she asked, 'What about your mum?' She hoped to hear something to Meg's disadvantage. She chided herself but even now she needed to know that Joe had made a mistake. Emboldened, she added, 'Do you think your parents have been happy?'

Alex considered the question. 'They've muddled along well enough.'

It was all that he had to say on the subject.

On the way home he seemed withdrawn and distracted. Grace had no idea what he might be thinking. She tried one or two topics of conversation but they soon dried up. She chided herself for asking about his parents. Perhaps he guessed her motives, its malice, and was angry.

Back at the cottage she offered him a brandy. 'Are you trying to get me drunk?' he asked. She blushed.

Seeing her discomfort he said, 'I was only joking, Grace.'

His misjudged humour only added to the unease. She poured him out a drink and they struggled through another half an hour before she could decently suggest that they went to bed.

'To be honest, I'm pretty bushed,' he said, picking up both glasses and taking them to the kitchen.

'Well, goodnight then.'

She stood up and grabbed her library book.

'Good night, Grace. Thanks for another good day. I'll sort that tree out in the morning.'

'Thanks.'

Suddenly tomorrow seemed like an epic journey that she would have to endure. This had been a mistake, inviting him here. Oh well, at least she knew now, knew who he was, saw that the fruit of Joe's loins had been made flesh.

She punched her pillow and forced herself to think of the maple tree. Planting it and visiting the churchyard—at least that might fill in an hour or two. Three more days to go. How the hell was she going to survive it?

CHAPTER EIGHT

In spite of the fact that she had drunk far less wine the evening before, Grace awoke feeling heavy and hung over. At the thought of her visitor sleeping through the wall, her limbs seemed incapable of movement. Something had happened last night to upset him. Whatever it was, she was anxious in case it was something she had said or done. At the thought of his silent, distracted presence she had no desire to see him. If she had a choice, she thought she would rather stay in bed.

She glanced at the window where the curtains were half parted. The sun sparkled with that fresh exuberance that suggested a fine day ahead. No good lying there; just get up and try to be a hostess.

Showered and dressed, she finally ventured downstairs to discover that the back door was ajar and, to her amazement, she saw that Alex was already at work. The surprise drew her outside and she wandered across the still dewy grass.

'You're up early.'

He stopped and stretched his back, leaning briefly on his spade. 'Got to get on. Can't stay in bed on a beautiful day like this.'

She gazed again at the hole, wondering if she should have consulted the nursery people about whether to put any particular soil around the new tree. Something grey and slender poked from beneath the earth. She wondered whether to investigate further but instead asked, 'Would you like breakfast?'

'That would be ace.' She returned to the kitchen to rustle something up.

Alex came in five minutes later, stopping to wash his hands at the kitchen sink, and she was reminded of her father. Perhaps the cottage regretted all those years when no man had stood where he now was. Inconsequentially, she thought a house needs a man, it completes it.

Alex dried his hands and came to the table. He said, 'Sorry if I was rather quiet last night. Thoughts, you know? To be honest, I'm not looking forward to going home.'

Grace resisted the temptation to say she understood. She had no idea whether she did or not. She knew her own regrets and failures, but Alex's might have been something else altogether.

'How long will you be in the garden?' she asked instead.

'An hour?'

'What would you like to do after that?'

'Well, if you'd like a day on your own I can go off somewhere?'

'Of course not—not unless you'd rather be on your own?'

'Of course I wouldn't.' He suddenly grinned.

113

'Let's make the most of this, shall we? This is such a beaut island. I'd like to take you out but I don't suppose there is anywhere local that you haven't been?'

She thought that he was probably right, then suggested that on the following day they should take the boat to Hurst.

'Sounds great. How about a walk on a beach somewhere today and a pub lunch?'

'Sounds great,' she echoed and relaxed. Everything was back on an even keel.

After breakfast, he went back to his task and as she washed up Grace watched him digging and bending. There was a rhythm to his stroke. After a few moments he stopped to take off his shirt and the sight of his naked back sent a disturbing ripple through her. Really, she thought to herself!

She was about to look away when she realized that he was bending down, peering into the hole. He moved closer, staring with intensity then he sat back and leaned forward again. She was reminded of the way the cat used to approach something alien, at the same time longing to touch but afraid of the consequences.

Alex was now standing upright, still staring at the hole. With a shake of his head he turned and hurried towards the house.

Grace was in time to meet him at the door.

'What's the matter?'

He shook his head again, in disbelief. 'I . . . I

think perhaps you need to call the police.'

'What?' She frowned her disbelief at him.

'The police. You aren't going to believe this, but over there, where I've been digging, over in that hole—I think I've found a body.'

*   *   *

The police car looked incongruous in the rural peace of the garden. It was parked across the gateway as if to prevent any attempt at escape. Grace and Alex stood side by side as two uniformed officers made their way to the wall, bending cautiously to investigate the hole, much as Alex had done earlier. After a moment they both stood upright staring at the site as if for inspiration. The younger of the two tilted his cap back and scratched his head. He began to speak into his radio, nodding at his invisible listener, while his companion mirrored his actions as if to add weight to his conversation. There was something lost about them, little boys in men's shoes. Grace found herself thinking of Agatha Christie mysteries, Miss Marple.

A series of cameos swept through her mind, a murderer shooting or stabbing his victim right there on her lawn and secreting the body beneath the wall. She tried not to consider that she might have been alone in the house and easily become a second victim. Although the cottage was detached and surrounded by quite a sizeable garden she had never felt any sense of isolation until now. In any case, until Edna's death there had always been a second person in the house. This was the first time that her vulnerability dawned on her and any excitement quickly dissipated. As if sensing her feeling, Alex put his arm around her shoulders.

'Are you all right?'

She nodded, not quite trusting her voice.

At that moment another car arrived, lights flashing and two more men emerged. By now the first two had erected a barrier of wide tape around the hole. One of the new arrivals carried a camera and proceeded to photograph the site from every angle. The second, who, from her passion for TV detective stories, she deduced was a police surgeon, pulled on a white all-in-one garment that reminded her of a babygro and stepped down into the hole to examine the contents. When he emerged, he merely shook his head and shrugged then, after a brief conversation, returned to his car.

Grace noticed that a straggle of people had appeared as if from nowhere and were craning to see what all the excitement was about. She could just imagine the gossip. Her neighbours would dine out on this for years.

For an age, everyone seemed to stand around, then one of the original policemen came across to them. He was big, burly, a

Mr Plod.

'Who discovered it?' he asked, looking from one to the other.

'I did.' Alex waited.

'Well, you realize that it isn't recent?' There was an edge of accusation in his voice, perhaps a hint that they were wasting police time.

'No. I just saw the bones and phoned you.'

'When I say it's not recent, I mean that it's ancient. It is almost certainly not a case for the police but forensics will tell us more. Meanwhile, a bloke from the archaeology department is on his way. They get touchy if we move the body without telling them first.'

Grace's overall feeling was one of relief. This act of violence, if violence it was, hadn't happened while she and Edna had been blissfully unaware in the cottage. She wondered what Edna would make of it and a surprise spasm of regret claimed her. Perhaps this was how it was going to be, unexpected times of grief just when she was convinced that she felt nothing about Edna's passing.

'Perhaps he should be on the other side of the wall,' Grace said aloud, 'In the cemetery.'

The officer shrugged. 'I couldn't say Madam. How did you come to find it?'

'I was digging a hole to plant a tree.'

Mr Plod nodded. 'Well, nothing to get too excited about. I'll just take down the particulars.' He took out a notebook and pencil flicked through endless pages and rested the book against his generous stomach. Grace half-expected him to lick the tip of the pencil before laboriously writing down their names and the address.

'You both live here?' he asked. Alex explained how he was visiting.

'You're from Australia?' He sounded as if he thought Alex might be making it up, some elaborate alibi. After several moments of staring at him, he looked back to his book.

'Anyone else in the house?' They both shook their heads.

'Well, apart from your digging, there's no other signs of recent disturbance.' He thought for a moment. 'Perhaps he does belong in the churchyard. They might have moved the boundary wall at some time.'

As far back as Grace could remember, the old wall had always been where it was, muted and grey and covered with ivy.

When he had finished writing down their 'particulars', as he called them, he thought for a moment before saying, 'Of course, your chappie might have been a criminal, someone not entitled to a Christian burial.'

Grace's own thoughts began to overtake her. Might he have been a warlock, someone practising the black arts? On the other hand, perhaps he was just a poor man who stole a sheep or a loaf of bread. Suddenly she was desperately keen to find out.

As if thinking along similar lines, Alex said,

'Perhaps he was a highwayman.'

Grace imagined him brandishing his firearms with Black Bess rearing up before they galloped off after the stagecoach.

'He's not Ned Kelly.' The officer gave him a glare.

Suitably chastened, Alex kept any other thoughts to himself. The constable sighed and closed his notebook.

'You aren't planning on leaving tomorrow?' he asked Alex.

Grace thought of all those stories where the suspect was told not to leave town.

At that moment an elderly van trundled down the lane and stopped at the gate. Someone dressed in grey cord trousers and a vivid red sweater climbed out. He was what they referred to as of wiry build and had a shock of grey hair. Speaking briefly to one of the policemen, he in turn went across to the hole and bent over to examine it, nodding to himself as if to confirm some theory. Briefly he spoke into some recording device then snapping it shut, pushed it into his pocket and clambered out, brushing soil from his knees. A short conversation with the uniformed men followed. They in turn nodded towards Grace and Alex, and the newcomer started off in their direction. Meanwhile, the uniformed men now produced spades from the boot of their car and began carefully to dig.

'Good afternoon. I'm Austin Morris.'

Before they could respond he added, 'I know, ludicrous name, isn't it. My father, whose name was John, was crazy about sports cars and had the audacity to name me Austin Healy Morris. How embarrassing is that?'

Alex laughed and held out his hand then, remembering that he was just a guest, turned to Grace. 'This is Grace Harrison. This is her cottage. I'm just a friend on a visit.'

Austin Morris shook her hand. 'Nice to meet you. For my sins, I'm from the County Archaeology Department. Anything over a hundred years old and the police pass it on to us. Yon laddie in that hole is certainly older than that.'

Grace detected the faint Scottish timbre of his voice. He had very pale grey-blue eyes that reminded her of the sea on a sunny day when it sparkled with diamond light.

'We're going to take him away now,' he said. 'Then we'll give him the once over.'

'Will you let us know what you find?' Under the keen scrutiny of his gaze she felt her face growing hot. 'I . . . I feel responsible for him as he was in our garden.'

'Quite understandable. Don't worry, I'll make sure you hear all the gory details.' He suddenly grinned. His lips twitched as if at some private joke and she gave an answering smile.

Out in the lane an ambulance had arrived, not a white one with flashing lights but a dark-blue vehicle, more like a hearse. Two men emerged with a stretcher and proceeded to load the remains. Grace began to wish that she had got a better look. Discretely, they covered him over before placing him in the ambulance.

Austin Morris stood quietly beside them, watching the proceedings. 'A bit of mystery,' he said, 'although the cemetery next door probably holds the answer. Given time, we'll see what we can come up with.'

Grace thanked him then, as the retinue prepared to drive off, she realized that she should have asked if it was still all right to plant the tree but somehow it no longer felt quite decent.

His arm still around her shoulders, Alex led the way back indoors. Outside in the lane the neighbours dispersed now that there was no more to be seen. Perhaps they had been hoping to be asked what sort of people the Harrison were and whether they were likely to have buried someone in the garden.

'Well.' Alex broke the silence first but there was nothing to say. Something amazing had just happened. Neither of them quite knew how to deal with it.

They abandoned the idea of looking around the church. Instead, they drove into the town where there was lots of activity and plenty of people. Alex decided to buy himself a new sweater in preparation for the coming Australian winter. More postcards, sand souvenirs, blown-glass trinkets were quietly amassed to deflect the sombre mood.

They walked a long way along the riverbank, stopped to watch the seabirds that ventured as far as the quay, whiled away each minute until there was really no excuse not to go home.

'What do you think?' Alex asked her, as they snacked on crackers and cheese and Alex poured out wine.

'I don't know. I can't believe that all the time I've been here someone has been lying buried just beneath my feet. It just feels wrong.'

'And yet over the wall there are dozens—hundreds—of dead people.'

'That's different. It's as if they got to the end of a natural journey and were accepted for who they were. This chap, our chap, feels outcast and desperate.'

He nodded. 'Perhaps you could plant the tree in his memory, whoever he was?'

'Perhaps I could.' She looked gratefully at him. He in turn was watching her. She couldn't interpret his expression.

'What are you thinking?' she asked.

He took a big gulp of wine. 'About you. I was just thinking how lucky I am to have come here. You might not know it but you have made me feel so much better—about everything.'

'But I haven't done anything.'

He smiled. 'Oh, you have. You have accepted me as a pathetic deserted husband quietly going to the dogs. You haven't once suggested that I should pull myself together.'

'Is that what you are, a pathetic deserted husband?'

'I think that's what I was before I arrived here.'

'But I haven't done anything,' she repeated.

'Perhaps you didn't need to. Perhaps just who you are has been enough.'

Grace gulped down more wine. She had no idea where this conversation was going but the warmth along her limbs wanted to follow it through.

Alex suddenly said, 'When was the last time a man kissed you?'

Grace's eyebrows shot up in surprise. 'I . . . I can't remember.' It suddenly seemed funny and she began to laugh.

'Then it is time somebody did—kiss you, that is.'

'Alex! You can't be serious.' She leaned away from him as he put his glass on the coffee table and turned towards her.

Her eyes grew increasingly large with disbelief as he said 'Oh yes, Grace, I'm very serious indeed. I don't know what this means but I have a very urgent desire to kiss you.'

She went to laugh again but the intensity of his presence stopped her. Instead she looked at his face, its contours, his amber eyes, his very kissable mouth.

She laughed again, uncertainly. 'This is madness.'

'Perhaps it is.' He moved closer, reached out to smooth her cheek and bent his head to touch her lips.

She had no idea what happened, no inkling that like some dammed river she was about to explode with pent-up feeling. Within moments they were struggling with each other's clothes, undoing buttons and buckles, shrugging arms out of sleeves and legs out of trousers. Suddenly, unbelievably naked, Grace gave herself up to the deluge of feeling. Somehow they had sunk on to the floor, knocked aside the coffee table. Now they lay panting and spent, flotsam mysteriously washed up on a distant shore.

'Phew!' Alex disentangled his limbs from hers, leaned up on an elbow and smoothed the damp hair from her cheek. 'Jeez, Grace, that was quite something.'

She couldn't speak. The suddenness of it, the unthinkable abandon and pleasure, it took away every thought.

'You,' he said, 'Are one hell of a woman.'

CHAPTER NINE

Grace awoke in the night to the familiar contours of her bed, only there was something different. A tidal wave of realization swept over her as she became aware of the body next to hers, the warmth emanating from beneath the covers, the regular rhythm of breathing. Her eyes jerked open.

It was still dark, probably about two or three o'clock. She lay still, trying to amass her thoughts. In any other circumstances she would have concluded that she had been dreaming but the man next to her was real enough. Besides which, her limbs ached as if she had climbed the Matterhorn. This was ridiculous!

Taking care not to disturb him, she climbed out of bed and tiptoed to the kitchen, dragging her dressing gown with her. She was naked— naked, her old body exposed to this vigorous man—who was young enough to be her son!

She tried to calm herself, to get a hold on the adolescent teenage tremors that enveloped her at the thought of their lovemaking. How had she allowed things to get so out of hand? Oh God, what would his father say? At the ludicrousness of the question she nearly burst out laughing. This was ridiculous in the extreme.

At that moment she remembered the other drama of the day before, the discovery of some poor man buried in her garden. More sober now, she wondered what it all meant. The police had been adamant that it wasn't a case for them and implied that there was no sign of physical violence, but she needed to know what had happened to him and how long he had been there. More important, who was he?

From habit, she plugged in the kettle, grabbed a mug and spooned coffee into it. On any other night she might have chosen warm milk to get her back to sleep but just at the moment the idea of returning to bed was impossible. She could, of course, creep back to the box room but what sort of message would that give out? Perhaps that was what she should do, pretend that the evening before had never happened, try to put their relationship back on to its original footing.

'Can I have one?' Alex wandered into the kitchen, tousled, boyish, now wearing just jeans. His bare torso looked vulnerable, inviting. He slumped down opposite her and glared blearily at the clock. 'Ten past three,' he announced.

Grace made the coffee in silence. She had no idea what to say. As she placed it in front of him he said, 'I hope you're not going to tell me you are old enough to be my mother?' The accuracy of her thoughts kept her silent.

He spooned sugar into his cup, stirred it

vigorously and set the spoon aside. 'I hope you aren't full of regret either.'

She shrugged. 'This sort of thing is outside of my experience,' she said.

He took a drink, put the mug back on the table. 'It might surprise you to know that it is outside of mine, as well. Since I married I have been a faithful husband. Even having been deserted and then set loose in Europe, I avoided any temptation. Then you come along.'

He smiled, teasing. She made a who-knows gesture, lost again for words.

'I can't imagine I'm much of a temptation,' she started, 'After all, I'm . . .'

The words faded as he finished her sentence. 'Old enough to be my mother? I knew you'd have to say it some time or other.'

'I just don't know what to think.'

'Then don't think at all. Look, let's go back to bed—to sleep if you insist although . . .'

Her ancient hormones were working overtime. When he reached out and took her hand she found herself moving magnet-like towards him. In bed, they made love again, a long, indulgent surge of pleasure. For the first time in her life Grace cried out with the joy of it. That had never happened before—not with Joe because she had been too inexperienced, not with the occasional men who had briefly engaged her attention when she had made excuses to Edna for her sudden outings. 'You be careful,' Edna's suspicions as always to the fore. They had been grey, faceless shadows, those men, hardly rousing a response from her lonely body, certainly no one important enough to leave home for. Then this. Perhaps its attraction was that it couldn't last. There could be no complications, no aftermath. Alex was leaving in a few days. There was no question of going with him, or of him staying behind. He lay heavily upon her, his cheek nestled into her neck. She thought, *Perhaps I am getting back at his father?* With a sigh of contentment she concluded that if this was revenge, it was worth waiting for.

They slept again, heavily, and by the time they got up the sun was shining an accusing light through the window, right on to the bed. Alex had hardly come out of the bathroom when there was a knock at the front door.

'I'll go.' Grace hurried into her dressing gown and went to answer it.

'Good morning, Austin Morris.'

Today he was wearing a vivid blue sweater. She thought that this must be his trademark, vibrant jumpers. Perhaps he was afraid of falling down a hole somewhere, and this way he was bound to be noticed. The blue of the sweater gave emphasis to the grey-blue of his eyes.

It must have been guilt, although for what she wasn't quite sure, but the thought of Alex, newly washed and with damp hair filled her with embarrassment.

'I . . . I was about to shower,' she said, stepping back and wordlessly inviting him in.

'Sorry to disturb you.' He stepped into the hall, wiping his feet although there wasn't even a speck of dirt on them. He glanced around at the hall. 'Lovely old cottage.'

She nodded. 'Would you like coffee?'

He shook his head. 'I just thought I'd pop in and tell you what I've found out about your body.' He was still looking around him as he added, 'I was curious so I got up very early.'

'You've already been to work?'

'I have indeed. I . . . I don't sleep very well.'

At that moment Alex came into the room, fully dressed, hair combed, looking cool and in control.

Acknowledging him, Austin Morris said, 'As we said yesterday, this isn't a case for the police. Your young lady out there must be at least three hundred years old.'

'Lady?'

'Yes, the skeleton is female. She was quite young too when she died, not more than eighteen.'

Grace did a double take. She had not for a moment considered that the body might be that of a woman. 'Do you know what she died of?' she asked.

'Not yet. I might be able to find out more.'

'What will happen to her now?'

Austin shrugged. 'For the moment she'll

probably be added to all the bones that are already cluttering up our offices. You might like to come and have a look sometime.' He backed towards the door, a busy man needing to get on. As he opened the latch he added, 'There was just one other thing. She wasn't English, your young girl. From the shape of her skull I'm pretty certain she was African.'

'African?' Alex and Grace echoed the word.

'What on earth would an African girl be doing here all that time ago?' Grace thought that even now strangers were comparatively rare in the village. Back then she would have been as alien as a Martian.

As he opened the door, Austin said, 'We could try and find out but I'm pretty sure that is something we will never know.' He handed Grace a card with his contact details. 'Just in case you want to get in touch,' he said. His eyes rested on her just a moment longer than felt strictly necessary then, with a wave of his hand, he was gone.

'Well.' Grace and Alex were both lost for anything more to say. The person in the garden was no longer a sheep rustler or a petty thief. Suddenly he, she was someone altogether different, a young, black girl, hardly adult, dying miles from home, denied a Christian burial. Not thinking of herself as Christian, Grace personally would not regret being buried outside the retaining walls of the churchyard, but back then it was about as rejecting as it could get. 'Poor little girl,' she said aloud.

She got up to head for the bathroom just as there was a second knock at the door. She and Alex stared at each other as if interrupted in the middle of some misdemeanour. 'I'll go,' said Grace, wondering who on earth it might be this time.

It was Molly. As Grace opened the door, Molly took in her undressed state, her head raised as if scenting prey. Alex had conveniently disappeared back into the kitchen.

'I came to see what on earth was going on yesterday,' Molly announced. There was an edge of reproach in her voice, a best friend not made party to the exciting events.

'Come on in. I'll put the kettle on.' From habit, Molly made for the kitchen and Grace followed with sinking heart, sensing that Alex was about to get the once over, but when her guest pushed open the door, the room was empty. He must have slipped out of the back door and into the garden. Indeed, Grace could see him over by the grave.

'I heard all about it from Mrs Gregory,' said Molly, also staring out of the window. 'She said the police were here and everything. What happened?'

'We discovered a skeleton in the garden. Alex—my visitor—was digging up that old plum tree for me and the skeleton was

131

underneath. It isn't recent. The police came but they aren't interested.'

'What's going to happen now then?'

'Nothing.' Grace didn't want to talk about it. She needed time and space to absorb all the implications.

Molly tilted her head to one side to avoid the window bars so that she could get a better look at the man in the garden.

'That him?' she asked.

Grace bit back the desire to say, 'Who else would it be?' instead answering 'Yes.'

'What's he like?'

'Very pleasant. Easy to get along with.' At the thought of how easy, Grace felt her face grow warm. The change was not lost on her friend.

'Cosy then, is it, having him to stay?'

'I don't know—'

'Come off it, you look like the cat that's got the cream. You haven't been—not you and young Lochinvar out there—have you? What would his father say?'

Suddenly they both exploded into laughter, friends again, sharing secrets. 'Shush, he's coming back.'

Alex came in, prepared to be charming to this unidentified woman.

'Alex, this is my friend Molly. She lives just down the road. She heard about the excitement yesterday and came to find out if there was anything she could do.'

'G'day. Alex Weston.' He held out his hand and Molly took it looking rather flustered. He added, 'My parents knew Grace and she's very kindly put me up for a few days before I fly home to Oz.'

'Enjoying yourself, are you?'

Wicked Molly, thought Grace. She turned to make a pot of tea.

'This is a lovely island,' said Alex, either ignoring or unaware of the innuendo. 'I'm hoping to see a bit more of it before I leave on Friday.'

'Do you think you'll be back?'

He shrugged. 'You never know with life, it turns up some unexpected things.'

Grace made tea for herself and Molly, coffee for Alex. She could tell that Molly wanted to get him out of the way so that they could talk. Clearly getting the hint, he gulped down his coffee then said, 'I'm going to pop down to the post office, send a letter. I'll get a newspaper too.'

Once he was gone, Molly said 'Tell me more—everything.'

'There's nothing to tell.'

As Molly looked disbelieving, she said, 'It just sort of happened—two lonely people and all that.'

'Well good for you. What's it like having a toy boy?'

A toy boy, Grace grinned. 'Actually, it's bloody marvellous.' Seeing her friend's expression sober, she said, 'We both know this is just a temporary thing, no strings and all that, but while it lasts, it's . . . '

'Bloody marvellous,' Molly added for her. 'Gawd, I wish it was with Reg. He's had me up half the night. He convinced himself he had to go to work and I had the devil's own job to stop him going out at two o'clock. That's when I saw the light on at your house. I nearly came over but I didn't want to disturb you. In the circumstances, it's a good job I didn't!'

'You must go to the doctor,' Grace insisted. 'Perhaps they can give Reg something to make him sleep, and anyway, they ought to assess the situation.'

Molly nodded, looking worn and distressed.

'I'd better go,' she said. 'Goodness knows what he is up to now. When—when his nibs has gone, come round and have tea, or lunch or something.'

'Of course I will—and don't hesitate to come over if you need anything. It doesn't matter if I've got a visitor. Anyway, he's very nice. He might be able to help.'

Molly nodded, not far from tears. 'Say goodbye to Lover Boy then—and you be careful. Don't go getting emotionally involved.'

'I won't. Honest.'

She saw Molly to the door and watched her walk down the path. As she was unlatching the gate, Alex came back and they stopped for a few words before going their separate ways. He carried an armful of flowers and for a second she felt pleasure at the thought that they were for her. She then remembered that they were going to visit his great-grandparents' grave. This must be what they were for. Seconds later he came back in.

'Your friend told me to take care of you,' he said. 'She looks like a canny old bird—whoops, sorry—about the old, that is.'

'She is canny,' Grace agreed. 'And she's fifteen years older than me, so I'll let that pass.'

'Right then, any more visitors, or can we have the rest of the day to ourselves?'

CHAPTER TEN

Alex was all for planting the tree that morning. 'We don't want to let it dry out,' he said, but Grace still felt that it was indecently hasty. Besides, she had been mentally planning to dedicate it to an unknown man and now that man had mysteriously changed into a girl. She needed time to think about it.

'I'd like to have a good look at the hole first,' she said.

'Why don't we both go and look in the graveyard? There might be some clue as to how she got there. Perhaps they did move the boundary. The vicar might know. Anyway, I've got plenty of flowers. I bought some for my grandparents' grave and your Dad's but you can always place some beside her resting place.'

Thoughtful Alex.

She doubted if the vicar would know anything. He was recent and besides, he had two other parishes to look after. In terms of longevity and history, this was his 'best' church but she didn't know whether he was in any way a local history buff.

While she showered, Alex rustled up the breakfast. This was good, having someone fussing over you. Grace couldn't remember when it had last happened, certainly not since Edna had become old and fragile. The caring had been all on one side.

She ate hungrily. All that nocturnal physical activity, she thought, and warmed at the memory, alarmingly ready for more. When she had finished eating she said, 'I'm just going to pop outside, just to take a look.'

'I'll wash up.' It got even better!

Outside, it felt like magic, a moist expectant coolness that could only herald the arrival of a warm, sunny day. Heavy dew still coated the grass and leaves with translucent emerald. Everything glistened, waiting for this wondrous bursting forth of new life. How wonderful it must be to be able to capture the colours, how the reds and oranges and purples all blended together in unlikely harmony. Grace thought for a moment of Austin Morris's jumpers. Did he have them in a whole range of rainbow colours?

As she approached the hole its emptiness grew increasingly awesome. She stood, head bowed, looking at the raw earth, the remnants of torn roots that Alex had wrenched away. 'I'm sorry,' she said to the spirit of the girl who had lain for so long in this forgotten place. 'I'm sorry that we disturbed you.' A thought occurred to her. 'Look, I'll make sure you are properly reburied.' She couldn't bear the thought of her bones lining some soulless shelf. She'd have a word with the vicar about putting her where she belonged in the churchyard.

'Ready?' Alex came over carrying some of the flowers. 'Let's have a look round next door then you can decide what to do with the tree.'

'Right.' She linked her arm in his and they went through the narrow wooden gate that led into the back lane and across into the graveyard.

'You never met your great-grandparents?' she asked, thinking of the Solomons ensconced for the last twenty years in the cemetery. It helped to keep her thoughts away from the dead girl.

'No, they wouldn't fly out to see us even though Mum and Dad offered to pay for them and this is my first visit to Europe. Dad came

137

over to see them—as you know.' He halted uncertainly and she realized that he was hazy about the circumstances of their meeting.

'What about your other grandparents?' she asked to keep them both away from the subject.

'Dad's parents? They're both dead now but I knew them quite well. Grandpop ran the winery with Dad. Grandma was fond of me.'

'She never came back to England either?'

'She wanted to when her parents got ill but the first time she was having chemotherapy and the second she broke her ankle. It was almost like it wasn't meant to be.'

If she had come I'd have met her, thought Grace. As it was, Edna had taken it upon herself to write to her on the progress of her parents. Gradually, a regular correspondence between the Harrisons and the Weston family had been established. When the senior Westons died and Edna became too frail to keep up the connection, it fell to Grace to write directly to Joe and his wife, only Christmas cards but it was enough to keep the memories alive, the wound from quite healing.

Alex said, 'I've got some photos of back home. I'll show you later. I guess you won't recognize the old man.'

The old man, her eternal lover.

They walked up the gravel path to the church entrance and Alex lifted the iron ring that rotated to lift the heavy latch. Inside it

138

was nearly dark, a huge, cavernous silence. The ornate, carved pulpit stood at one end, polished rails separating off the chancel from the main body.

They both wandered around separately. Alex stopped to read the plaques on the wall, stooping to consider the burials marked with stone slabs beneath their feet.

'This is one beaut church,' he commented.

There was no one else around. They spent a long time looking at arches and windows, reading the visitors' guide, and Alex put some money in the box to help with restoration.

'Are any of your relatives buried in here?' he asked.

'No, they were far too humble to be allowed inside'

'I don't suppose there are any of mine?'

'I don't think so.' She hesitated. 'We always thought Mr Solomons was Jewish although he couldn't have been because he ran the Sunday school and the youth group and just about everything else.'

'Perhaps he was a convert, not a natural-born Christian—whatever that is.'

Grace didn't know either.

'The churchyard?' He raised his eyebrows and took her arm.

She took him directly to see the plot where Mr and Mrs Solomons were buried. Strangers lived in their house now. Only very rarely did she remember those journeys around the block so that she could walk past and hope to catch a glimpse of Joe.

Alex was reading the inscription on the headstone. 'Asleep at last in the bosom of the Lord,' it said. Mrs Solomons had died eighteen years ago, Mr Solomons five years before that. It was another era.

Alex was silent and she knew that he must be thinking of the family he never knew. 'Do you think it would be morbid to photograph the headstone?' he asked. 'I'd like to show it to the folks back home.'

'I don't think it would be morbid.' She waited while he checked on the position of the sun, bent with easy grace to focus on the grave. His flowers lay in abundance on the surface. Grace went to fetch one of the jars by the graveyard tap and filled it with water. She couldn't bring herself to leave the flowers to die of thirst.

She showed him her own family graves, the Harrisons, the Dores, the Millmores, the Galpines. They were all linked by marriages stretching back through the ages. She placed a swathe of flowers on her father's grave, regretting the recent neglect. Silently she told him, 'I'll get Mum's ashes from the undertakers soon, then she can be with you.' For a treacherous moment she thought how good it would be if Alex was still around to perform a simple ceremony with her, scattering Edna's ashes on to Gordon's grave, but he wouldn't be, so she put the thought out of her head.

He took her hand as they read more epitaphs, 'Gone to a better place', 'At peace at last', 'A faithful servant rewarded in heaven'. Her dad's grave merely bore his name and the date of his death, 17 February 1967—such a long time ago. Perhaps she should have put some words of love on the stone. It was such a natural thing to do. She thought of the girl in the garden, her grave unmarked, her name unknown. In spite of the sun, she shivered.

'Shall we go?'

They walked back past the Solomons's cottage and Grace told him everything she could remember about his great-grandparents. He stopped to photograph the cottage where his own grandmother had grown up. This would no doubt stir up more family memories.

Grace was glad to get back to the cottage. 'I suppose it is too late to take that boat to Hurst Castle?' Alex asked and she realized that so far he had seen only a fraction of the locality.

'It is. Perhaps we could go tomorrow.'

He nodded. 'You realize that tomorrow is my last full day? I'll need to leave at lunchtime the next day for the flight home.'

She felt the knee-jerk reaction, the realization that all of this was going to end so soon. Keep calm. Don't show any emotion about it. We're both grown-ups. We knew that this was only an interlude.

Seeking some solitude, she collected up the rest of the flowers that he had left in the kitchen sink. 'I'm just going to put these in water and place them by the grave,' she said.

'Can I start some lunch?' When she hesitated, he added 'I'm a dab hand with the frying pan.'

'OK.'

She took the bouquet outside. Would it be sensible to plant the tree this afternoon? She thought that if they didn't, the time might slip away and he would leave without doing it. She could manage well enough on her own but somehow the tree might not only be a memorial to the young girl, but also to him and their brief time together.

The boundary wall behind the grave was covered in ivy. Grace wasn't sure what made her do it but at the thought of all those epitaphs she parted the ivy and examined the surface. To her surprise, unlike the roughness of the stones on either side, the area looked smooth. A flat piece of stone had been inserted into the fabric. Scrabbling to remove the ivy a thousand tiny roots gave up their toeholds, tearing beneath her hands. Underneath it was still damp and myriad wood lice made a dive for shelter. She shuddered at the thought of touching them, perhaps squashing them, but after a few seconds they had all disappeared. Breathlessly she ran her fingers over the surface. Surely it wasn't her imagination, there were markings here, indentations in the stone that couldn't be random? She went to run into the house and get a brush to clean it off but then stopped. This was a moment she wanted to herself. If there was something here she wanted to discover it on her own.

Wiping her hands on to the damp grass then drying them down her jeans, she began to trace the outline again with her fingertips. Yes, she was certain of it; there were words on the stone. Perhaps the lonely stranger hadn't been forgotten after all!

Now she hurried into the house. Alex was cracking eggs into a bowl.

'Omelette?' he asked then stopped what he was doing as he saw her expression.

'What is it?'

'I've found something. On the wall.' She went to the sink and filled a pail of soapy water, dug an old scrubbing brush from the kitchen cupboard and prepared to go back out again.

'Shall I come and see?'

'If you like.' It touched her that he didn't take it for granted that he should be involved. Her heart was thumping as she returned to the site and climbed into the hole, the better to reach. She felt a shudder at the possibility that some small part of the girl might remain in the hole—a toenail perhaps, a tooth? She physically drew herself up to be as unintrusive as possible.

Dirty soapy water trickled down into the grass behind the grave. Where she scrubbed as the water dried, marks appeared in the stonework. She still couldn't work out what they were. Close behind her, Alex said, 'It might just be coincidence. Perhaps they are natural markings in the stone.'

'But why would they put the stone here? The rest of the wall is just plain rocks and boulders.'

Another idea occurred to her. She hurried back to the house returning with a towel to dry the wall properly, some greaseproof paper and an old crayon. 'Brass rubbing!' She said setting to work to trace the outline of the indentations.

It was difficult to get into the corners but some sort of pattern was definitely emerging on the paper. When she had finished she climbed out and held it up to the light.

'Can you see what it is?'

Alex stood just behind her, leaning over her shoulder. She couldn't stop herself from moving back towards him, some hidden magnet connecting her to his body.

'It looks like some sort of monogram, letters intertwined. Let's take it indoors and have a proper look. I think there are some numbers as well, a date perhaps?'

They hurried back to the cottage. The broken eggs formed an abandoned swirl of yellow, white and orange in the bowl.

The deciphering was still uncertain but after much tilting and staring they arrived at a consensus. At the top were two letters, an *R* and an *H*. Below them, intricately curling towards them was a single letter *P*. Underneath, they were pretty certain that it was the date, 1689.

'This is amazing. We have her initials and the date she died.'

'Well . . .' He sounded cautious, pouring cold water on her excitement. 'The initials might have belonged to two people, an *RH* and a *P*. Or they might not be connected to the grave at all.'

Grace dismissed this immediately. 'Perhaps P was the wife—*R* and *PH*?'

'It could be.'

'Perhaps we could go to the Public Record Office and see if they can identify it?'

'When?'

'After lunch?'

He glanced briefly out at the grave before saying, 'OK.' Then after a pause, 'I could always plant the tree when we get back.'

She guessed that he might have preferred to do something else on this bright spring afternoon but the urge to find out was too great.

After lunch they drove into Newport to the record office. It was housed in a lofty Victorian building with a view across the valley and over the town. In its heyday it must have been a sought after place to live, a stone's throw away from the quay. Now, a non-stop stream of traffic trundled past the top of the road. Grace parked the car and they both stopped to take in the view. The parish church dominated the skyline in competition with the ugly scar of County Hall. The River Medina, once the town's lifeblood, emitted blinding shocks of sunlight when glimpsed between the houses.

Inside, the building felt quite Dickensian, large old tables that might have come out of Victorian boardrooms, bookshelves filled with outsize tomes, Debrett, County histories, Kelly's directories, a range of books of local interest. Rows of filing cabinets lined the walls housing a largely outdated card index system. Much of the stock was computerized but the real joy was the store of original documents, maps and personal letters.

Grace wasn't sure what it was that she was looking for so she showed the monogram to the girl at the desk and told her about the burial. The young woman looked at it for several seconds, her lack of movement suggesting that she wasn't really sure what to say. 'Well, you could look through the burials for that year to see if you can find it,' she finally offered.

'But we don't have a name.'

This threw the young woman who then said, 'Well, you could look through all the deaths beginning with *H* and try and find someone whose first name began with *R*—or *P*. You might just strike lucky,' she added, seeing Grace's face.

It seemed to be the only way. They were directed to the cabinet holding the death records and to the drawer containing the *H*s. Being in alphabetical order, Grace fingered her way along until she came to the first of the *R*s. She couldn't believe how many there were—Richard Habrook, Robert Hambleton, Robert Hamellock, Richard Harbour, Robert Harbour, Robert Harcourt—this was going to be a terribly long job.

Beside her, she was aware that Alex was less than enthusiastic. 'So what exactly are we looking for?' he asked.

'Someone whose surname begins with *H* and whose first name is either *R* or *P*, or even better, both, and who died in 1689.'

His eyes widened in that questioning look that said this is a waste of time but if that's what you want . . .

Grace felt that she should abandon the idea. Now. It was a lovely day. She should be taking Alex somewhere inspiring—the marshes at Newtown, the beach at Compton? Instead, she turned away from him and began to wade through the first line of cards.

In spite of her plan of action, she kept being sidetracked by life's tragedies. There was Robert Harding who died at the age of sixteen,

147

or Robert Harvey, son of Robert Harvey, collar maker of Newport and his wife Jane, who was born at the House of Industry, poor child, what a start to life.

Alex was dutifully ploughing through the *H*s starting from the other end. As he worked, Grace was aware that he was making faster progress, not distracted by anything. The minutes ticked by and after nearly two hours they met, not in the middle as he had worked faster than her but at least they had exhausted the possibilities. There were only four possible burials and none of them appeared to have any connection with the village.

'This is hopeless,' he whispered.

She was inclined to agree but the desperation to know made her stubborn. At that moment an older man came out of the office and turned towards one of the works of reference. He had an air of quiet certainty and Grace found herself saying, 'Excuse me, I wonder if you could help us.' She showed him the monogram and explained about the skeleton.

He was a softly spoken man with a pleasant face. After a moment he said, 'In view of the circumstances of the burial being outside the boundaries of the church it might be that the death was not recorded.' Grace felt that they had just wasted two hours. 'Where did you say you found this?' he asked.

Grace explained where her cottage was

and he nodded, clearly knowing the neighbourhood. 'At that time, nearly half the island belonged to a man called Robert Holmes. Your cottage would certainly have been a part of his estate.'

'So you think that this *RH* might be him?'

'It could be, but it could be a hundred other people.' As an afterthought, he added, 'If your young lady died in her teens, it might be worth looking at the births and marriages for the possible years as well.'

Grace felt heavy at the prospect. Aware of Alex gazing absently through the window, she knew that now was not the time. Another day she would undertake the wearisome task of looking through more endless cards. This would, of course, be when Alex was no longer here. She did not want that time to come and certainly she shouldn't be wasting the present in this way.

'Thank you very much,' she said to the curator, preparing to go. By now however, he had become interested.

'Holmes was Captain of the Island and based himself at Yarmouth Castle. He built himself a house, now the pub next to the castle, and he installed his daughter at what is now Thorlea Hall.'

'His daughter?'

'Her name was Mary.' Grace felt the thud of disappointment, she had hoped she might be Priscilla or Patience.

'My girl was African,' she volunteered.

'Really? That might tie in with the fact that Holmes travelled to Africa and the Caribbean.'

Alex made some small, impatient movement behind her, bringing Grace back to the present.

'I'm afraid we must go.'

The curator bowed his head. 'Well, check up on Robert Holmes. You might find that he is just the man you are looking for.'

CHAPTER ELEVEN

Outside, it was still sunny although the heat was fast fading. Grace took Alex down to the quay to watch the ships and swans and to give herself time to absorb the afternoon's discoveries, or rather the lack of them.

She struggled to free her thoughts from the skeleton and the hope that this man, Robert Holmes, might hold the clue. She would have liked to go immediately to the public library and enquire about a biography or any other information that might be available but Alex had that faraway look in his eyes that comes from polite boredom and she knew that it was time she considered his wishes.

'Let's go out to eat this evening,' she suggested, having a small country pub in mind.

The food was excellent, lots of freshly cooked vegetables and a wide variety of other dishes.

'If that is what you would like to do,' he answered.

'What would *you* like to do?' She glanced at him, fearing that he might be in a bad mood, but he simply looked distracted. 'What are you thinking about?'

He shrugged. 'I was just realizing that in three days I'll be back home. I've been away for five weeks and already the whole place seems to have become an irrelevance.' He raised his shoulders as if he did not know how to explain.

Grace remained silent. She had no idea what his feelings might be. Perhaps it was time for him to break away from his life so far? She quickly warned herself that encouraging him to do anything could have unforeseen consequences. There was no question of him staying here, no question of them having any sort of future. None. Whatsoever.

Still, he had said he felt trapped by the winery even before the crazy events that had taken place between them. She thought of her own entrapment, years ago. How much did she regret it? What other lives might she have led? It was unanswerable.

She squeezed his hand to show that he had her attention. Along the river a sailing dinghy was tacking towards them. Its bright yellow sail created a perfect picture. Further along the bank the path petered out and water lapped the muddy edge. Trees that reminded her of mangroves rose from near to the water. She wondered what it would be like if they had alligators on the island.

'That would make a lovely photo,' she observed, hoping to distract him. He seemed to deliberately bring himself back from some distant place, digging out his camera and taking several shots.

'Go and stand over there.' He indicated a place nearer to the bank.

She began to shake her head but nevertheless moved to the spot he indicated. 'Right then, look at me—and smile. I want to remember this place, this moment.'

Her smile tightened at the thought of how insubstantial all this was.

When they reached the point where the path stopped they turned back. Grace scrambled around for anything to say to escape the sudden cloud that had descended upon them. This was how life was, one moment busy and happy, the next . . .

'We'll definitely go to Hurst tomorrow,' she offered. He nodded absently.

'Do you still want me to plant the tree when we get home?'

Did she? It would give him something to do, some physical exercise to drive away whatever was bothering him. She thought that perhaps she should encourage him to use his physical energy up before bedtime. Perhaps they should stop the lunacy. Last night, for the first time in her life, she had taken a man's penis into her mouth, caressed it, felt the sensitivity of the tip, in turn abandoned herself to his exploring tongue. Her face blazed at the memory. Why was it that in the cold light of day these acts seemed so ridiculous? Last night, a sense of well-being she would never have believed possible had settled upon her when their lovemaking finally burnt itself out. Well, whatever the future held, at least she had experienced this—finally.

'Shall we stop off somewhere for a drink?' she suggested, the future of the tree sidestepped.

He shook his head. 'Perhaps we should get back, so that I can do the planting?'

Clearly this was what he wanted to do. She acquiesced. They drove home via a different, meandering route through villages that would have been at home on rural calendars. She gave him a running commentary to keep the silence at bay.

When they got back he went immediately into the garden. She turned on the kettle then reached instead for the wine bottle. Steady on, she would be driving later if they were going out to eat. She poured herself not quite a full glass and drank thirstily.

Alex seemed to be working with excessive energy. His spade drove into the hole, deepening it then he removed the polythene from around the roots of the tree and leaned it against the wall.

Coming over to the cottage he called out 'Do you want to come and witness the planting—like one of those royal visits where HM tips a trowel of soil into a hole and declares something or other dedicated?'

'OK.'

The image brought a smile to her face and she realized too that he seemed to have driven out some unwelcome ghost. He heaved the tree into the hole and she held it upright while he packed it around with earth. Tamping it down, he glanced at her.

'Want to say something?'

'If we were religious we could say a prayer. As it is . . . ' She took a deep breath. 'I dedicate this tree to the unknown girl whose resting place we disturbed. May we find out who she was, and one day soon may she again rest in peace.' She made a mental note to see the vicar about her reburial.

'Ah-bloody-men,' Alex finished for her. She smiled at him and he put his arm around her shoulders. 'Sorry for the mood.' He kissed the top of her head and like some heat-seeking missile she found herself nestled against him.

She heard his intake of breath. 'Oh God, Grace—bugger going out for a meal. Let's go indoors.'

It was back, the wild, illogical, crazy feeling

that defied any sort of normality. Hardly inside the door he had his jeans unzipped, pressed her up against the table, the cooker and then grabbed her hand to head for the bedroom.

'Jesus!' she thought. 'Whoever would have imagined this!'

*　　*　　*

Neither of them had the energy to think of going out again. There were oven chips, a pizza, some rather limp salad. Grace cobbled the meal together while Alex laid the table.

Afterwards, he went to the bedroom and came back with a folder.

'Photos,' he said.

She dried her hands and came to sit on the sofa beside him. She wasn't entirely calm at the prospect of seeing the connubial bliss of his family life.

'This is our place.' He held out a picture of a low, rambling dwelling fronted by shrubbery. It seemed to rise out of a valley, nestling on the brow of a gentle rise.

'Great-grandfather Weston purchased the land and planted the vines.' He handed her a view of the front entrance with a board announcing Evergreen Winery. 'Is it evergreen?' she asked, for something to say.

'Luckily we seem to get our share of whatever rain there is.'

Several photos of rows of grapes followed

while Alex explained the different types and their attributes.

'This is my unit.' He produced a photograph of a modest oblong building with a quaint wooden veranda. Near to the door stood a woman, clearly caught unprepared as she appeared to be deadheading roses. 'Susie.' He said shortly. 'I'd forgotten this one.'

She was a slim, athletic looking girl, her look challenging him to go away. Grace glanced covertly at him to try to assess his thoughts but his expression was neutral. The next photo followed.

'Ah, we had the neighbours over just before I left for a sort of farewell barby. There's the old man there, and Mum.'

Grace scanned the faces. One man was poking the barbecue, another holding up a glass, a third simply staring at the camera. Which one was Joe? With disbelief she realized that she did not recognize him. Coming to her aid, Alex said, 'There's Dad doing the cooking. Dab hand at the barby he is.'

She stared at the balding, rather solid man looking out at her. Something faltered inside of her. Why had he shown her this? Why had she not managed to hang on to her own image of forty years ago? Now it would be forever superimposed by this, this travesty.

Hanging on tightly to her equilibrium, she asked 'Which one is your mum?'

'There, putting the food on plates.'

Margaret Weston looked neat, trim, the sort of woman who has her hair done regularly and wears make-up during the day. She would probably be unfazed at the prospect of meeting Grace. Here was the woman who had lived forty years of Grace's life, but with a man who now looked more like Mr Blobby than Superman. It was an unkind comparison and she didn't want to dwell on it.

More photos followed, a koala in a garden pond, kangaroos stretched out on the lawn. Other photos of Joe, perhaps clearer, exposed a little more of the man she remembered although still well hidden behind a robust frame, his head barely covered by wispy hair the colour of bleached straw.

Grace thought of the photos that Alex had taken that afternoon. Would he show them to his parents when he got back? What would Joe think of the grey-haired woman staring back at him—what would he think if he knew what had happened between her and his son? However you looked at it, it was a revelation.

Perhaps in sympathy with the mood, the room began to feel chilly and Grace lit the fire. The last of the winter's logs from a dead elm in the neighbouring copse crackled and flared and threw out a welcome warmth. Alex poured out two glasses of a carefully chosen Syrah and sank on to the sofa.

'How did you come to end up living back

here?' he asked. When Grace didn't answer, he added 'You went away to work, didn't you, up in London?'

'Yes.' Images of that year began to form in her head, its early misery as the truth about Joe hit home, the numb reality of moving to London now that it seemed to have lost its point. There would be no Joe at the end of the rainbow, just the prospect of a lonely, empty existence.

'I don't think you should go,' Edna had said. 'It's obvious that you don't want to. Goodness knows what put the idea into your head in the first place.' But go she did.

Grace realized that Alex was watching her and she said, 'I got a job in the Civil Service, a tax office of all places, and my mother fixed up some accommodation with the vicar's cousin.'

Alex grinned. 'Not a lot of room for hanky-panky then.'

She shook her head and drank more wine. 'I . . . I was trying to get over a broken heart.' She smiled briefly to show the foolishness of youth.

'Really?' She saw his mind working but she didn't answer his unspoken question.

She didn't tell him that was because Alex's conniving mother had got herself pregnant and had stolen her lover away. If it wasn't for you, Alex Weston, she thought, my life would have been very different. But there again, thinking of the last few days, things had turned out very different indeed.

She had no idea what, if anything, Alex knew about the circumstances of his parents' marriage. It wasn't up to her to enlighten him. In any case, the marriage could only be judged by its success or otherwise and the couple was still together, which must indicate something.

Perhaps picking up on her thoughts, Alex said, 'My mother has had a lot of bad health. She's had treatment for cancer twice. She's been really brave.'

Grace looked back at the photograph of the barbecue. 'She looks like a nice woman,' she observed, for something to say.

To get things back on to safer ground she said, 'I spent just over a year in London. In some ways I loved it. Our office was very central and during the lunch hours I would rush down to the National Gallery or the Tate or the Portrait Gallery and just look at everything. After the quiet of the island it seemed wonderful. On sunny days I bought sandwiches and sat in St James's Park.' Her mind wandered again, those sandwich bars that sold exotic fillings, things she had never before encountered, like salami and avocado. At home, a sandwich was nearly always filled with paste.

She said, 'I hardly ever went out in the evening. I was staying out in the sticks in a place called Elmer's End. By the time I got back to the digs each night it was quite late and at weekends I used to go home.' She regretted the wasted opportunities.

Having Alex's attention, she continued: 'At about this time my Dad was taken ill. Mum couldn't really manage on her own so I came home. After he died, I just stayed.' She gave him a c'est la vie shrug.

Rather hesitatingly he asked, 'You never married?'

'I never quite got round to it.' She thought for a moment. 'I never met anyone I even considered marrying.' Reading his mind she added, 'I had a few flings, tepid affairs, nothing to write home about.'

He nodded that he understood, although whether he had any true concept of her life, she had no idea.

Alex got up from the sofa. 'I've got something to give you.' He left the room and was gone for a few moments then came back with a small fancy envelope. 'This is for you.'

She took it from him and opened the flap. Inside was a small box. Lifting the lid it revealed an opal pendant on a fine gold chain.

'My goodness, it's beautiful!'

'They mine the opals down near Adelaide.' As he spoke he took it from her, undid the clasp and slipped it around her neck. She remembered the kangaroo brooch all those years ago, now hidden somewhere in a drawer. A similar thought occurred to her, that Alex couldn't have bought this with her in mind because when he left home he didn't even know that he was going to meet her.

With some embarrassment he said, 'Actually, it was Dad's idea. He wondered if I might see you. If I didn't, he asked me to post it to you.'

She nearly laughed out loud. After all these years! Her thoughts roamed back over endless Christmases, polite cards, falsely jolly messages jointly to her and her mother—and now this. How very bizarre.

'Well, thank him for me,' she said.

He took her hand. 'I'm feeling pretty bushed. How about an early night?'

Remembering that there was only one more to go, she said, 'An early night it is.'

CHAPTER TWELVE

Grace awoke to near total darkness. Even before she could turn over she knew that she would have trouble getting back to sleep. She had noticed before that if you drank wine in the evening you quickly fell asleep but the booze had a nasty habit of stimulating your imagination at about two o'clock in the morning. With thoughts of their earlier conversation about London, her memory was already racing.

She must have worked on the mainland for

more than a year, for it was October and they were particularly busy at work. A few weeks earlier she had been temporarily transferred to an office in Frith Street. From the front windows the frenzy of Shaftesbury Avenue distracted the tax officers from their work but it was to the side view that Grace's attention was constantly drawn, to the prostitutes plying their trade from the opposite doorways. This was a way of life she had not even heard about before she came to London. She had no concept of what their lives might be like. Hanging about, occasionally exchanging words with fellow workers, they smoked and paced and then, following some barely seen exchange, they went off with a man in tow.

Grace was no longer a virgin. She knew what they did, but any connection with her own romantic yearnings for Joe and this casual exchange was beyond her. How could they do it? Why did they do it? It was a thought that frequently taxed her mind along with the revenue returns.

As she was stapling together some documents, Mr Chaucer, the head of section, came into the room.

'Miss Harrison, there has been a telephone call.'

Grace remembered that jolt of anxiety, the fear that she had done something so terrible that unknown powers outside the office were aware of it. He said, 'Your mother telephoned to say that your father has been taken ill and she would like you to come home.'

Her thoughts went immediately to their little house. They did not have a telephone so Edna must have gone next door and asked to use theirs. She could imagine her struggling with the machine, trying to explain to the person on the switchboard at the other end.

'Is he . . . ?' The awful truth dawned on her.

'I believe that he has had a stroke. You had better go now.'

She did so, wondering what would happen about her job and, more immediately, what she would find when she got home.

She was shocked when she saw her father. He looked so small, neatly tucked into the hospital bed, his usual berry-brown skin faded to parchment as if some invisible force had sucked out his blood. This was not the person she knew.

'Give Daddy a kiss.' Edna nudged her towards the narrow bed. In spite of his pallor there was a strange, stale, unpleasant heat about him and his mouth sagged alarmingly to one side. A dry crust formed around his blue lips.

'He can't speak,' said Mum. 'He's lost the use of his right side.' Lowering her voice she added, 'They don't know if he'll ever get any movement back. I don't know what I'm going to do.' She caught her breath, fighting down a sob.

Edna was always the strong one, the one issuing the orders. In the face of this sudden frailty Grace was at a loss. Stiffly she bent and kissed her father's cheek. 'Hello Dad.'

His eyes, watery and colourless, registered something. Was it her presence? She didn't know.

Dutifully they sat around the bed. Grace tried to think of a one-sided conversation but instead her thoughts drifted to all those unanswered questions. Would they send her father home or put him somewhere? Would he be in a wheelchair? Did he wet the bed? How soon could she get back to work? At her side, her mother chatted on about his allotment.

'Your beans have been a treat this year, Gordon. I've already salted down more than last year. I've pickled some beetroot too. You'll like that when you come home.'

Was Edna pretending or would he really come back in this state? After an eternity, a nurse ordered them away while she 'saw to him' whatever that meant. Waiting outside the curtain Grace felt a sort of horror creep over her.

They travelled home on the bus, Edna clutching a bag of dirty washing. 'I don't know what I'm going to do,' she said. 'I really don't.' When Grace did not respond, she added, 'I won't be able to manage him on my own.'

'Won't they—put him somewhere—just until he's better?'

Edna gave her a look. 'You've seen him. Does he look as if he's going to get better?'

There was nothing to say. They completed the journey in silence.

At the end of the first week Grace telephoned the office. They told her somewhat grudgingly that she could take another week. If she didn't return after that . . . the alternative was not spelled out.

Grace felt like the proverbial fish out of water. For the moment her life was on hold. The village where she had grown up and had friends now seemed tiny and empty. Like her, her friends had left for pastures new.

She went shopping with Edna in the nearest town. In the time she had been away a newly opened Milk Bar had shot up where once the cobbler's shop had been. It sold variously flavoured milkshakes and American Kunzle cakes. Desperate to break the monotony, Grace suggested that they should pop in for a drink but Mum said, 'Don't be silly. I wouldn't go into a place like that if you paid me You shouldn't either. There's such a lot of riffraff about.' Inside, a group of bored youngsters were playing records and indulging in some complex ritual flirtation. Looking through the door, Grace felt like an interloper, someone from another planet.

As the second week drew to a close, Gordon was getting up each day, being dressed and encouraged to drag himself a few steps across the room. He was supposed to feed himself but what with having to use his left hand that had mysteriously developed a shake most of the food landed down his front. The toilet was a problem too. He couldn't undo his fly buttons or pull his trousers down.

'He's going to need a lot of looking after,' the nurse forecast. A lot indeed.

As Grace prepared to remind her mother that she really must return to London, Edna dropped her bombshell.

'I've been to see Doctor Maguire and explained to him how we are fixed. He's written a letter to your office telling them that you are needed here and that you can't go yet.'

'But . . . '

Visions of her real life, her independence, everything began to slide ever further out of reach.

'You shouldn't have done that! If I don't go back I'll lose my job.'

'No you won't. The doctor has explained. They'll put you on unpaid leave.'

As Grace's anger spilled over, Edna began to cry. Between sobs she mumbled, 'Go on then, if that's what you want. Never mind about Daddy and me. We don't matter.'

Even as the words were uttered, Grace knew that she was defeated.

Another week passed then on Thursday afternoon as they visited the hospital, the matron told Edna:

166

'We've decided to send Mr Harrison home. There isn't anything that we can do for him here that can't be done elsewhere.' She turned to him, slumped in his chair and spoke slowly and loudly as to someone both deaf and daft.

'You want to go home, don't you Gordon?'

His speech had still not returned and he responded with a strange animal noise.

The short notice kept Grace and Edna busy. His bed had to be brought downstairs, shopping needed to be done and Dr Maguire was to be notified.

When the ambulance arrived at the door the two men half-carried Gordon Harrison inside the house. 'Nasty steps,' said the driver to him. 'Guess you'll have a bit of trouble with those, old son.'

Her father was dumped into his armchair and the men brought in a few accessories, a commode, some ominous looking pads and a Zimmer frame. They had another call to make so they didn't hang around.

It was cold for the time of the year so Edna lit the fire and sent Grace to fetch coal from the bunker. As she shovelled it into the hod a terrible sense of hopelessness settled upon her. Her life, any hope of escape, seemed further away than ever.

At that moment her nighttime ramblings were disturbed by the distant ringing of the telephone. For a moment she felt disorientated. Was she dreaming? At her side,

Alex gently snored. The insistent call of the phone continued. Now she looked at the luminous hands of the clock—ten past three. She felt a surge of anxiety. Telephone calls at this time only meant trouble.

Stumbling in the dark she made her way to the tiny hall where the phone stood on a table. 'Hello?' Her voice croaked slightly.

'Grace? It's Joe. I know it must be some unearthly hour over there but I do need to speak to Alex. It's his mother, she's been taken really badly again and they've rushed her into hospital. I know he can't do anything from this distance but, well, he might like to try for an earlier flight or something.'

Grace could hear the anxiety in his voice. 'I'm really sorry,' she said. 'I'll go and wake him up.'

She did so, shaking him soundly on the shoulder and gently repeating that his father wanted to speak to him. She followed him back into the hall, listening to his side of the conversation.

When he rang off, he said, 'It's Mum.'

'Your Dad said. What do you want to do?'

Still half asleep, he looked lost and she put her hand out to touch his shoulder. 'I'll make us some coffee.'

He sat hunched over the mug, waiting for his brain to catch up with his body. Finally he said 'I'd better see if I can change my flight. If I can get one today . . .'

Of course this was what he must do, but Grace, hugging her own mug of coffee, felt the dark shadows of loneliness waiting to envelop her.

*   *   *

After about an hour on the telephone Alex managed to bring his flight forward by twenty-four hours.

'That means I'll need to leave here at lunchtime,' he said, looking to her for her reaction.

She nodded. 'I'll run you to the ferry. Or if you like, I could come with you to the airport?'

He shook his head. 'I'd rather you didn't. Saying goodbye is going to be bad enough as it is—not that I won't be back sometime, you can be sure of that.'

She remained silent. For the moment she couldn't think of anything but the practicalities of getting everything ready. Keep busy. At all costs, keep busy.

Alex packed. They went into the garden to inspect the tree. As they stood by the burial place, he reached out and took her hand.

'You will let me know, won't you, what happens about the girl?'

'Of course I will.'

'I'll write as soon as I get back.'

'Fine.'

The morning dragged and yet passed too

169

quickly. At midday they had a quick snack then while Alex piled his luggage into the car Grace checked around to make sure that he hadn't left anything behind. As she came out of the bedroom he came back into the hall.

'Grace . . . '

'Don't. Everything is all right. You get home and see your mother.'

He nodded. Stiffly she accepted his attempt at an embrace. Not now, she couldn't let her guard down and snuggle close to him, it was too much to face, too much to lose.

Taking her hand he led the way out to the car. In silence they drove to the ferry terminal and Grace waited while he sorted himself out. The ferry was already boarding.

'Well, I hope you find your Mum better by the time you get home.'

'Thanks—and Grace . . . '

'There's no need to say anything.' She found a smile from somewhere—'It's been nice having you!'

They both smiled at the craziness of their situation.

She hustled him toward the barrier, gave and accepted a fraternal kiss and stood back while he struggled up the gangplank with his belongings. Before stepping into the ship he stopped to wave.

That, she thought, might be the last time I ever see him.

She drove home in some sort of cocoon. Even her shoulders felt hunched up as if to avoid contact with anything around her. She dreaded going home yet longed to be there, safe inside the house, hidden from the outside world.

Once inside, she made straight for the bedroom and began to strip the bed—no foolish curling up in the place where he had been. They had both known that this was an interlude. It had finished rather more abruptly than they had expected, that was all.

She put the sheets in the washing machine, washed up their lunch things, wondered whether to ring Molly but immediately dismissed the idea. She was too unsteady to talk about the last few days. Instead, she rang the vicar.

Rather surprisingly, he was at home. 'Sorry to trouble you but I was wondering about my mother's ashes. I . . . I think I would like to scatter them on my father's grave.' She had nearly said 'sprinkle' but that sounded rather like icing sugar.

'No problem, dear lady.' Good, that was that out of the way. Before he could ring off, she added, 'There was something else. As you probably know, we found a skeleton in the garden, right by the church wall. The archaeology people have it at the moment but, when they have finished with it, could we

171

arrange for a proper burial for her in the churchyard?'

To her surprise there was an awkward silence. 'Well,' the minister began, 'that rather depends on why she was in the garden?'

Grace didn't know, but she went on to say that as far as she was aware, she was a young girl and a foreigner.

'In that case, it wouldn't be permissible.'

For a moment she thought she had misheard. 'How?' she asked.

'Well, for some reason she wasn't thought eligible for a Christian burial whenever she died. Whatever that reason was, it would still apply now.'

'What? You still deny people burials?'

'Of course not—exactly. My suggestion would be that you telephone the council and see if they can find her a space in a civic burial ground.'

'Thank you.' She put the phone down quickly, shaken that some sort of seventeenth-century mumbo jumbo should still apply.

While she was mulling over the implications she heard the door knocker wrap smartly against its metal base. Now she didn't mind if it was Molly, because she was sufficiently affronted to want to let off steam.

As she opened the door it was to find not Molly, but Austin Morris.

CHAPTER THIRTEEN

Grace must have looked surprised to see him, for Austin Morris appeared to be embarrassed.

'I do apologize for dropping round uninvited,' he started. 'I'm actually on my way home and, as I have made one or two more discoveries, I thought they might interest you.' His voice was pleasantly modulated, suggesting that he was well educated rather than simply well bred.

'Of course, please do come in.' She stood back and he stepped into the hall, wiping his feet with care. The sun had been shining since early morning and today he wore an orange T-shirt with the logo *'Bomb Disposal Expert. If I start to run, try to keep up.'* She smiled.

It was immediately clear that Austin was shorter by a head than Alex, who had frequently had to duck inside the house. In spite of his eccentric choice of shirts and jumpers, he was what Grace would have called dapper. His abundant wiry hair framed a face with regular features, made noticeable by his mouth that looked forever on the verge of smiling.

Grace led the way to the kitchen and Austin looked about him as if searching for Alex.

'My visitor left today,' she announced,

amazed at the casual way in which she could deliver the news.

'Nice chap,' said Austin, taking the seat she offered him.

'Coffee?' She reached for the tin automatically. Alex drank only coffee and within those few days she had developed the habit of making it as he liked it.

'Tea, if you don't mind.'

She put the coffee back and reached for the tea caddy. For most of the day tea was her usual drink.

'Well now,' Austin declined a biscuit and sipped at his drink. 'I can say with some certainty that your young lady had given birth, quite soon before she died I would guess. The shape of her pelvis indicates this.'

Seeing Grace's expression, he added, 'There was no sign of a baby buried with her so we must assume that the youngster survived.'

Another aspect to the case that she had not even considered. The thought of this baby born to a girl who seemed to have been ostracized by the locals seemed heartbreaking. Was it a boy or a girl? Aloud, she said, 'I wonder whatever became of it?'

He shook his head. 'If you have no objection, I thought I would look in the parish records to see if I can locate a baptism at around that time, although in the circumstances, it's a long shot but it might help.' After a moment his words echoed her gathering thoughts, 'I wonder if there might just be someone around here who is descended from him or her?'

The thought was gripping. Perhaps they could DNA the whole village to see if anyone had an African ancestor. She found herself telling him about her discovery of the monogram and subsequent visit to the Record Office.

'Might I see the spot?'

He finished the rest of his tea and Grace led him out into the garden.

'That is a beautiful herbaceous border.' He stopped to admire the long bed that stretched the length of the boundary wall. New growth was pushing its way past the detritus left from last summer.

'I have to thank my Dad for that. He took care of it for years. It needs some work. I've tried to keep it up but I don't have his flair. Are you a gardener?'

'I dabble, but my wife was the gardener.' There was a moment's hesitation before he added, 'She died three years ago. In fact, she is buried right there in the churchyard.'

Austin gazed across the wall and his face looked wistful. Grace could think of nothing to say. Pulling himself back from some private place, he turned his attention again to the garden.

At the site of the grave he took in the maple tree. Remembering how they had planted it only the night before, Grace felt the maudlin nostalgia lurking and quickly suppressed it. Meanwhile Austin stepped around the tree and bent down to examine the wall. It was a few moments before he delivered his verdict.

'From the style of the lettering I'd guess that it is contemporary with the burial.' He stood up and smiled at her. 'Perhaps someone loved her enough to put up their own memorial after all.'

'I hope so.' She began to tell him what she had, or had not, found at the Public Record Office, ending with the suggestion that the RH might be the Robert Holmes who had once owned her garden.

His eyes were focused on the wall but he nodded to show that he heard what she was saying.

'I have a biography of Holmes. You might like to borrow it?'

'Thank you, I would.' She waited, wondering if he might have any other suggestions, but he remained silent then, marshalling his thoughts, he said, 'This is just the sort of mystery I like to get my teeth into. I hope you won't think that I am interfering but I can look up the records in the archaeology department and see what I can come up with.'

'Please do.'

With an intake of breath he said, 'Well, I'd better be going. My dog will be tired of waiting for me. I often take him to work but I had several visits to make today so I left him at home.'

'What sort of dog is he?'

'A mongrel, an RSPCA special. Nice chap, his name is Columbus—a bit of a wanderer. He was my wife's.'

She walked with him to the gate and he stopped again to look around the garden. 'Such a perfect setting.'

She smiled and said, 'It's called Palma cottage. I don't know why. The Parish Council did a recent survey of the village and it was definitely here in the seventeenth century.' She would have liked to help with the survey but at that time Edna had reached a stage where she couldn't be left.

'Maybe a palm grew here once,' he offered. 'The climate is mild enough.'

'Perhaps it did.' She realized that they might have planted a palm instead of the maple tree.

Austin interrupted her thoughts. 'Right then, I could drop the book in on the way to work tomorrow. No need for you to get up or anything; I'll just put it through the letter box.'

'That's all right,' she said, 'I'll be up,' and she knew that she would be.

*　　　*　　　*

Grace made herself a sandwich for tea and started to read a detective story. Books were such a useful weapon against having to think and just for the moment she had no desire to go over the events of the last few days—either the arrival and departure of Alex, or the discovery of the skeleton. Inevitably they both kept creeping into her mind.

The phone rang at about seven o'clock and it was Alex. At the sound of his voice her legs propelled her into a chair and ridiculous tears welled up. Damn it, she was not meant to feel like this.

'I'm at the airport,' he said. 'Just thought I'd let you know I got here all right. I've booked in. We board in about half an hour.'

She fought to sound calm. 'Have you heard anything more from home?'

'I phoned just now but there's no reply. I guess Dad must be at the hospital.'

When she didn't reply, he asked, 'What have you been doing?' I stripped your bed, she thought so that I wouldn't be curling up in your sheets like some love-struck teenager. Aloud, she told him about Austin Morris's visit and that the young girl, P, was already a mother when she died.

'Plenty to find out then,' he observed. Breaking the next silence, he blurted out, 'I'm really missing you, Grace. I'll be back some time, you can count on that.'

Her feelings lurched, dangerously near a chasm. This was not how it was supposed to be, just a bit of fun then back to normal, except that normal was coming to terms with being alone and not knowing what to do with the rest of her life.

For a terrible moment she thought that he might say that he loved her. She remembered what he had concluded about his marriage, that he and Susie didn't know each other. It was only the sex that was exciting and when that wore thin . . .

'Let me know when there is any news of your mum,' she said 'And have a good flight.' As an afterthought she added, 'Give my good wishes to your father.'

'You take care, Grace. Write to me. Phone me.' She nodded by way of reply, a futile gesture but once again she couldn't trust her voice. In the background she heard the distorted public address system at the airport and Alex said, 'They're calling my flight. I'd better go.'

'Goodbye then, Alex.'

'Goodbye—take care.'

*   *   *

That night she drank too much wine and had a good cry, although she couldn't decide what for. It was an overwhelming sadness connected to nothing and yet everything. She was free but it was an empty freedom. She could have nearly anything she wanted and yet she had no idea what that was. She could go anywhere and yet she wanted to stay at home and hibernate.

179

She seemed to be in an impossible place.

When it came to bedtime she realized that she hadn't made up the bed so, feeling queasy and light headed, she staggered back into the box room hoping that she wouldn't suffer the indignity of being sick. She lay on her back, very still, and eventually the dizziness subsided and at last she escaped into a dreamless oblivion.

It was the sound of a thump in the hall that woke her. Warily she opened her eyes, blinking them against the shaft of light that enveloped her pillow. It was broad daylight and outside she heard the click of the garden gate and then the sound of a car's engine. She squinted at the clock and realized that it was 8.30. She scrambled out of bed and peered round the door and into the hall. A book-shaped package lay on the door mat. Austin Morris had already been. With a head that felt like the night after the party, she was glad that she hadn't seen him. Now at least she had something different to read, something to advance any knowledge there might be to be gleaned about P.

Grabbing her dressing gown, she stumbled downstairs and plugged in the kettle. Two mugs of tea might go some way to restoring the damage to her head. While she waited for the kettle to boil she opened the bag containing the book. It was a hardback with a picture of a sailing ship on the cover and, in

180

one corner, a portrait of a solid, bewigged man with an arrogant mouth and knowing eyes. Slipped inside the front cover was a note. *I hope you will find this useful. It is an entertaining read at the least. I will telephone if I find out anything useful. Regards AM.*

With her tea and a slice of toast to soak up last night's excesses, she sat by the French windows that led into the garden bathed in the beam of sunshine and began to read.

Although Grace was not familiar with seventeenth-century history, as she devoured the pages the essence of Robert Holmes the man emerged. He was not someone she would have chosen as a friend. Bombastic, seemingly insensitive to the finer feelings of others, he was courageous to the point of being foolhardy. A man who cared little for his own safety, he had scant sympathy for anyone weaker than himself.

Grace stopped to make more tea, pondering what she had discovered so far. If—and it was still a big if—a young African girl had been in his power, what must she have felt about her situation, and most of all, about him? Grace knew enough about to slavery to imagine the misery of a woman placed at the mercy of an alien, white master. But perhaps P wasn't a slave? Was it possible that love had been involved here? Quickly she reined back her imagination and tried to envisage a picture of the situation based solely on the facts.

Returning to the book, she gleaned that Holmes was the third son of an Englishman living in Ireland. Not born an aristocrat, he seemed sensitive about his background, but when civil war broke out in England he put himself forward as a Royalist soldier, serving under King Charles's nephew, Prince Maurice. It seemed that the king's sister had a brood of children and Maurice was one of them. When the war went against the king, Holmes, along with Maurice's brother, Prince Rupert, set off on what could only be described as a piratical sea voyage. Inevitably their travels took them to Africa and here Grace's senses heightened. Was it here, on his voyage, that P had come into his hands?

The jar of the doorbell broke her concentration and she hurried to see who might be there. It was Molly.

'Come in.'

By way of greeting Molly said, 'I've just come from the doctor's. He's going to send Reg for assessment and see if they can get him into a day centre. I've got to take him to the hospital tomorrow morning.'

Grace stepped back and Molly made her way to the kitchen, plonking herself in her usual chair. Automatically Grace boiled the kettle.

'Where is he now?' she asked.

'Asleep in his chair. He was up for much of the night and now he's exhausted.' Molly turned bleak eyes on her friend. 'To tell you the truth, I'm worn out too. I don't know how long I can keep this up.'

Grace was silent, remembering her own desolation as Edna grew increasingly feeble, but at least Edna had always retained her marbles.

'How are you going to get to the hospital tomorrow?' she asked.

'We'll take the bus.' Molly had given up driving since she had had a prang with the dustcart.

'I'll take you in.'

'No, really, we can get the bus.'

'I insist.'

Molly looked relieved. She drank her tea, still smarting from her situation. Eventually she said, 'What about lover boy, then?'

'He's gone. He had to leave a day early. His mother is ill.'

Molly nodded thoughtfully. 'What are you going to do now? Now that he's gone?'

Grace didn't want to talk to Molly about Alex, or about her latest quest for Robert Holmes. It needed too much explanation and besides, Molly wasn't really a history person. She wished that she would go but, remembering how her friend had always been the one to come and help with Edna, she chided herself and said, 'If you want a break, you just let me know and I'll stay with Reg.'

Molly hesitated. 'He can be really difficult

at times.'

Grace wondered whether he might be growing violent. She had read somewhere about mild, benign people who, in the grip of dementia, could change their personalities.

'I could pop round later for a cup of tea,' she offered.

The relief on Molly's face said it all. For a while she seemed to be mulling something over in her mind then she said, 'I know you haven't been married and you might feel that now you're free . . .' She stumbled for the right words. 'Well, you might—you know, meet someone. I'd just say think very carefully. And if you do ever decide to do it, pick someone younger and healthier than you. If there's any looking after to be done, make sure it's not you doing it.'

Grace acknowledged her words. With a smile, she said, 'It's a bit early for that. I don't even know anyone that might be a temptation.'

'It doesn't always happen when you expect it,' Molly advised. 'Look at me 'n' Reg. I was quite happy working in the corner shop. I'd learned to cope after Bill died and wasn't looking for another man, then one day he comes in with a bunch of flowers and says how he's always admired the way I coped with things. The next minute he's asking would I like to go on a day trip that was going up to the Tower of London. Well, I'd never been there before so I said yes, and look where it's led.'

She sighed dramatically. 'Just you mark my words. You think before you jump.'

CHAPTER FOURTEEN

When Grace arrived back from taking Reg to the hospital it was to find the answerphone beeping. She pressed the button as she took off her jacket and after the usual preliminaries she heard Alex's voice.

'Grace. Just thought that I should let you know that Mum died yesterday morning. I'm afraid I arrived too late.' There was an interval and she knew that he was fighting down his emotion. When next he spoke his voice was under control. 'She died peacefully and Dad was with her. I'm glad about that. Anyway, well keep you informed. I miss you. Bye.'

The shock of any death causes the heart to lurch, whether in sadness or sympathy. Grace sank into the chair, thinking of the two men, father and son, united in the loss of a wife and mother. She thought of her own recent turmoil when Edna finally reached the end of the line. So many conflicting feelings had claimed her: relief, regret, lost opportunities, guilt and something larger about the enormity of life, its living and dying and her own mortality. She glanced at the clock. They were somewhere between nine and eleven hours ahead in

Australia, she never had been able to remember what happened when the clocks went forward and back. Whichever, it was the middle of the night over there. She would have to wait until later to respond.

She made a sandwich and took it with the Holmes biography into the conservatory, now bathed in the warmth of the spring sunshine. In spite of her anxiety to finish the book in the hope of finding any clues, she could not concentrate. Instead her mind kept drifting to the time when her father had finally died, nearly two years after the stroke that had changed all their lives. It was a relief, of course it was, not least for Gordon, who had made only the slightest improvement since he had lost the use of his right side and his speech. Under her mother's supervision, Grace had helped to care for him. She thought of the cream she nightly massaged into his dry, spindly legs and the periodic trimming of his toenails. This fell to her because Edna could not get down on her hands and knees to do so. Their hard yellow crust appalled her.

The toilet was, of course, the worst, helping him to the commode, girding herself to empty the contents. She shuddered. Not for the first time she hoped that either nature would deal with her kindly and wipe her out at a stroke— either literally or metaphorically—or that she would still have the ability and courage to take the step herself when things got too bad.

This was no good, dwelling on such morbid scenes. With an intake of breath, she picked up the book and began to read.

Holmes's life had all the ingredients of a seventeenth-century adventure story. War and ambition sat cheek by jowl with courage and unquestioning lawlessness. Her attention was engaged when Holmes sailed off to West Africa, making his way up the Gambia River only to be ambushed because, in a moment of gung-ho piracy on the coast, a canoe manned by Africans was overturned with the loss of life. Marched through the jungle, he eventually came face to face with the chief in whose hands his life rested. Did he beg or negotiate? Of course he didn't. Fortunately for him, on the coast Prince Rupert was making plans to come to his rescue, handing over the now captive survivors from the canoe in return for Holmes's life. Undeterred, the voyage continued across the Atlantic, zigzagging its way among the islands. Grenada, Martinique, Guadeloupe, Montserrat, the names were as exotic and magical now as they had been then. Then, in a full-scale drama, while the others stood by helplessly, a storm of terrible proportions claimed the ship captained by Prince Maurice. What became of him no one ever knew. There were tales that he was taken prisoner by the Spaniards and sold into slavery but the reality was probably that he simply drowned. Surely this of all their adventures must have affected them the most?

Grace assiduously made notes of dates and locations, recording anywhere where the party might conceivably have taken on board a young black girl. For the moment, their chief prizes were a string of Spanish ships loaded with silver, mahogany and spices. But by now their own craft, the *Swallow*, was barely seaworthy. The ship leaking badly, they limped their way back to France. For Grace there was one glimmer of hope. Among those on the return journey was the young son of a Moorish couple who had been pursued by Prince Rupert and his companions. The child became separated and, unable to reunite him with his parents, the party brought him back to England. Grace felt her confidence grow, realizing that such a scenario was not impossible. Might P have been rescued in similar circumstances?

She began to feel chilly and realized that the sun had disappeared behind a lowering black cloud. Angry droplets of rain began to assault the glass of the conservatory. April showers. It descended with sudden force, a diagonal downpour lashing the daffodils. Reluctantly she fetched a cardigan. The house did not feel much warmer and she lit the fire, a focus of warmth and comfort in a suddenly lonely place.

Somehow she whiled away the time until she was confident that it would be morning in

Australia and then, with a deep intake of breath, she dialled Joe's number. The phone rang a few times before it was answered and there was Joe's familiar voice made flat by sadness.

'Joe, it's Grace. I just rang to say how sorry I am.'

'Thanks, Grace. How did you know?'

'Alex called me.' She hadn't thought of that, not considered that Alex might not have mentioned his call to his father.

'Right. Anyway, as you can imagine we're . . .' Grace felt his distant grief and in a moment of clarity realized that just because his marriage had not been planned all those years ago, it didn't mean that he had passed the decades in resentment and regret. They had been a couple, sharing not only a bed but also companionship, family decisions, their very lives.

'I'm so sorry,' she said again. She wanted to speak to Alex but didn't know how to ask. The problem was solved for her when Joe said, 'Alex has gone into town to register the death. There's such a lot to do.'

'When is the funeral?' She said it for something to say.

'Friday, we think. Of course there's a PM but it should be routine.'

'Well, just to say how sorry I am.'

'Thanks. Well . . . we'll be in touch. Oh, and thanks for looking after Alex. He's come back

189

a different man. His mother would have been so relieved.'

That said it all, really. With a hushed goodbye she replaced the receiver and wondered again at the confusion known as life.

*   *   *

Suddenly it was Easter. With its usual contrariness, April delivered a cold spell with biting wind and rain. Across the churchyard, Grace saw the faithful entering the church, heard the Easter hymns she remembered from childhood. She tried to recall the details. Good Friday was a day of mourning, the death of a prophet (she couldn't bring herself to believe that Jesus was really the Son of God, it seemed too much like Greek myths and Roman folklore). Whichever, it was surely evidence of man's inhumanity to man. *'When I survey the wondrous cross.' 'There is a green hill far away.'* She heard the melodies drift across, thought of that Easter with Joe, all the new possibilities, the wonderful discovery of love, its potential. This present feeling of loss and regret wasn't good. Since it was too wet to go into the garden, she returned again to Holmes, still hopeful that somewhere she would find the clue that solved the mystery of P.

The phone rang late on Friday morning. 'Grace?'

'Alex! How are things. How was the

funeral?' She remembered what time it was over there, what had been happening half a world away.

'It was OK. Mum was quite religious, you know? It was pretty traditional stuff. I'm glad it's over.'

'What are you going to do now?'

'I'd like to leap on a plane, come straight back to England.'

'You mustn't!' She felt sudden alarm at the intensity in his voice. 'You need to stay and help your Dad.'

He sighed loudly. 'Susie is here. She came for the funeral.'

Susie, the errant wife. Grace wondered if she had come alone or with the new man in her life. Alex said, 'I think the guy's dumped her. She doesn't seem in a hurry to leave.'

There was nothing she could say.

He said, 'Look, I'll give you my phone number in my unit. The only trouble is I'm not there very often, but if you can't get me, write, won't you?'

'Of course I will. I . . . I've discovered a few things about that man Holmes who owned the cottage.'

'Write and tell me about it—please?'

'I'll write today.' She had nothing else to do to fill the hours.

'Right. Well, I'd better go. Dad and Susie are in the kitchen making sandwiches.' As an afterthought he added, 'Dad's always had a soft spot for Susie. Mum never really liked her.'

'And you?'

By way of reply he gave a short snort of amusement. 'God knows.'

They said their goodbyes and Grace wandered into the living-room. She remembered the photo of Susie in the garden, trim, challenging. Was that old chemistry at work between her and Alex? And if it were, if they got back together again, how would she feel? He hadn't dismissed his estranged wife's presence as being too late, no longer of any interest. A pang of longing claimed her. For Alex? She didn't know. It was for someone, anyone who might fill the emptiness of her life. Just let something happen soon.

* * *

Christ the Lord is risen today!! The Easter Sunday music emanated again from the church. Strange that in the past she had hardly noticed it. It was beautiful in its way, the melodies, the words that spoke of faith and wonder, even if Grace could find no reality in the stories. Such certainty must be a comfort, but the dark side was the very assurance it gave to the faithful, the confidence of being right at the expense of everyone who thought otherwise, Christian versus Jew, Christian versus Muslim. Along with greed, it was surely the cause of all ills. Then there was the magic and miracles and they were difficult to swallow. The very concept itself amazed her.

As the church was emptying the sun put in an appearance. Suddenly she knew that she had to get out of the house. What were other people doing on Easter Day. Sharing Easter eggs, cooking Sunday roasts, entertaining friends, escaping for the weekend, going for walks? A walk was what she needed. She wished that she had a dog to keep her company. Dogs gave shape to the days, getting you up in the morning, either shadowing your every move or snoring in the doorway, right where you would probably trip over them. A dog, though, it was uncomplaining, accepting and above all company. Perhaps she should seriously think of getting one. She remembered what Austin Morris had said, 'An RSPCA special, a nice chap.' Yes, that is just what she could do with, a nice chap.

This weekend, Molly and Reg had visitors so she was spared the sense of duty that she should visit but perversely she missed Molly's lighter moments, her irreverence and humour, although lately they were well hidden beneath the burden of caring for Reg. Well, the visitors were here for another couple of days so she must make her own amusement.

Putting on her walking shoes, she glanced out of the window. The two-timing sun was shining benignly at her but towards the east rain clouds scrambled over each other to reach the top of a growing black mountain. She watched for a moment but could not tell in which direction they were heading. She fetched a waterproof jacket.

Outside, the temperature was noticeably warmer but everything was still damp from a recent downpour. She walked along the path to the back gate and into the lane skirting the churchyard. Looking over the wall, she noticed that the flowers she and Alex had placed there had already been defeated by the elements.

A dog sat by the church gate. At her approach he stood up and wagged his tail uncertainly. He was large, grey and shaggy with a self-deprecating air. 'Hello boy,' she smoothed his head.

For a moment she wondered whether Fate had been listening to her earlier and had sent him along to be her companion. For a second she imagined recounting the incident, how, like Moses in the bull rushes, she had found him abandoned, waiting for her.

'Good afternoon!'

Her daydream was interrupted and she looked up to see Austin Morris coming out of the churchyard.

'I . . . I've just been putting some flowers on my wife's grave,' he said. 'I see that you have met Columbus.'

She smiled, embarrassed by her own fantasy of adopting the dog. Today Austin was soberly

194

dressed, a grey sweater visible beneath a dark-blue jacket. She realized then that the vivid jumpers were hand-knitted. Had his wife lovingly created them for him and did he wear them to keep her memory alive? How long had he been a widower? She thought that he might have mentioned three years. She wondered what he would do when they wore out.

'Are you going out? Well, obviously you are.' He smiled at the foolishness of his own question.

'I thought I should get some exercise.'

'I'm just going to take Columbus up to the Monument. As you can see, he's an athletic chap. He needs plenty of exercise and up there I can let him run to his heart's content.'

Grace nodded. For a second he seemed undecided then he said, 'If you would like to, we'd be delighted for you to join us.'

Grace in her turn hesitated. 'Well—yes, that would be very nice.'

That decided, they set off in the direction of the Downs, along a treelined lane now heavy with blossom. Underfoot the ground was spongy and in places riddled with puddles. With abandon, Columbus lolloped through them, indifferent to the mud and leaves sticking to his coat. He gave off a nearly forgotten damp dog smell.

They crossed the road and set off along another path, now climbing steadily up towards the brow of the Down where a towering stone monolith cast a shadow towards them. Grace found that she was short of breath and cursed herself for being unfit—and for agreeing to the walk, thus exposing her weakness to her companion. A few yards ahead he stopped. He was panting almost as much as the dog.

'I'm really not very fit these days,' he admitted.

'Me neither.' They both silently cast around to take in the view. This was indeed breathtaking, a patchwork of fields made the more flamboyant by the emerging splashes of yellow as the oilseed rape began to flower, alternating with a blue hint of the flax to come. The distant hazy grey-green of the sea framed the panorama.

'I can't think of anywhere in the world that could beat this,' Austin announced.

'Have you travelled a lot?'

'A fair bit. I went on several archaeological digs in the Middle East and North Africa and my wife loved to holiday abroad.'

While Grace was taking this in, he asked, 'How about you?'

I've never been abroad, she thought. It felt like a shameful confession, an admission that her life and by implication her attitudes were narrow, lacking in experience. 'Hardly at all,' she finally said, thinking of a holiday in Dorset, a weekend in Bath with a brief lover. That had been a disaster. They had wanted to see different things, the sex was awful and she couldn't get home fast enough. This was after Dad had died but she had still been marooned on the island.

When they finally reached the monument they found a dry, sunny spot on the south side and for a while sat on the grass to indulge in the view. Near to, the pillar was even more impressive than from a distance. Austin told her about the man who made his fortune trading with Russia and erected this memento to record the visit of a Tsar to England. He gave an embarrassed laugh. 'Please forgive me, I can't help lecturing about anything historical. It seems to be in my blood.'

'Not at all, it's interesting.' To keep the conversation going she asked 'Where were you born?'

'Near Naseby. That's probably what gave me a lifelong fascination for the past. As you probably know, one of the most decisive battles of the Civil War took place there. You could say it decided the king's fate.'

Before she could comment, he asked, 'And where were you born?'

'In the cottage where I now live.' She felt her cheeks grow pink at the confession. 'I've not been very adventurous,' she admitted, thinking that had things been otherwise, she might have been very adventurous indeed.

'I rather envy you the continuity. That's the great thing about an island, you know exactly where the boundaries are.'

At that moment Columbus returned from one of his sorties, clearly checking to see that they were still there before setting off in another direction.

'That dog is my sanity,' Austin said quietly. 'When Percy died I think I went a little mad.'

Percy? Grace did a double take. Was Austin gay? If so, he had confused her by the talk of a wife when he might have said partner. Into her silence he said, 'Her parents had flights of fancy about the Gods and called her Persephone. Quaint, don't you think?'

'Ah.' She nodded, hoping that he hadn't noticed her confusion.

'I expect you know the story,' he started. 'How she was abducted into the underworld and was doomed to spend a quarter of each year there. Her absence symbolized winter when nothing would grow.' His thoughts seemed to overtake him and he fell silent. Eventually, as if realizing where he was, he asked, 'How are you getting on with Holmes?'

She was glad to be on what felt like safer ground. 'His life seems pretty amazing. I haven't found anything that might tie him in with the girl in the garden, though.' As an afterthought she asked, 'Did he marry?'

'He didn't.'

Grace felt him settle back to recount another tale.

'Holmes was undoubtedly a great

womanizer. There is one story that he tried to seduce Elizabeth Pepys, the wife of the diarist. Not made of such heroic stuff, Pepys was afraid to challenge him because he knew that Holmes wouldn't think twice about challenging him back—to a duel. What Elizabeth thought about it, we don't know.'

'So he had no children, then?' Grace asked.

'Well, he might well have had dozens but there was only one that he acknowledged and that was a daughter born when he was in his sixties. Who her mother was is something of a mystery. There is some circumstantial evidence that she might have been the child of Grace Hooke. Grace was the niece of Robert Hooke, the great scientist and architect. You do know that he came from the island?'

Grace nodded to show that she did, although she knew little enough about him. Satisfied, Austin continued.

'When Robert's brother died he took the girl—Grace'—he paused to acknowledge that they bore the same name—'into his household in London, but also, it seems, into his bed. Anyway, there came a point when Grace came back to the island, by which time Holmes was the governor here and living at Yarmouth. Rumours reached Hooke that Holmes was showing too much interest in his niece. Jealousy apart, perhaps he had a right to be worried, for certainly Grace was away from his house long enough to have given birth to a child. She eventually returned to London but the poor girl died young. As for Holmes's child whoever her mother was, he took the girl into his household and indeed built her a mansion on the outskirts of Yarmouth in the now landlocked Thorlea. I expect you know it?'

Grace had driven past the fine hall on many occasions but never considered who might have lived there. In fact, she had no idea who lived there now.

'Who does it belong to?' she asked.

'Some pop singer. Made his fortune in the sixties and retired there.'

'Do you know who?'

'Sorry, I can't remember.'

The clouds had now moved noticeably nearer and they both stood up, aware that the ground beneath them had been damper than they had realized. Columbus appeared from amongst the gorse bushes and they set off on the return journey. By the time they were back in the village it had begun to rain.

'Would you like to come in for a cup of tea?' Grace offered, frantically trying to remember what sort of state the house was in.

'I think I should get back home before the weather gets any worse. But thank you, some other time I'd be glad to.' There was an awkward moment then Austin said, 'Perhaps you would like to pop into my office? Your young lady is in a box on the shelf. Why don't you come and visit her?'

Grace thought of the girl, now reduced to a few bones. In a strange way she felt like her next of kin.

To Austin she said, 'Thank you, I will.'

CHAPTER FIFTEEN

Grace felt healthily tired when she got indoors. She decided to make do with cheese on toast for tea and switched on the electric fire for comfort. Lighting a coal fire for the few remaining hours of the day seemed unnecessarily extravagant.

As soon as she had finished eating she sat down to write to Alex, wanting to share with him the details of Holmes's life. After a while her thoughts wandered to Persephone Morris. She wondered what she had been like. With a name like Persephone, she could not imagine her knitting stripy jumpers. Perhaps it was the burden of their names that initially drew them together: Austin Healy Morris and Persephone someone. Whatever, the poor woman must have died relatively young. One thing was for certain though, she had been loved by her husband. A certain wistful regret settled upon Grace. How good it must be to be loved like that, unconditionally.

Her thoughts were interrupted by the telephone. It was Alex. She did a quick calculation and realized that it must be about four o'clock in the morning.

'Are you all right?' she asked.

'Depends what you mean by all right. I . . . tell me, what did my father mean to you?' By the slowness of his speech she guessed that he was drunk.

'Alex?' In response to his desperate tone her heart lurched. 'I don't know what you are on about. I knew your father more than forty years ago.' When he didn't respond she added, 'I really can't see that it's any of your business. What's all this about?'

The words came tumbling out. 'I don't know what to think, about my feelings, about his, about yours.'

'There isn't anything to think about.' She felt alarmed. Trying to be calm, she said, 'Alex, we agreed that whatever happened between us it was just—two ships passing and all that.'

'Grace, I think I love you.'

'You don't. You can't. It's just . . . look, you've been through a lot lately. Why don't you give yourself time?' As an afterthought she asked, 'Is Susie still there?'

'Yes.'

'And?'

'And what?'

'Well, is she going to stay?'

She could imagine him shrugging. Making a stab in the dark, she said, 'If you need my blessing to get back with your wife, then you have it.'

The silence was overlong. Eventually he said, 'It would be the easiest thing all round. Dad would be pleased.'

'What about you?'

'I don't know what I want.'

'Exactly. Try not to worry about it. Give it time and it will sort itself out.'

What am I talking about, she thought? I sound like some agony aunt when in reality I have a very big role in this. During the next silence, she wondered what would happen if Alex came back. The idea was crazy—or was it? Of course it was. They had both become involved when their lives were in limbo. What did she know about him, his thoughts and feelings? He was a nice guy but what did that tell her?

Aloud she said, 'Honestly Alex, just be patient. Everything will sort itself out, you'll see.'

After another silence she said, 'It must be very late, you should try to get some sleep. Things will seem better in the morning.' More platitudes. As she sensed that he was preparing to ring off, she resisted the temptation to say, 'Remember me to your father'. In the circumstances it did not seem like a good idea.

'Look, I'll write to you,' she said instead. 'Try not to worry.'

She sensed that he was nodding his head,

tired and defeated. 'Just go to bed then, OK?'

'OK. Grace, I'm sorry.'

'There's no need to be sorry for anything. Goodnight.'

With that she put the phone down.

With a sigh she sat back at the table. Her letter lay in front of her and she knew that it was no longer appropriate. The chatty tone jarred with the desperation she had heard in Alex's voice. God, this was a mess. Instead, she found a note card with a view of Carisbrooke Castle and wrote briefly:

Thinking of you at this difficult time. I am sure that things will seem better when you have had time to reflect on all your options. Meanwhile, take good care of yourself. With fond wishes, Grace.

This seemed totally inadequate but she didn't know what else to do. Even the picture of the castle might be a mistake, reminding him of the happy hours they spent exploring. Not wishing to be alone with her thoughts, she turned on the television and, when she ran out of options, escaped into sleep.

The next morning she knew that she must keep focused and over breakfast she read more of the Holmes biography. It decided her to visit Yarmouth Castle where he had made his base during his governorship of the island.

Yarmouth was almost too small to be called

a town, and yet town it had been since the Middle Ages. The castle had been built on the orders of Henry VIII who, having upset the Catholic nations of Europe over his break with the Church, feared retribution from all sides. From the outside it wasn't much to look at but once through the gates it was easy to imagine the succession of bored gunners who had been posted here but never fired a shot in anger. The view from the upper platform was bracing, with the restless sea on three sides. Ferries ploughed their regular furrows from Lymington three miles away across the Solent. She was the only visitor and she closed her eyes, trying to imagine it as it must have been three hundred years earlier trying to pick up some link with the distant past. Still, Holmes might not have spent much time here. Instead, he had purloined some of the castle land and built himself a fine house next door. It was now a rather classy hotel.

She bought a postcard of the castle thinking that she could safely send it to Alex with a truncated account of her discoveries and then ventured next door, planning to have coffee.

The narrow street fronting the two buildings had probably changed little in recent times. Three pubs dominated the town centre. A fine old town hall and a little further south a parish church completed the kernel of the town. Other buildings were irrelevant to her quest. Beneath the tarmac of the road she could still see the outlines of old cobbles. For a moment she could almost hear the rattling of carts, the resonance of horseshoes.

Inside the hotel, the first thing that greeted her was a large portrait of King Charles II, saturnine and wearing a wig with luxurious black curls. She had read only that morning how the king had three times visited Holmes as indeed had his brother James when he in turn became king. For a man with modest roots, this Holmes had scaled the heights. She glanced curiously at the fine old staircase, remembering that upstairs Holmes's own room had been lavishly lined with yellow damask. His daughter Mary's room had been altogether more modest. Whatever else, she knew for certain that Mary was not the P who had lain for three hundred years in her garden.

Nobody seemed to be about in the vestibule so after a quick look around she decided against having coffee and stepped outside again. A narrow beam of sunshine lanced the street and she stopped for a moment on the hotel steps to absorb the fleeting warmth. There was one other place to visit before she left the port: the parish church.

It seemed unlikely that Robert Holmes was religious although of necessity he had no doubt observed the niceties required of him. His one gift to the town of Yarmouth was not an act of charity but a life-sized statue of himself, installed inside the church. The story went that King Louis XIV of France had commissioned the statue from an English sculptor but insisted that his head should be carved in France. While the torso was in transit, the ship was wrecked and the headless body recovered. Holmes acquired it and had his own head modelled to complete the work. She couldn't help but admire his arrogance.

As with the castle, there was no one in the church. Her footsteps echoed along the aisle, stepping over the resting places of the great and good buried beneath. She found the statue at the far end, protected behind a metal grill. She stared through the bars at the white marble, wondered at the Latin dedication extolling his virtues. Modesty was not one of them.

She thought that this was the closest she was likely to get to the man. He appeared shorter than she had expected but then, of course, the body was intended to represent the Sun King, not a renegade Anglo–Irishman. How true the head was to his actual features she had no way of telling. She felt pretty sure that he would not subscribe to Oliver Cromwell's view that he should be represented warts and all.

After a few minutes she wandered outside again into the sun. She didn't want to go home, back to an empty house. For a while she wandered around the town, buying a pasty for her lunch, then she remembered Thorlea, the house that Holmes had built for his daughter.

It was only a minor detour. It would delay her return home and perhaps there would be some other clue as to the essential Holmes.

The route from Yarmouth passed through extraordinary countryside, across a marshland that during winter flooded to create a lake suggesting bottomless depths as it reflected the ever-changing sky. Here, waders and seabirds sent out melancholy cries that must have echoed down the ages. She stopped the car near a bridge and got out to soak up the stillness. A little further on, across a field, stood a solitary chapel, once a place of worship, then a mortuary and now a storeroom. She climbed the stile and picked her way over the hillocks between grazing sheep that shifted a few steps to keep their distance. Where are you, Mr Holmes? She silently called. And where is your daughter Mary?

What sort of a person might she have been, this Mary, damned for her illegitimacy but courted because her father was powerful? Had anyone given her any maternal love? Certainly not her mother, who must have been banished, whoever she was. The girl's situation could not have been a happy one.

The house was just over the wall and Grace turned around to study it. This must surely be what they called Jacobean? Great sash windows broke up the muted yellow of the walls. Stout chimneys proliferated across the steeply pitched roof. As far as Grace knew, the house was never opened to the public so there would be no opportunity to see inside.

'Did you want something?'

The voice made her jump. A man mounted on a splendid black horse was on the other side of the wall. Clearly, he had ridden across the grass verge, otherwise she would have heard him.

'I . . . I was just looking,' she said lamely, feeling as if she had been caught out in some wrongdoing.

He was dressed in faded jodhpurs, a polo shirt and well-creased riding boots. He was thin, tall and bareheaded, his greying hair tied back at the nape of his neck.

Grace watched as he dismounted, landing lightly on his feet and tucking the stirrups into the leathers. The horse's neck was curly with sweat, as if they had ridden hard. The man's face was long and aristocratic but marked by hard living. He looked familiar. Grace frowned. Austin Morris had said something about a pop star living here and at the time she had thought of boy bands, then her eyes widened in disbelief. Duke Jamieson!

Here was the ultimate icon of her generation, the wild, crazy lead guitarist of Anarchy who had played with the likes of Hendrix and Dylan. She was so confused that she simply stared until he said, 'Who are you?'

'Grace Harrison.'

'Edward Jamieson, generally known as Duke, and don't tell me that you like my music.'

I like your music, she thought. I more than like it, it sustained me through my teenage years and across the lonely decades. It represented the sort of liberation that I longed to escape to.

'Well?' She detected impatience in his voice.

'I . . . I was interested in the house. I'm interested in Robert Holmes, who built it.'

'Why is that?'

'We . . . I think that he might have buried a woman in my garden.'

She saw his eyebrows flick up in surprise. That got your attention, she thought, gaining her composure.

He ran his hand absently along the horse's neck. 'Do you now? You'd better come and have a look, then. Can you hop over the wall?'

Grace glanced quickly at the four-foot-high wall with a deeper drop on the other side. This felt like some sort of challenge. Duke Jamieson was about three years older than she was. From his athletic performance, on the horse however, it didn't seem that the wall would cause him any problems. Quickly looking around, she found a metal bucket, upended it and stood on it so that she could climb over. She dropped awkwardly at his feet.

Immediately the air was rent by sound as three dogs came hurtling from the back of the

210

building, barking as if their lungs might burst. She stood her ground because there was nowhere to run to. She liked dogs, but these looked formidable. She glanced quickly towards Duke who appeared to be enjoying the spectacle of her dilemma. To the two deer hounds and the Great Dane he said, 'Calm down, girls.' Boisterously they gathered around Grace and began to lick her hands.

As if in response to the noise, a young woman poked her head around the door from one of the outbuildings. Duke gave a brief nod of his head and she came across and took the horse. In silence, they both watched her lead the animal away, a small, neat girl with thick brown hair and a behind that swayed provocatively as she walked. Duke did not speak to her. For a moment Grace wondered if she might be his daughter, then realized that she was far more likely to be some sort of live-in servant or lover or a combination of both. What was he—sixty-three? No one thought twice that he might be sleeping with a girl young enough to be his granddaughter. Why was it then that she had such anxieties about the age gap between her and Alex?

There was no time to pursue her thoughts because Duke said, 'Well? Are you coming?'

She followed him across the yard, the retinue of dogs dancing behind her. At the door they stopped and slumped down, ready to wait for their master's reappearance.

Inside, it was much as she expected, lofty, dark. Their footsteps resounded on the stone flagging of the corridor. As they emerged into a hallway, light funnelled from above, polishing the wooden panelling, softening the grey of the flagstones.

They stopped in the hall and he pointed to a portrait hanging opposite.

'There's your man.'

Grace recognized the figure whose picture was on the front of the book cover, the same pugnacious thrust of the head, eyes gazing arrogantly back at her. It must have been painted when he was in his forties. The face was strong with a prominent nose, a slightly downturned mouth and heavy chin. Superficially the statue in the church had captured something of his heaviness but the painting showed so much more of his self-assurance, a complete confidence in himself.

'Well?' Duke was watching her. He looked amused.

'Hardly a sensitive man,' she said.

'Probably not. Would you like a drink?'

She thought he meant coffee but he opened the door of some sort of armoire stretching the length of the wall to reveal a selection of bottles.

Some Victorian delicacy made her uneasy. Even by today's standards, Duke was notorious. He made no secret of the fact that he was bisexual and he had once famously announced that *if it moves, I screw it.* His drug addiction had been legendary.

Seeing her hesitation, the already familiar, wry smile played across his face.

'I'm driving,' she said, humiliation colouring her cheeks.

'Water then? Still? Fizzy? Laced with something?'

'Just plain water.'

He took out a heavy crystal glass and a bottle of spring water and poured her a measure. For himself he poured an equal measure of what might have been gin or vodka. He splashed the water briefly into his glass.

As Grace took the glass her hand brushed against his and her senses went haywire. Once, as a naïve teenager, she had daydreamed about this, meeting Duke Jamieson, living in a big house and owning lots of horses. Her image of what it would be like and the reality of what it would have been like were planets apart.

She looked again around the room. The other three walls were packed with wall-to-wall books. For something to say she asked, 'Do you read a lot?'

He smirked. 'If you're asking are these just for show, the answer's no. Some of them are collector's items, first editions, rare copies. That doesn't stop me from reading them.' His speaking voice was soft, middle English; she

213

thought of his husky, erotic singing voice that had melted her in the privacy of her room.

Seeing her looking at a section of island books, he said, 'Have a look if you want to. I have to go out in about twenty minutes.' With that, he put down his glass and glanced at his Rolex.

Grace suddenly remembered that she had her camera in her bag. She glanced at the portrait and, as he went to leave, she asked, 'Would you mind if I took a photo of—'

'Yes, I would.' His voice was suddenly hostile. 'Bloody journalists use all kinds of tactics to get in here.'

Do I look like a journalist? thought Grace. Aloud she said, 'I'm not a journalist. I only meant might I photograph the portrait.'

He eyed her for what seemed a very long time, taking a cigarette from a box on the table and a lighter from his pocket. He had very slim hips, the jodhpurs were tight and he scrabbled to get a grip on the lighter. Grace remembered him gyrating with what then seemed awful daring and Edna's snort of indignant outrage.

He drew long and hard on the cigarette before saying, 'OK then, snap away at the old man, but if I see one picture printed, one article written about this place—'

'You won't.'

She was about to thank him when he said, 'If you're really interested in Holmes, there's a box down there on the bottom shelf with some papers in it. There might be something connected to him. Anyway, I'm just going to change. You'd better be ready to leave when I come back.'

As soon as he shut the door she grabbed the box, feeling a surge of excitement. She was torn between taking the photo and looking at the contents. The box won.

On the top were various letters written in the early twentieth century. She resisted the desire to look at them because time was so short. She knew already that he would not invite her back. She caught sight of wires running above the door. The whole place was probably under surveillance. Here was a man who valued his privacy.

Letters, invoices, they seemed to go in chronological order so she dug further down. Near to the bottom she found several documents, one relating to the purchase of a parcel of land adjoining Thorlea Hall, another a bill of sale for *One harp with fine gilding*. They related to a later Holmes, called Henry.

Going right to the bottom she found letters clearly addressed to her Holmes. The first started 'Your Honour', but the writing was so convoluted she couldn't read it. Another was addressed to 'Dearest Robin', and appeared to come from a naval officer, but again she could only interpret the odd word.

All the time the minutes were ticking by. In desperation she pulled out a slim volume at the bottom of the box. It was leather bound and the pages were brittle and brown with age. Large, bold writing filled each line. It appeared to be some sort of record, notes and details about breeding sheep, recording weather patterns and a few more personal jottings. Luckily it was more legible.

She turned a page and read: *'Today, sorely plagued by the gout. The remedy does little to ease my suffering,* and a little further on *'I passed the night in some agony. Only the application of my own piss to the affected parts brings relief.'*

It dawned on her that this was Holmes's personal diary. The dates seemed to start at around March 1682. At the realization, her throat constricted. With trembling fingers she looked at the last entry, dated 17 June 1683. She hardly dared to acknowledge what she was thinking. Would there, could there be an entry for 1682 that would throw some light on to P and what had befallen her?

She fumbled with the pages as the door opened and Duke put his head around. 'Ready?' It was an order rather than a question.

'Would you mind waiting for just one minute?'

'Hurry up. I'm already late.' His voice was sharp. He went back outside.

By now Grace was in a panic. Her eyes raced across the pages—March, April, May

1682, page upon page of short entries. Then, there it was, 18 May.

With disbelief, she read: '*This day, the black girl died in childbirth. I have named the infant Paloma in remembrance of her mother.*'

'Are you coming?' Duke's voice seemed to come from another world.

'Yes.' She shut the book and dropped it into the box.

'Leave it there. I'm going to be late.'

In a daze, she followed him back into the hall. She had nothing to lose. Dragging out the camera she started to flash away at the portrait without having time to focus. With luck something would be OK.

'Come on!'

'I'm coming.'

She followed him out. Ignoring her, he walked across to a Land-Rover and climbed in. She began to walk ahead down the drive, focusing on the implication of what she had found. Some sort of electronic device closed the wrought iron gates behind them and he drove past her, not acknowledging her. A few yards further on he slewed to a halt and waited for her to catch up.

Out of the window he asked, 'Do you want to come to a party on Saturday?'

'I—' She was so surprised she couldn't think.

'No need to worry about drinking or driving.' He added enigmatically.

217

What did that mean? Surely he couldn't be inviting her to stay the night? Surely he wasn't propositioning her!

'Listen, I've got to go. Come if you like. I'm interested in this Holmes who owned my house. You can tell me about him.' As he put the car into gear, he added, 'If you're worried about your reputation, I've invited a friend who is some sort of history freak. He doesn't drink much so he could drive you home, that is, if you want to go home. Otherwise . . .' A sudden provocative smile transformed his face and she found herself smiling back.

As the car raced off in a cloud of dust she wandered towards her own modest vehicle, stunned by the turn of events. Until last week she had been a typical, unfulfilled—yes frustrated—spinster. Since then she had had abandoned sex with a man twenty years her junior and was now perhaps being propositioned by the notorious Duke Jamieson! Madness, she thought, pure madness, but she was smiling.

CHAPTER SIXTEEN

When Grace got home she couldn't settle. The events of the morning had been too bizarre. She badly needed to talk to someone but there was only Molly and that would take too much

218

explanation. Besides, what would Molly think? Grace was in no mood to be lectured. She tried to imagine telling her friend that she was going to a party at Duke Jamieson's but the idea was preposterous. She decided to keep it to herself.

The only other person she could think of, who would be interested in what she had discovered about Paloma, was Austin Morris. He would certainly like to know what she had found out. His telephone number was on his card beside the phone. In a decisive moment, she actually picked up the receiver, but then she realized that it was one o'clock and there was a good chance that he would be at lunch. Anyway, she needed to calm down. If she had to mention where she had found the information then the excitement in her voice might give her away and how humiliating would that be. She felt annoyed with herself for responding like an over excited teenager. The only other thing to do was to write to Alex, and she sat down to do so.

There was too much to say to fit on the card of Yarmouth Castle so she wrote a letter instead, informative, friendly and, she hoped, reassuring. She did not mention Duke. It must have been the thought of Alex, but for a moment she was certain that she could smell his aftershave and an answering quickening in her womb reminded her of what they had shared. As if trying to get away from herself, she put her pen aside and went out into the garden.

Evidence of Alex's visit was everywhere, the maple tree and across the wall the cemetery with his great-grandparents' graves, memories that attacked her at every turn. Irritated by her emotion, she tried to concentrate on Paloma, the name that Holmes had given to his—his what, his lover, his charge? She sank on to the garden bench in the sun. The rays were soothing. Was Holmes the father of Paloma's child? There was no way of knowing. If he wasn't, what was it about the girl that had made him have the wall beside her grave inscribed so elaborately? She wondered why he had not simply insisted that both mother and child should be baptized and then Paloma could be buried in the churchyard. Perhaps, though, even with his influence, the clergy would have found it a step too far. There was still so much that she didn't know.

A more sober mood settled upon her. Even across the centuries she felt the girl's loneliness, a maternal ache enveloped her for the abandoned young woman and her motherless daughter. Now they had no one except her to be curious about them. Well, at least she could see that the first Paloma was properly laid to rest. As for what became of her daughter—all those questions again.

Still trying to calm herself, she went back indoors. After her eyes adjusted to the gloom

220

she returned to Alex's letter. She wished she could think of the right things to say, to admit that she missed him without owning up to the fact that she would welcome him back. This was too dangerous. Her feelings were liable to change from minute to minute. She thought of the certainty with which she had told him that his own feelings were unreliable, that time would alter them. She needed to take a page out of her own book.

As she was sealing the envelope the telephone rang.

'Grace?'

It was Austin. At the sound of his voice she sank down on to a chair, feeling that there was some strange alchemy going on here. Had he known that she had wanted to talk to him? She dismissed the thought as stupid.

'Grace, it's Austin Morris.'

I know who you are, she thought.

'This is just to let you know that I looked at the baptismal records for the time that the young woman died and there is no record of a child being christened in the parish.'

'Thank you. As a matter of fact, I have some news. I discovered something this morning, a document that actually mentions a black girl dying in childbirth.'

'Really, how very fascinating.'

Fortunately, he didn't ask where she had got the information although at some point she would probably tell him. Instead he said,

'Might I suggest that you have a look at the deeds of your house. It is just possible that there would be something there that would help. That's assuming that isn't where you got your information today?'

'Er, no.' She sidestepped the question, saying instead, 'but thank you for the suggestion. The deeds are with the bank but I can always phone and request them.'

'Well, if you come up with anything more . . .'

She had the impression that he wanted to say something else. After some hesitation he continued, 'I don't suppose you go to the cinema, or the theatre at all? I . . . I sometimes I get tickets passed on to me and I thought you might like to come if it was anything you might like.'

Oh God, was he inviting her out on a date? She hesitated a moment too long before saying, 'That's really kind of you.' Did she want to go out with him? No, she didn't. There was nothing wrong with him. In fact, he was a very pleasant companion and she liked his humour, his interests, but life was already too complicated. As for what she liked, what did she like? She had no idea what he had in mind, the cinema, an opera, a musical, Shakespeare?

He said, 'As a matter of fact, I have got tickets for a play on Saturday evening but unfortunately I'm otherwise engaged. I don't suppose you would like to have them, take a friend perhaps?'

A sigh of relief—he wasn't asking her out, just being considerate. 'Thank you, but I'm already going out on Saturday,' she replied. Was she? Was she seriously considering going to Thorlea Hall or was it just an excuse? As Austin expressed regret and rang off, she thought, 'I can't go—can I?' But already she suspected that she would.

By Saturday she had convinced herself that she wouldn't go. How could she possibly just turn up like some ageing groupie? She visualized his house bursting with pretty young girls, older men smoking, drinking, snorting coke or whatever they did. She really had little idea about the drug scene other than from TV dramas and, anyway, she had no wish to be part of it. Like a tennis match inside her head, two voices tried to score points. One voice suggested that Duke might actually play some of his hits. Other members of the band might be there, those who had survived. Two had died young, one in a car crash, the other from the inevitable overdose. Her adventurous self admonished her, 'Don't be such a stick in the mud. This is the freedom you have been longing for, for decades. Get out there and sample life—to the full.'

While she was agonizing, there was a tap on the back door. She guessed correctly that it was Molly.

'Just thought I'd pop round and see what

you've been up to.' She looked perkier than the last time Grace had seen her. 'How are things?' she asked.

Molly plonked herself down at the kitchen table in what Grace couldn't help but think of as Alex's chair. Molly said, 'It's been a relief having other people around. Good news, too. Reg is going to the day centre twice a week. It will give me a break.'

'That's great.'

Molly looked around the room as if trying to detect any changes. 'Been doing anything interesting?' she asked.

'Not really.'

'Do you want to come round for supper this evening?' There was hope in Molly's voice, a hint that she needed the company.

Just as Grace was about to reply the telephone jarred.

'Just a minute.' She picked up the receiver. 'Hello?'

'It's Edward Jamieson. I'm sending a car to pick you up at eight this evening.'

'What?' The news stunned her into silence.

As if he was picking up on her thoughts, he said, 'I found out where you lived from the telephone directory.'

'Oh.'

'Right. I'll see you later.'

Before she could object, he had gone.

'Who was that?' The ever-astute Molly picked up on her surprise.

'No one—just a friend.'

Molly's expression was difficult to interpret. 'Tonight then?' she said, preparing to get up.

'I'm afraid I can't. I'm going out.'

'Are you now? Where are you gallivanting off to, then?'

Grace couldn't say. Detecting Molly's disappointment, she said, 'I'm really sorry about this evening but I promise that I'll come round tomorrow and tell you all about it.'

Molly nodded, reassured. 'Come to Sunday lunch then.'

'I will. I promise that I will.'

*   *   *

The question of what to wear occupied her for much of the afternoon. At one level she chided herself for being so shallow. At another she knew that she needed all the help she could get to maintain her courage, and if it meant wearing something special, then so be it.

The wardrobe did not offer a lot in the way of choice. Grace had got into the habit of buying a few good-quality clothes and they lasted. She never went out often enough for them to wear out. She was tempted to fly into town and buy something new but there wasn't really much time. Besides, she didn't really trust her judgement when it came to choosing something appropriate and her grown-up self was already lecturing her on her foolishness.

225

She decided to wear trousers so that she could wear comfortable shoes. That was a start. In her wardrobe was a stand-by black velvet pair. Now all she needed to do was choose a suitable top. She'd wash her hair, put it up in the way that Alex had commented on, wear long earrings, dig out her largely neglected make-up bag and then simply hope for the best.

She wondered who might come to pick her up. Did Duke have a chauffeur? He could certainly afford one. His records were still played almost daily and recently there had been a renewed flourish of interest in the band because one of their pieces had been chosen as the theme music for a new television series. And all the time he had been living a few miles away!

Inevitably she was ready far too early, so to keep herself occupied she read some more of the Holmes biography. It was nearing the end of his life. A soldier turned sailor, he still managed to start a war with the Netherlands and then destroy their navy. But it all took a toll on his health. Increasingly, he was to be found in fashionable Bath in pursuit of relief by taking the waters. Fighting until the end, on 18 November 1691 he died. Grace felt an answering sadness, a sense of loss that even from this distance acknowledged the end of an exceptional if difficult man.

For a while she simply gazed into space,

then it occurred to her that a copy of Holmes's will was probably held at the Public Record Office. She made a note that on Monday she would go and look at it.

The book made no further mention of his daughter Mary or, of course, of the first or second Paloma. Grace sat quietly, trying to imagine the two daughters. Did Mary know about the other girl? Was it just possible that Paloma had been in the same house—as a servant, of course, but it might still be possible to find out something about her. At the thought of Thorlea Hall her pulses quickened. In less than an hour she would be there, perhaps standing where young Paloma had stood. She was glad now that she was going.

Her reverie was interrupted by a knock on the door. Quickly she pushed the book aside, grabbed her bag and hurried to answer it. Her heart was beating too fast and she felt flustered. Back-tracking, she thought that even now she could send the driver away, say that she hadn't been consulted about a lift and that she wasn't coming.

A young woman was waiting on the doorstep. Grace did not think it was the same girl that she had seen before. Inevitably she was pretty, with dark wavy hair and rather startling blue/black eyes. She wore a short denim skirt and cotton top, the colour enhancing her eyes. She had lovely long legs.

'Hi, I'm Virginia.' Her smile was wide and

disarming. Grace gave a rather nervous smile in return and followed her down the path.

'Do you often get jobs like this?' she asked.

They had already reached the car, a rather superior-looking Citroën and Virginia opened the back door for her.

'I'd rather sit in the front, if you don't mind.' Grace decided to assert some sort of control over the situation.

'Sure.'

As she slipped into the passenger seat, Virginia said, 'I get all kinds of jobs. That's what's so great about being with Duke you never know what is going to happen next.'

Being with Duke—that must, of course, imply that she was his mistress? And who could blame him? As Virginia started the engine, Grace echoed the girl's words in her head—she had no idea what was going to happen next.

CHAPTER SEVENTEEN

The electronic gates at the entrance to Thorlea Hall stood open as they drove in. Already, several cars were parked at the front of the house.

Virginia had been quiet during much of the journey, not volunteering any information, but Grace detected that she was relaxed and confident. Grace occupied herself by trying to imagine what her relationship with Duke might be. As the images grew too vivid, she simply looked out of the window.

They pulled to a halt and Grace felt increasingly nervous. How did one behave on an occasion such as this? What was the occasion? Perhaps Duke had such gatherings all the time and it was nothing special. Perhaps they had drug-fuelled sex orgies? At the thought, she nearly laughed. Before she could undo her seatbelt, somebody opened the car door.

'Welcome.' She looked into the face of a tall, slender young man with dark Byronic hair and designer stubble.

Feeling flustered, she clumsily heaved herself from the seat. The car was low to the ground and an elegant exit seemed impossible.

The young man took her arm to help her. 'I'm Quentin,' he said. 'Welcome to Thorlea.'

'Thank you.' She extricated herself from his grip and turned towards the house. Beautiful girls, beautiful boys, it all fed into the myth that surrounded Duke Jamieson's lifestyle.

This was the first time she had seen the house from this side. An extravagant stone double staircase led up to a first-floor balcony that stretched the length of the house. Huge French windows stood open and from inside she could hear that they were playing 'Time is Running Out', one of their all-time successes.

She wondered if it was live music or a recording.

Around her people were milling about, mostly older people, soberly dressed. The women had a certain chic, the men the self-satisfied look of success. At that moment she spotted Duke. He was dressed in dark trousers, a black shirt and a sequined waistcoat. With the setting sun behind him he looked slender, strangely sensuous, almost ethereal. Virginia was talking to him and his head was bent towards her as if to hear over the hubbub. He patted her arm to show that he understood and seconds later he was coming down the steps and across the lawn.

'Good. You've come. I thought you might say no.'

Grace felt a moment of confusion that he should care whether she was there or not. 'What's the occasion?' she asked.

'I'm not really sure. That time really is running out? That my son is here?'

His son—Quentin Jamieson! His mother had long since disappeared but she remembered that the boy had gone into fashion design. With those looks, no wonder he was a success. She suddenly felt dowdy in her velvet trousers and plum-coloured top.

'You look good,' Duke said, as if reading her thoughts. 'Come and get a drink.' He half turned and smiled. 'Don't worry about getting home; I'll make sure you get back safely, honour intact.'

Her face flushed. She suddenly felt foolish again, to imagine that he might fancy her. Once more she wondered about Virginia and the girl who had taken the horse. Anything as mundane as marriage was unlikely in this setting.

She asked for vodka and tonic and it came in a tall crystal tumbler. A slice of lemon trembled on the surface of the bubbles. She took a gulp and the sensation was pleasing, almost decadent.

'Let me introduce you to some people. There's someone I particularly want you to meet but he isn't here yet.' He suddenly snapped his fingers and yet another young girl appeared. 'Candice, look after Grace; make sure she has someone interesting to talk to.' With a wave, he stepped away and went back inside.

Candice waited politely. 'Do you like Duke's music?' she asked.

'I grew up with it.' Grace felt embarrassed at the admission that she was so old. 'How about you?' She tried to deflect the attention away from herself.

'Yeah, it's great.'

'Do you work for Duke?'

Candice shrugged. 'Not work exactly. He . . . you know, he sort of took us in.'

Grace didn't know at all. 'You live here?' she asked, more for something to say than because she expected to work out all the relationships.

'We do now.'

Who was 'we' she wondered—Candice, Virginia, the girl with the horse? Were they some sort of harem? Candice smiled at her. 'We owe a lot to Duke. He knows what it's like to be on the streets. He took us in, gave us a home.'

'So you're—?'

'We're all sort of his family now. For most of us, he's like the dad we never had.'

'The dad? How many of you are there?'

'Four, no, five.' She gave a laugh. 'He's not our real dad. Everyone thinks he's wild and terrible, but he isn't. He's kind.'

Here was another surprise.

They had wandered into the room and its beauty distracted her from more conversation. It was sparsely furnished but the length and breadth of the space, the light coming from three sides, gave it a feeling of floating elegance.

Candice stopped by a group of people, two men and a woman. 'This is a friend of Duke's,' she said, indicating Grace and that she should join them. They widened their circle to let her in.

'I'm James Stanforth, solicitor. This is Greta and this is Roland. They're business associates.'

Business associates—what did that mean

she wondered? 'I'm Grace Harrison.' She offered no explanation because she didn't have one. Inevitably, the conversation went along the lines of have you known Duke long and where do you live? Behind her, the tone of the room was changing. People began to look towards the far corner where drums, guitar and bass rested against the wall.

'Duke's going to sing,' said James Stanforth. 'He usually gives us one number if we're lucky.' They all turned to face the corner.

Grace couldn't see the man on the drums. It was Quentin who had picked up the bass guitar but it was the other man, his father, Duke Jamieson, who held all eyes. For a while he stood very still as if gathering himself, then magically, he began to play. The notes encircled the gathering, ricocheting across the room. Then he started to sing 'Requiem for Rori'. The audience was silent, spellbound.

Rori Doherty had been the original bass guitarist, killed when his car went off the road near Brighton. The song reflected that the young man would always be twenty years old, that anything was still possible in a life that didn't have an ending. Grace felt the pathos and an answering tear welled in the corner of her eye.

As the performance came to an end there was again silence. People were touched by the enormity of the feelings. Only after a moment to collect themselves did they start to clap.

Grace slipped away from Stanforth and his companions. She had nothing to say to them. She felt surrounded by sadness. She wanted to get away and be alone. The garden would be the place to go and she started towards the French windows but a voice called out to her.

'Grace, come and meet the friend I was telling you about.'

Grace turned to see Duke still acknowledging the praise for his performance. Behind him, the man who had played the drums was replacing the sticks, easing himself off the chair. He looked around to see who Duke was talking about.

Grace actually faltered. Her mouth fell open and she felt something inside of her jerk her to a halt, for behind the drums was Austin Morris!

'Well, I never!' His surprise seemed to equal hers.

'What are you doing here?' she asked. From their conversation about the house she recalled that he had said he didn't know who owned it. Now here he was playing drums as if he was always here.

Austin looked confused as he turned to Duke 'Edward, I was wanting to introduce you to Grace but I was waiting for the right moment. I had no idea that you already knew her.'

'We're recent acquaintances,' Duke replied, then turning to her he said, 'Tell him about this house and what you have been looking for.'

'He already knows,' she said. 'I had no idea that he knew you.' She looked accusingly across at Austin, who bowed his head.

'Sorry, but I never let on that Edward and I are old friends. People were always looking for introductions and it's hard to get any privacy when you're famous.'

Briefly Grace wondered if she had known, whether she too might have been angling for an opportunity to meet the great man. She didn't know what to make of the discovery. Austin Morris, something in the archaeology department, reticent, unexceptional, was a friend of one of the most celebrated, wild guys of British music.

Duke did that finger snapping movement again and someone appeared with a tray of drinks, vodka and tonic for her, something similar for Duke and a very dark ale for Austin.

Taking his glass, Duke said, 'You two go off and talk about history, or whatever it is you do. I'll see you later.' They were left alone.

Austin said, 'I'm really sorry if I surprised you. Edward and I were at university together.' He gave a short laugh. 'I wasn't always a grey academic, you know.'

She thought of his stripey jumpers, the vivid T-shirts. Whatever else he might be, he wasn't grey.

'Shall we go outside?' he suggested. 'The gardens are quite something and, as you can see, the paths are lighted with lanterns. Besides, I ought to just check on Columbus.'

'He's here?'

'Over in the stable with Edward's menagerie.'

Together they set off down the staircase, across the gravel and on towards the back of the building. Austin said, 'When you said you were going out this evening I had no idea—'

'Me neither. I nearly didn't come.' She explained how she had happened to see Duke when she was eyeing the house from the outside. 'You didn't know that he had documents here about Holmes?' She asked.

'I didn't. I thought that all of the historical stuff was in the Public Record Office.'

They reached the stable yard and the dogs abandoned their cease fire and set up a cacophony of barking. Grace thought that indeed it sounded like a battlefield.

'Hey, enough of that.' Austin called out and unfastened one of the stable doors. Duke's three dogs and Columbus tumbled out to greet them.

'Oh, I'm sorry, I forgot about your clothes.' Austin tried to quiet the enthusiastic quartet who were happily circling and jumping around them.

'It doesn't matter.' She patted an assortment of heads and after they calmed down Austin ordered them back into the stable. To her surprise they obliged.

'Have you seen Duke's farm?' he asked.

'No.'

'Well, farm is probably the wrong word. Sanctuary would be more appropriate. He is always taking in lame dogs, two and four legged.'

'I met a couple of girls this evening—they seemed to have been "adopted"?'

'That's more or less it.' She could tell that he was choosing his next words carefully. 'Duke is always surrounded by young people. He has such a reputation for sex and orgies, but it isn't like that any more. It never was, really, not like the Press represented it. Anyway, he had a serious illness some time ago. Don't you dare say that I said it, but he's virtually celibate.'

Like me, thought Grace, and possibly like Austin who seemed still to be grieving for his lost wife.

She followed him down by the side of the stables and then through a gate into another yard. Various animal sounds carried across the space. Looking over a door, Grace came face to face with a donkey who appeared to be annoyed that his sleep had been interrupted. Other animals were similarly housed, a pony that clearly had trouble walking, a cow, two goats leaping up at the door and waving their horns with scant regard for her extended hand.

Austin said, 'The dogs might look like a designer breed but they were rescued from a puppy farm. That pony there has deformed legs so was destined for the meat industry but Edward wasn't having that. He's got this affinity with anything abused or abandoned.'

There were so many revelations.

Austin said, 'We could go into the house and have a look at those papers if you wanted to.'

As they started back, she explained about the diary and how she had only managed to glance at the entries. She was about to say that she would welcome a chance to look at it properly when they heard the sound of feet running along the gravel and toward them.

'Austin! Austin, are you there?' It was Quentin Jamieson.

Austin opened the gate to go back outside. 'What's wrong?' he asked.

The boy was gasping for breath but even in the gloom they could see the shock on his face. 'For God's sake come quickly. It's Dad—I think he's dead.'

CHAPTER EIGHTEEN

They began to run up the path towards the house. All the time, Quentin's words pursued them. Of course Duke couldn't be dead. Half an hour before he had been singing, ushering them out into the garden. As Grace grew increasingly breathless, wild scenarios of shootings or attempted kidnappings bombarded her. Could someone have broken in, in front of all the guests, and attempted to exact some sort of revenge? Had some drug-fuelled guest pulled a knife and tried to stab him? The party hadn't been like that but still she reverted to her image of Duke Jamieson, the bad, exciting boy of pop. Anyway, it must all be a panic for nothing.

Austin and Quentin were already a long way ahead. They both took the steps two at a time up to the first-floor drawing-room. Grace fought with her bursting lungs to try to keep up with them.

The scene inside the room looked like a theatre set. Guests stood in a semi-circle, still and silent, and in the centre someone lay on the floor. One on each side, Virginia and Candice knelt like the two Marys at the foot of the cross. Their faces were shocked, looking for help and reassurance.

Austin pushed Candice aside and fell to his knees, feeling for a pulse, talking to Duke, shaking him. 'Have you called an ambulance?' he asked the air.

Someone said yes. They seemed incapable of movement.

Austin began to give the prone figure the kiss of life. As he worked, he talked to him between breaths. 'Come on, mate, don't do this to us.'

Grace watched in fascinated horror. Perhaps this was some sort of trick Duke played on his friends, one of those famous pranks of his, except that no one was laughing.

She became aware of a distant wailing. Moments later there was the sound of gravel being swept aside by a braking vehicle. Two men came running into the room, carrying medical equipment. Austin stepped back to let them work. His face was stark, his eyes black tunnels of anxiety.

The paramedics went through their routine, asked what had happened, checked for vital signs, slipped an oxygen mask over Duke's face. Within two minutes he was loaded on to a stretcher. Quentin went with him. Austin promised that he would follow by car.

As they departed, the rest of the party looked helplessly at each other. No one seemed willing to go home, as if by staying they could undo the events of the past half an hour.

'What happened?' someone asked. Clearly he had been out of the room at the time.

'He was talking to the Emersons. He took a drink and then just suddenly he looked strange then he dropped the glass and fell to the ground.'

'You don't think he could have been poisoned?'

Several guests rounded angrily on the questioner. 'Of course he wasn't poisoned. He's had a heart attack,'

'Or a stroke.'

'I'm sure he'll be all right.'

'Perhaps we should go home?'

The suggestion seemed to spark them into action. People began to move towards the doors. There was a certain reluctance in their steps, as if they needed to stay and be a part of whatever was happening. But gradually the numbers in the room decreased. Outside, the sound of car doors slamming and engines starting preceded the departures.

Grace wondered what to do. With no obvious way of getting home, she said to Virginia 'Do you mind if I use the phone to get a taxi?'

Virginia stood up with an effort. 'I'll give you a lift.'

'No, you won't.' The girl was white and clearly in shock. 'I'm sure he'll be all right,' Grace said. 'Why don't you and the others go to bed?'

Virginia shook her head. She began to cry. Across the room, sitting alone on an elegant Regency chair, Candice was chewing the edge of her finger. Grace knew that she could not leave them.

'I'm going to make tea,' she announced, knowing that it was the age-old, if misnamed treatment for shock.

As no one answered, she went to find the kitchen. A few days ago she had stood here with Duke while he told her about the portrait, the box of papers that might help her search. Please don't let him be dead!

She managed to find mugs, boiled the kettle on the huge Aga, located the fridge, found teabags, sugar and spoons, and took a tray to the drawing-room. Nearly everyone had now left. Grace placed the tray on a rather beautiful table, agonizing in case the heat should mark the wood, and took two mugs of sweet tea to Virginia and Candice. They accepted it meekly, like children, and Grace's heart went out to them. For all their sophistication they were little more than children.

Looking round the room, she decided that the best thing was to keep busy. Taking the now empty tray she began to collect up glasses. Peering into an anteroom she saw that food had been laid out for the guests. One or two attacks had been made on it but for the most part people hadn't got around to eating. Feeling suddenly hungry, she grabbed a canapé, then another. There was the taste of asparagus then roast vegetables. Grabbing one more for luck, she picked up the used plates and headed once more for the kitchen.

Nobody came to help her. A few stubborn guests remained but she guessed that downright nosiness rather than concern kept them there. She ignored them.

The kitchen had a huge, deep, old-fashioned sink. She filled it with hot, sudsy water and enjoyed the process of washing the glasses. They were nearly all crystal, tumblers, wine goblets, elegant champagne flutes. Upended on the draining boards, they sparkled in the light. When she had finished washing up she fetched the food and began to pack it away. There were two huge fridges and she found space to store it. For good measure she finished up some savoury rolls.

It was 4.30 when Austin and Quentin arrived back. They had no need to say anything. As they came through the door, Quentin was shaking his head as tears tumbled down his cheeks. Duke was dead. Numbed by the news, Grace returned to the kitchen and made more drinks for the returning duo.

'I'm so sorry,' she said.

Neither of them spoke. They looked exhausted.

'You get to bed,' Austin exhorted the younger man. 'You and the girls, go to bed, take a couple of paracetamols, try and get some sleep. I'm going to take this lady home and I'll be back in the morning.' He looked at Grace and gave her a tight smile.

'I think you should stay,' she suggested. 'I can always get a taxi.'

'At this time of the night? Around here? I don't think so.'

He was right. Local taxi drivers were family men. They didn't provide a twenty-four-hour service.

'Look, I'm fine. I'll just drop you off then I'll come back.'

She suddenly felt exhausted. The late hour and the shock were beginning to take their toll. She didn't argue with him and after he had finished his drink she went with him. The young people had disappeared upstairs.

'What about the dogs?' she thought suddenly.

'We'll let them out. They usually sleep in the old scullery. They'll be fine there.'

On the way to the car they made a detour to the stable block. A few hours earlier they had been here discussing Duke. How could he have left the world so suddenly?

As they drove, Austin said, 'There will be an inquest of course—sudden death and all that. I don't know when the funeral will be. I have to go to Bath on Monday for a couple of weeks to run a course. I hope it's sorted before then.' They continued in silence for a while then he said, 'I know Duke left instructions in his will. He's . . . he was, very well organized. The kids, the sanctuary, are all provided for.' He sighed. 'I still can't believe it.'

Grace reached out and touched his arm. The shot silk shirt he wore felt smooth beneath her fingers.

'I'm so sorry,' she said. 'I feel as if I have

244

lost a friend too. Even if I had never met him I would still feel his loss because he was my teenage idol. Lots of people will feel like that. I still think his music is better than anything else I know.'

'He was at our wedding,' Austin announced. 'He gave us tickets to Bali, hotel reservations, everything. People didn't have honeymoons like that then.'

She realized that silent tears were running down Austin's cheeks. Again she touched his arm, helpless in the face of his grief. It occurred to her that he was remembering not only his friend but that honeymoon and the wife he had lost.

As they drew up in her lane, he did not get out. 'You go on in, try not to dwell on what's happened. I'll call you tomorrow.'

Instinctively, she leaned forward and kissed his cheek. 'You drive carefully.'

'I will.' He turned the car in the lane, a tight three-point turn, and began to drive away. As she watched him go she thought that she had never felt so lonely.

*   *   *

She was too tired to do more than slip out of her clothes and seek the sanctuary of her bed. It was well after five and the dawn chorus had already been rehearsing for an hour. Mercifully, sleep came quickly, a dense,

245

dreamless escape from the shock and pain of the evening. When she awoke vivid sunshine was blazing through the curtains. Bit by bit, the events of the evening returned and she longed to turn over and blot them out again but they had already found a foothold. There was nothing for it but to get up and make tea.

She had no idea what to do with the day. It stretched like a prison sentence, isolating her from the people with whom she had shared the last evening. She needed to be with them to compare notes, reassure each other and secure friendships that would see them through the dark days.

After two cups of tea she showered and dressed. Her black velvet trousers and top lay abandoned on the floor. Her feelings hit a new low as she picked them up and put them on hangers. She should put them in the laundry but just at the moment she couldn't face washing away the link with last night.

The phone called her back to the present. When she lifted the receiver, she heard Molly say, 'Lunch is in half an hour. Come on over and keep me company.'

Oh God, she'd forgotten all about the promise. She thought quickly but there seemed no way to get out of it. Say she wasn't coming, and she'd have to come up with a reason. Tell the truth, and Molly would insist that she shouldn't be on her own.

'I'm just getting dressed,' she said.

'You lazy stay-a-bed.'

She agreed. It was the easiest thing to do.

Half an hour later she knocked at Molly's door and walked in. The smell of cooking assailed her and she realized that she hadn't had any breakfast. Her treacherous stomach was hungry for food.

'Come and sit in the kitchen. Reg is watching the snooker—at least, it's on. I'm not sure how much he is taking in.'

Grace sat down. Inside, she was struggling with what to say, where to begin. Molly was busy making gravy the old-fashioned way in the roasting pan, sifting flour and meat extract into the juices. It reminded her of being young, coming home to Edna.

For the first time, Molly looked at her.

'Are you all right? Whatever's the matter?'

Grace shook her head, the words evading her. 'Such a lot has happened,' she finally managed to say.

'What sort of things?'

Then it all came tumbling out, the skeleton, Alex, Austin, the amazing invitation to Thorlea Hall that had ended last night in Duke's death.

'I heard about that on the radio,' Molly interjected. 'They said he died from a drugs overdose.' She made her familiar disapproving sniff that reminded Grace of Edna.

'He didn't! He had a stroke.' She felt angry at the sensationalism of the press and with

247

Molly for being so quick to judge. It included anger with herself, for she too had fed into the myth that Duke Jamieson was a hell raiser.

For once Molly didn't seem to know how to respond. Grace heard the pop of a cork, the glug of wine into a glass. Her stomach felt acid but she accepted the glass, forced down the first gulp and the rest followed.

'How long had you known him, then? You never said anything.' Molly sounded disappointed not to have been let into the secret that Duke was a personal friend of Grace's.

'I only met him a couple of days ago, by accident.'

'And he invited you to a party? And you went?' Molly's tone implied that Grace must be mad.

'It wasn't like that. It was a very sober affair.'

'Hmm.' Molly didn't sound convinced.

Grace began to explain about Paloma but she knew that she wasn't taking Molly with her. The idea of forming a bond with a dead pile of bones clearly didn't spark any interest in her friend. She wanted to go home, to get away from everything, but Molly was draining the vegetables, clattering plates on the kitchen table.

'Be a love, take in the cutlery and see what Reg is up to.'

Grace did as she was asked. Reg was asleep

in the chair. He was leaning at an uncomfortable-looking angle but he seemed oblivious. On the television, the velvet voice of an Irish commentator explained the intricacies of the latest snooker shot and how it had gone wrong.

'Hello, Reg, lunch is ready,' she said loudly.

He jerked awake and looked totally lost.

'It's Grace. I've come to have lunch with you.'

He gazed blankly at the screen as if the game was some new mystery puzzle.

When Molly came in, together they heaved him out of the chair and up to the table. Molly had put his dinner in a bowl and it was cut up small, as if for a toddler. Again Grace felt relief that she hadn't faced this particular hell with Edna. Perhaps she should have appreciated more that Edna had managed to keep control of her senses. No way of telling her now, though.

'What are you going to do now?' Molly asked once they sat down.

'About what?'

'About everything. Are you planning on going to Australia?'

'Australia?'

'Yes, Australia.'

'No, of course I'm not.'

'Well, your lover boy is free now, isn't he?'

For a moment Grace wasn't sure whether Molly was referring to the recently separated Alex or the even more recently bereaved Joe.

Either way, it was the last place that she wanted to go just at this moment.

So the meal continued, Molly asking questions, Grace fending them off. It seemed that no subject was safe.

'How is Reg getting to the day centre?' she asked in an attempt to steer the discussion away from her.

'They're sending a car for him.'

Good. Grace needn't feel guilty if she didn't offer to take him.

Molly said, 'Perhaps one day while he's there, we could go into town, have a spot of lunch?'

'Yes, of course.' No doubt the present mood would pass. Grace knew that she was in shock, the delayed shock of Edna's death and the crazy interlude with Alex, but also last night's sudden death, just when a new episode in her life might have been opening up.

As soon as she decently could, she excused herself.

'I'm not sure it is good for you to be over there on your own,' Molly said.

'Really, I'll be fine. I've got letters to write.'

'Ah.' To one, or both of the supposed lovers no doubt. Molly remained silent.

The cloud lifted as Grace walked up her pathway and opened the door. She was greeted with the beep of the answerphone. Pressing the button, it was to hear Austin saying, 'I called round earlier but you weren't there. Could you give me a call, just to let me know that you're all right?' He reeled off a number that Grace guessed was at Thorlea Hall.

She sat down and kicked off her shoes. For an age she simply sat in the chair, fielding the emotions that seemed to well up from nowhere and everywhere. At last she got up and went to the phone.

It was answered by a young, female voice, tight with unhappiness.

'It's Grace from last night,' she said, 'Is Austin there? He's been trying to get me.'

There was a brief silence and then he came on the phone.

'Grace? Are you all right?'

'Yes, I'm fine. How about you?'

'We're all OK.'

We. She suddenly wished that she was there, sharing the shock, being part of something. A family? She said, 'Any news?'

'Not about the funeral, no. It will be a very private affair, Duke's instructions.'

'Did he . . . did he have any idea that something like this might happen?' she asked, thinking that she had never bothered to make a will, always somehow convincing herself that there was plenty of time. Apart from Cousin Joan, she had no obvious next of kin.

'I don't think he expected to die suddenly, but he has a huge estate and a fortune in money. The last thing he would want would be

251

solicitors making themselves rich while others argued over it.'

She didn't know if Quentin was his only child, or at least the only one that he acknowledged. It reminded her of Holmes and Mary.

'Well, I'll be thinking of you all,' she said.

'I've got to go away tomorrow. I can't get out of it. I'll come back just for the day for the funeral, then—'

'What happens to Columbus?' she asked.

'He stays here with Duke's dogs.'

'Ah, of course.'

He cleared his throat. 'This might not be the time to say this but . . . the funeral will be private but there is going to be a memorial service and I guess it will be pretty huge. Entrance will be by ticket only. Would you like me to get you one?'

When she hesitated he added, 'It will be in London and I'd quite like your company if you wanted to be there.'

'Then I would, yes please'

Again there was a long pause before he continued. 'Duke wants his ashes scattered on Afton Down, where the pop festival took place. It seems appropriate somehow.'

It did. Grace remembered the occasion, their village suddenly swimming with young people with tents and sleeping bags strapped to their backs. All those long skirts and long hair on both the boys and girls, the suddenly

252

strange smell of what people called wacky baccy.

Edna insisted that the house must be locked up like Fort Knox. 'It's warning you on the news. They won't think twice about breaking in and pinching things. They even—you know—in the garden.' She bristled with indignation, even suggesting that they should get a guard dog.

'Mother, don't be so paranoid. They are only young people enjoying themselves.' Grace could still feel the pang of envy.

'You don't know anything about it, young lady, all those drug addicts and drop ins.'

'It's drop*outs*, mother, and anyway, most of them go to work. It's a bank holiday, remember?'

But Edna was right. She didn't know about it, not what it was like to be free and liberated. She had never smoked pot, never even been drunk. She suddenly felt terribly old, although many of the people wandering the streets could have given her several years. But unlike them, she was trapped. She remembered that even Duke, one of the headliners on the main stage, was three years older. It had taken nearly forty years before Grace finally got to see him in the flesh, and then he had to go and die.

Quickly, she pulled her thoughts back to the present. 'Right, well, I'd better go. Please give my good wishes to Quentin and the girls.'

'I will, and Grace—thank you.'

'What for?'

'For what you did yesterday. For . . . well, just for being you, really. Goodbye.'

As she put the receiver down she felt the first disturbing realization that this was turning into more than a mutual interest in Paloma's past.

CHAPTER NINETEEN

The postman called on Wednesday morning. His arms seemed to be full of mail. 'Your birthday or something?' he asked.

Grace smiled and shook her head, looking at the large brown package he was clutching. She dutifully signed for it, accepted it and a handful of letters and went back indoors.

On top was a gas bill and beneath that a circular for double-glazing. She put them both aside and regarded the rest. A postcard and two envelopes both bearing airmail stickers with Australian stamps, completed the delivery. Sitting down, she felt uneasy and wondered which to look at first. The postcard was marked Bath and bore a picture of the eighteenth-century smart set preparing to take the waters. She turned it over and read the message.

Thought this would give you some idea of what it was like here in Holmes's time. A beautiful city. Have you ever been here?

Funeral on Friday. I will just be popping down for the day. Here for another two weeks after that I'm afraid.

Hope that you are well.

Austin

His writing was strong and clear. She imagined his voice reading the message, the smallest hint of Scotland among the English vowels. She had asked him about it and it turned out that his mother was Scottish. Holidays had always been spent in Oban. Partly as a joke, he had said, *'I know something of what it is like to have dual nationality. The Scots and the English have always been at war. I never know which side I am on.'* She thought of Paloma's daughter. She couldn't have known who she was either, an African girl, probably with an English father, in a remote English community. Many second-generation immigrants throughout history must have faced the same dilemma.

The two Australian letters were addressed in different writing. She looked from one to the other, wanting and yet not wanting to read them. They could only complicate her life, and just at the moment all she craved was peace. With a sigh, she opened the larger of the two. Inside was a card with a colourful depiction of an Aboriginal dream-time, with symbolic people and turtles, snakes and kangaroos. It was from Joe.

Dear Grace,
I can't tell you how much it means to me to have heard from you. This has, of course, been a terrible time for us both. Everything seems very unsettled at the moment. I think Alex would like to go away from here altogether so I have to remind myself that he is a free agent. If he wants to go, he must do so. I didn't have the courage to leave when I was his age. I seem to be coming out of a very long tunnel—one you might say that has lasted for years. Mine hasn't been an unhappy life: quite the contrary. What has made it hardest is knowing that I made you unhappy all those years ago. Perhaps, someway, somehow, I'll have a chance to make it up to you.
Thinking of you,
Joe

Phwew! Grace put it aside and tried to interpret all the hints and innuendoes. What did he mean that he had wanted to leave when he was Alex's age? Had he thought of walking out when he was forty? Had his marriage not even been tolerable? Had she still really been in his thoughts all that time? Until now, in her heart of hearts, she had believed that the

256

memories were only hers. In moments of honesty she chided herself for not letting him go. Joe had married, had a child, moved on, put the past behind him. If he hadn't . . . She didn't know what to think.

Her hands felt tingly as she opened the second envelope. Inside were pages of airmail paper covered with Alex's writing. With sinking heart she scanned the lines.

Dearest Grace,
I feel that I was such a fool to phone you the other night. I had had too much to drink, as you probably guessed. They do say, though, that in wine you speak the truth: In vino veritas is it? That being so, when I said that I wanted to come back to England—and to you, I meant it.

Nothing seems certain here. I've tried to talk to Dad about going away, even for a holiday but he seems incapable of thinking about anything at the moment. I'm longing to get away but I can't just walk out on him. And what about you? What are you thinking?

I really appreciated the card of Carisbrooke Castle. That was such a happy day, wasn't it? It was for me, anyway. Susie has gone back into town. I know she wanted me to talk about getting back together but I can't, not at the moment.

Grace, why don't you come out here?

You don't have any ties and you could come and see what it is like. There is such a lot that I want to show you, to share with you. Please think about it.

I hesitate to say it again, but you are really important to me. There are things that have to be worked out.
Alex

Grace put her hands over her mouth and breathed out heavily as if to expel some burden. What was she to do?

She sat for ages, gazing at nothing, feeling nothing. Finally her eyes turned to the package the postman had delivered and she shrugged off her anxieties. These were the deeds to her house. Perhaps here she might find an answer to some of the unsolved mysteries surrounding Paloma.

Casting the wrapping aside, she placed the pile of documents on the table, starting from the top. She knew that the solicitor was in the process of sorting out her mother's estate and that the house would, of course, be coming to her, but at the moment he hadn't completed the work. The top document in the bundle was therefore a transfer of the deeds of the house to her mother. It took her by surprise that it was in Edna's maiden name, Edna Galpine, and seemed to have belonged to her since 1937. It had come to her through her own widowed mother, Eliza Galpine.

For a moment, Grace put the paper aside. Clearly, when Edna and Gordon married they must have moved into a house that was already in Edna's family. Grace knew nothing of her maternal grandparents but she had always assumed that she came from a long line of agricultural labourers. Perhaps Grandpa Galpine had been more successful? She wondered what he had done for a living and what he would have thought about his daughter marrying Gordon Harrison, a common gardener? But there, at the time of the marriage Edna had only been in service and, thinking about her, she was hardly one of the aristocracy!

She leafed through a few more papers. A few years before, around the turn of the century, the Galpines had sold off quite a lot of land that had originally belonged to Palm Cottage. This, of course, was the time that Queen Victoria had virtually taken up full-time residence on the island and people were moving here in droves. Behind the garden, away from the church and hidden behind a hedge, was a row of Victorian dwellings. Clearly, they had been built on land that had once belonged to her family. Grace stopped to ponder the mystery of these events, now out of reach. She regretted never having talked to Edna about her childhood or her parents. She wondered what had happened to any money made from the sale of the land. Such a pity

259

that she didn't know more about her mother's ancestors.

Undeterred, she moved on down through the documents. Before Eliza Galpine had owned the house it had been in the hands of George Dore, and before that Lionel Milmore, then Frederick Jolliffe, Amos Bush, William Godfrey, Bernard Gosden and, the first entry, Rufus Stone. The Stone documents were difficult to read but they bore the date 1690. Had he bought the cottage then, not knowing that someone had been buried in his garden? Regretfully, there was no reference to Sir Robert Holmes.

The disappointment was tempered by the realization that Grace now knew the name of every family that had lived in her house for three hundred years. Here, they had cooked in her kitchen, cultivated the garden, slept in her bedroom, made love, dreamed, suffered loss and disappointment. She felt exhausted by the morning's discoveries. She stopped for lunch.

The day offered nothing in the way of distraction but it then occurred to her that these same people were probably buried in the churchyard opposite. She brightened up. This afternoon she would make a point of seeing how many she could find. With a regretful glance at her morning's correspondence, she swept them into a pile and heated the kettle.

It wasn't an ideal day for looking around a graveyard. A biting wind blew from the east and the sky looked angry. Grace dug out the coat she had hoped not to wear again for several months, retrieved a scarf and gloves from a drawer, and set off down the path. In her pocket she had a list of all the house owners and a notebook and pencil to record what she could about them. As she passed her father's grave she stopped for a moment, just to think about him and send out some message of love across the ether. She really must fetch Edna's ashes, unite her parents in death.

The churchyard was a big one and there was no obvious place to start. Probably the sexton or someone would have a register of all the burials and could point them out but she didn't know who he was or how to contact him. Besides, this solitary search seemed preferable.

After a while she found a headstone bearing the name Frederick Jolliffe who had died on 10 December 1802. Beneath his name was another entry, *Elizabeth, wife of the above, born 2 June 1769, laid to rest 21 October 1805—* Trafalgar day. How soon afterwards might the local people have heard about the battle and what, if anything, might it have meant to them?

She continued to wander. Many of the tombstones were too eroded to be able to read the inscriptions. She found a couple more people, George Dore who died in 1873, closely followed by his wife Frances. There were several other Dore graves dating from around the same period. From their ages, some might have been George's brothers and others his sons. Whichever, quite a few of them had died at around the same time. She knew that tuberculosis had sometimes been rife in farming families, or perhaps there had been an outbreak of cholera. Thank goodness for modern drugs and sanitation. She shrugged off the speculation and realizing how cold she was, returned to the house.

The letters from that morning still lay on the table and seemed to accuse her, waiting for a response. She had no idea how to reply to either of them. Perhaps if she didn't, both father and son would think better of it and not get in touch again, except that she knew this wouldn't happen. Waiting for the kettle to boil, she wondered if she lost touch with both of them how would she feel? In one sense, both of them were strangers, their personalities largely constructed inside her own head, to turn them into the sorts of people she would like them to be. How many years had she clung to the daydream of Joe? Did his letter hint that a future might be possible, and if so, how would he view the complication that she had slept with his son? It was simply too fraught to contemplate.

With some amusement, she thought instead of Shakespeare's Portia. As far as she could remember, her suitors had to choose between caskets, the winner getting her hand. She couldn't remember the details except that happily the one she fancied made the right choice. Perhaps she should try something similar, set Joe and Alex a test and then decide which one passed. Ludicrous as it sounded, it was no crazier than the situation that now existed. The letters remained unanswered.

On Friday morning, her first thought was that it was the day of Duke's funeral. Although it was unreasonable, she felt excluded. Of course, she had no right to be there. It was a family affair, Duke's son, his adopted daughters, perhaps a few distant relatives and family friends—and Austin. She wondered what sort of service would take place. From local radio broadcasts she had already learned that many fans had arrived to gather outside the house and to hold their own wake. Some of them might have been at the pop festival all those years ago. Like her, many of the women might have daydreamed about knowing him, being his girlfriend, sharing the unconventional life that from the outside had seemed so glamorous. In spite of her restlessness she was not tempted to go near Thorlea. Her communion with the dead man was personal, not to be shared with strangers.

Her telephone rang at about six o'clock.

'Grace, it's Austin. I just thought I'd let you know that everything went off well today.'

'Good.' She was aware of a sudden

263

quickening of her heartbeat.

'Are you all right?'

'Yes, I'm fine.' Her curiosity got the better of her. 'What happened?' she asked. 'What did you do?'

'Well, there was a short ceremony at the house. Everyone had their chance to say their piece, remember Edward and of course we played his music.'

'Of course. Who was there?'

'The kids, Dino Reece, Gerald Grant—his manager.'

Dino Reece, a former keyboard player with the band, had spent much of his life in therapy. He had been the plain one that no one quite remembered.

Austin said, 'We had difficulty getting in and out of the house. The fans have arrived in force. Edward's still here. His body is going to the crematorium tonight, when the crowd has gone home. Apparently there have been more people there as well, waiting for him to arrive.'

'Well, I'm glad it went well,' Grace said.

'I'd better go then. I have to get back to Bath tonight.'

'You're driving?'

'Yes.'

'Then do take care.'

'Thanks, I will. As soon as I get back, I'll ring you.'

'Thank you. Goodbye, then.'

'Goodbye, Grace.' His voice sounded

gentle, tender, and there was a void when he rang off. Already, she feared that he was another complication.

Grace put a ready-made pizza in the oven and escaped first to the television and when that failed to her book. Now that she had finished the Holmes biography there seemed no way forward with her research. The deeds to the house had produced nothing. Preparing for a restless evening, she thought that perhaps, after all, there was nothing to find.

CHAPTER TWENTY

Over the weekend, Grace found two postcards of local views and sent one to Joe and one to Alex. The messages were short and friendly, pointedly sidestepping their correspondence.

On Monday she arranged to take Molly into Newport on a shopping expedition while Reg was at the day centre. It was a pleasant, uncomplicated trip. They toured Marks and Spencer looking for new summer clothes, shopped in the food hall for something indulgent to cook at home and lunched in a pub with a spectacular view north towards the Solent.

Molly was in good form, almost back to her old self. Reg was going in for some tests shortly so he would be in hospital for at least a week.

'I shouldn't feel so pleased, but I do,' Molly confessed. 'Although if anything ever happened to Reg I'd be full of guilt.'

Grace thought that for *if anything ever happened*, read *when something happens*, or more specifically, *when Reg dies*. Clearly, in spite of herself, the prospect brightened Molly's future. After a thoughtful sip of tea, Molly added, 'Perhaps next week while he's in hospital we could go to the cinema.'

'Why not?' The idea was not particularly appealing but Grace reminded herself that she must get out more.

'P'raps we could go and see that film about the two gay cowboys,' Molly suggested. 'They say it's good although the thought of two men doing that . . .' She pulled her prune face. 'Still, it's supposed to be good.'

Grace guessed that the thought of two beautiful young men exposing themselves might have something to do with the attraction. She was noncommittal because in her own way she was enjoying her space. Her freedom was too new to fill it with appointments.

The day before, she had cleared out Edna's room, keeping a few of her possessions, packing the rest away for the charity shop. At some point she would have to think about collecting Edna's ashes, also do something about Paloma's bones, but that would have to wait until Austin returned from Bath. He might already be back. She wondered if she should ring him, or wait for him to make contact. She pictured him on the night of Duke's death, the way he had stepped in and fought for his friend's life. In spite of the existing complications, there was something about Austin that made her hope that he wouldn't just go away.

Thinking of Paloma, it seemed only right that she should go back into the garden, back by the wall that acknowledged her life. The thought of having her as a neighbour was comforting in a strange way. She still hoped that against all the odds something would turn up to reveal the details of her life.

'S'pose we should be getting home.' Molly interrupted her thoughts. Reg would be back from the day centre in half an hour. Together they left the café, Molly to her duties and Grace to her welcome solitude.

The last unpredictable days of April produced a mass of white blossom. Grace took to walking the lanes just to absorb the scent of hawthorn and soak up the beauty of the season. She was in love with the banks of cow parsley, the way it blurred in the breeze. Here and there, fragile patches of Milkmaids spread in patches along the grass while the pungent scent of wild garlic completed the landscape. This was the season of green and white. Everything seemed to be on the move, even the static plants reaching towards the sun. It made her feel restless but at the same time strangely content.

She had just finished eating one of her M and S meals after such an outing when the telephone rang. She answered it to hear an Australian accent and she realized with shock that she wasn't sure whether it was Joe or Alex.

'How are you?' she asked, hoping for a clue.

'I'm good.' There was a pause. 'What are you doing tonight?'

'I've just been having my dinner.'

'Well, come and meet me.'

For a second she thought that she had misheard. When she didn't respond the voice said, 'I'm here, down in some posh hotel in Yarmouth. I arrived this afternoon.'

The news was so shattering that her legs gave way, delivering her into a chair. 'I don't understand,' she started. 'Whatever are you doing here?'

'What do you think? I've come to see you.'

With increasing panic she realized that she still wasn't a hundred per cent certain who it was. It seemed to be the sort of thing that Alex might do, just turn up, but surely he would come to the house? Besides, the voice—she was almost certain that it was Joe.

'This is madness,' she heard herself say.

'I know it is but it's happening just the same. How long will it take you to get here?'

268

'I'm not—'

'Don't say you're not coming. I've flown half way round the world to see you. I'll expect you in half an hour.'

When she didn't respond, the line went dead.

Grace was too shocked to even think of changing her clothes. Whatever was going on, it was getting out of control. She wasn't ready for anything like this. She hadn't even asked which hotel he, whoever he was, was staying at but it had to be the one next to the castle, Holmes's old house. If it was Joe, then he knew nothing about her discovery unless Alex had told him but she doubted that Alex had taken in so much detail. If it was Joe, then it was just a coincidence. She doubted that Alex would stay in an expensive hotel no matter who had owned it. The mystery remained unresolved.

God, this was a disaster!

There seemed to be nothing for it but to drive to Yarmouth and see what happened. At the roundabout, a bus nearly ploughed into her. The driver blew his horn and glared down at her. Sorry, she mouthed. Her hands were shaking. For the rest of the journey she concentrated solely on the road.

As she got out of the car she realized that she had forgotten her jacket, and the sea breeze quickly reminded her that summer was still a long way off. Trying to swallow down her anxiety, she marched up to the hotel steps and went inside.

She saw him immediately, sitting at the bar with a pint in front of him. He had lost weight since Alex had shown her the photos of the barbecue. No doubt his recent bereavement had taken its toll. What remained of his fading hair was sandy grey but he still looked fit, muscular, and his face was, in its way, still handsome. As he looked towards the door, she could see that the vivid blue of his eyes had been clouded by experience.

Seeing her, his face relaxed into a smile of such joy that she felt tears threatening her. He eased himself off the barstool and came towards her.

'Grace Harrison—you look wonderful!'

'Nonsense.' She couldn't help but smile, and his embrace was easy. In spite of all her reservations he felt male and comforting.

'I reckon I gave you a bit of a turn,' he said leading her to a nearby table.

'You could say that.' A voice in her head warned her not to be carried along by his bonhomie. His being here was a mistake. Somehow she must let him know that.

'What are you drinking?'

'Nothing. I'm driving.'

'I'll get you a taxi home. Come on, we can't not celebrate seeing each other after all this time.'

'Joe, I'm not sure about this.'

'Relax. We're just old friends meeting up after a very long time. I'm not going to make a fool of myself or anything. It is just such a strange sensation, being at liberty to do what I like, when I like.'

This was something she recognized, but to fly half way round the world . . . ? She asked, 'How's Alex?'

'He's OK. He's gone straight to France. He's got some bee in his bonnet about buying a French winery.' He frowned. 'You don't know if he met some girl when he was over there do you? He's been like a teenager in love since he came back.'

She shook her head feeling the guilty heat of her face. The true implications of what had happened between them took on new proportions. At one point it had seemed like a joke, her sleeping with Joe's son, but now that he was here, everything was so much more complicated.

He spoke to the barman and moments later the man came back carrying a tray bearing a bottle of champagne.

'Come on, indulge me. I promise I'll see that you get home safely.'

There seemed to be nothing for it. Besides, she needed a drink. The waiter opened the bottle and poured the liquid into two rather elegant flutes. She noticed the label, Veuve Cliquot. Joe was certainly pushing the boat out.

'So how are things?' she asked, not really sure what she was referring to.

Joe took a speculative mouthful of the champagne. It was only at that moment that she remembered the business he was in. As she watched him, the essential form of his body, the subtleties of his face and his expressions, seemed to metamorphose and become real and remembered. She found herself taking it all in, the colour of his skin, a few curling hairs showing just above the vee of his shirt. Her eyes wandered to his hands. He wore a wedding ring. This symbol of his past gave her a bit of a jolt.

'Tell me about you,' he insisted. 'I was sorry to hear about your mum.'

'It's strange being—' She didn't finish the sentence. To say either that she was alone or free had dangerous implications.

He asked, 'What are you going to do now? You can do anything you want to, can't you?'

She raised her eyebrows, a gesture that implied life was not always that simple.

'How about you?' she asked again.

He settled back in the chair and drained the champagne. 'Alex has been encouraging me to sell up. I must admit that sometimes I'm tempted.'

'Where would you go?'

He put his glass down and looked at her. 'That's just it. Like you, I can go wherever I want to. Where I end up might depend on a lot of things.'

She looked away, thinking Joe, don't do this.

He reached out and placed his hand on hers. 'Grace, relax. I've never had a chance to talk to you about what happened, all those years ago. It might seem a bit late now but I feel I need to clear the air.'

When she didn't respond, he went on. 'When I went home, I couldn't wait to come back. I was looking forward to going to uni but most of all I wanted to get back to you. Well, everything seemed just fine at first. I don't know if Meg suspected that she was pregnant but she didn't say anything for several weeks. To be honest, since I got back I was trying to avoid her. Anyway, perhaps her mum noticed something was wrong. I don't know. Once her family realized, they came straight to my dad and he hit the roof—really hit the roof. I couldn't see any way out. Perhaps I should have simply run away, but where to? I had no money of my own and besides, it would have broken my parents' hearts if I'd shamed them like that.'

He gazed into some distant past. 'So, I let them get on with planning the wedding and everything. Meg was pleased. If she noticed I wasn't happy she never acknowledged it. Strange, really, she never did in all the years we were together.'

'But you stayed.'

He shrugged. 'There was the business, then Alex, and just when I thought he might be old enough to understand if I left, my dad got ill and I couldn't pull out.' He sighed again. 'It seemed as if it wasn't meant to be.'

'Perhaps it wasn't—isn't.' She added quickly, 'But you must have felt something for Margaret—Meg?'

'Yeah, she was a nice enough woman. I guess she deserved better.'

They were both silent, then he turned to look at her. 'Have you got someone else? I expect you have.'

She didn't know what to say. Finally she said 'At the moment I'm not in the market for getting involved.'

'Fair enough. I wouldn't want to hurry anything, but, might there just be a chance that one day we could . . . pick up where we left off?'

'Joe, it's too soon. You've only just lost your wife. You were together for over forty years. You can't just shrug that off as if it doesn't have any meaning.'

He nodded his head silently, pouring more champagne and said, 'I'm only here until tomorrow then I'm going out to meet Alex. He's inspecting some winery and insists that I come out and have a look. After that, we're both coming back here for a few days.' While she was digesting this, as an afterthought he said, 'Who knows, he might be waiting to introduce me to whoever he met while he was over here.'

Grace's heart lurched. Too quickly she said, 'Joe, don't jump to conclusions. It was probably just a casual thing, ships passing in the night and all that.'

'Perhaps you're right. Susie came to see us for the funeral. I think she would like to get back with him. That would be best, really.' He broke his train of thought and turned to smile at her. 'Do you want to come and have a look at my room?'

She knew without being told that it would be Holmes's bedroom. There weren't many guests staying and Joe would clearly have asked for the best. At any other time she would jump at the chance of seeing it, but tonight, what an irony.

'I don't think so. Look, I ought to be getting back home.'

'Can I see you tomorrow, then?'

She wanted to say no, but as he had said, he had come half way round the world to see her. Perhaps a few hours in her company would convince him that he was living in cloud cuckoo land.

'If you like.'

'We could go back to some of our old haunts.'

'No! Let's go somewhere different. Let's forget about the past for the moment, shall we? Let's just see what happens.'

'If that's what you want.'

'I think it's best.'

After a moment he said, 'Actually, there's somewhere I would like to show you. I'd like your advice.'

'OK.' She stood up and he accompanied her to the door.

'Grace—'

'It's all right, really it is. I'll see you tomorrow.'

'Let me get you a taxi.'

'There's no need, I've only had one glass.' Actually she had had two but she knew from experience that there wouldn't be any taxis about and she didn't want to give him an excuse to encourage her to stay.

'Shall I come over tomorrow?' he asked.

'No, I'll pick you up about 10.30.'

She kissed him on the cheek. 'Sleep well.'

'I don't think so.' He grinned, nodding his head ruefully. 'But promise you'll come tomorrow?'

'I promise.'

'Then you sleep well.' As she stepped out into the cool spring evening she thought that was as unlikely as a snowball surviving Hell.

CHAPTER TWENTY-ONE

Of course Grace had trouble sleeping. Her life was beginning to feel like an avalanche, gathering momentum and with no way of stopping it. She lay in the dark listening to the screech of a vixen, finally getting up and opening the curtains so that she could look across the garden. Something solid moved in the shadows by the wall near to Paloma's grave. The fox was silent, watching. There was an expectant quality to its stance, still and yet ready to pounce at a second's notice. At some time in the past one of its ancestors might easily have dug Paloma up and they would never have known about her. Grace shivered and tried to think of something more cheerful.

It was almost dawn before she finally fell asleep and then she dreamt about going into a cavern and stepping into a dark, icy, bottomless pool. Although she struggled to reach the sides there didn't seem to be any. She awoke with a gasp, fighting for breath, clutching the duvet as if her life depended upon it. Panting, she lay still, unnerved by the feeling of panic. Freud would no doubt have had some explanation but whatever the reason, the feeling added to her sense of being out of control.

In the tree by her window a collar dove was

telling the world to *get your own sticks*. She listened to the repeated call, clinging on to its normalcy, wondering if by some enchantment she was really interpreting the words. Another assortment of coos, quarks, jacks and trills quickly proved her wrong. It was spring, the essence of each call was clear for all who bothered to listen.

At that moment she heard the rattle of the letterbox. She glanced at the bedside clock. It was 8.30, too early for the postman. Heaving herself up, she went to the window in time to see Austin Morris open the garden gate and step out into the lane. Groggily she went through to the hall. A sheet of paper lay on the doormat and she picked it up. It bore a brief, scribbled message.

Grace,
Just to let you know that the memorial service is on Friday and that I have the tickets. As it will be a long day I wonder how you would feel about staying the night in London? I'll call you later or perhaps you can call me.
Regards, Austin

Instantly she regretted saying that she would go to the service. At the time it had seemed an appealing idea. Famous people would almost certainly be there. It would be a new experience and there would be something

278

adolescent and romantic about saying a public goodbye to Duke. Instead, the thought of two days in Austin's company loomed like the face of the Eiger. If it went wrong she might find herself plummeting into a bottomless crevasse.

While the kettle boiled, her thoughts turned back to the more immediate prospect of spending a day with Joe. She felt troubled by the fickleness of her feelings. This was the man who had dominated her life for four decades. Now that he was free, the first thing he did was to come and find her and, instead of rushing into his arms in the way any self-respecting heroine would do, she was in a state of terror. Perhaps it was time to admit that all those years she had been kidding herself, hiding behind the illusion of lost love so that she wouldn't have to do anything positive about her life. Well, now the present was here in force and she knew with certainty that whatever she said or did, she would regret it. How could her motives be so treacherous?

She showered and dressed. When Alex had been here she had agonized about looking her age, worried about her shape, wrinkles, hair colour, everything. Today she felt a defiant need not to hide the signs of ageing. What if her chin did sag? What if her stomach fought back against the constraints of her denim jeans? Looking in the mirror, she lectured herself. Grace Harrison, you are nearly sixty years old. You're behaving as if you were sixteen. In fact, at sixteen you probably had more sense.

The time was ticking on. Before she left she rang Austin's number. A woman answered the phone and she could hear her say, 'There's a woman for you.' Seconds later he came on the line.

'Thank you for your note,' she started.

'Grace, good of you to call back. I don't know what you think about Friday?' His voice was disconcertingly comforting.

'Um.'

'We could always take in a play in the evening, or go to a concert or something. If you'd rather not, we could come back on a late train, but I know a nice hotel and I could book us rooms.'

Rooms, he said rooms. That was reassuring.

'That would be fine,' she heard herself say.

'Good.' He hesitated. 'I was going to suggest that you might like to come over to our centre today and have a look round. I've cleaned Paloma up nicely.'

'I'm afraid I can't. I have to meet someone.'

'Some other time, then. About Friday, I could pick you up at eight o'clock? I have a friend who lets me park the car near the ferry terminal.'

'Thank you.'

'Right. I'll see you then.' He rang off and Grace was left with the dead receiver. Perversely, she wished that she was going to his office rather than to Yarmouth to pick up her first lover. Lover, the word seemed so ludicrous that she laughed.

In spite of herself, she changed her clothes twice before leaving the house. A very expensive scarf about her throat added a certain chic to her appearance, boosting her confidence. It had been a present from her office when she had been forced to give up work to look after Edna. The office had never been the place she wanted to work. In fact, it was probably the last place she would have chosen.

When Gordon died she had ventured to suggest that perhaps she could now return to London and take up her post with the Inland Revenue. Edna had put on her hard done by face and said, 'Go ahead, if you're so desperate to get away.' For once, Grace was prepared to rebel but when she took matters into her own hands and contacted the Personnel Department she learned that her position in Shaftesbury Avenue had been filled. Another door of opportunity slammed in her face.

After an awkward silence, Mr Grey, the officer, told her that there actually was a vacancy at Newport on the island. 'Talk about luck,' he said. 'It came up only last week and they were planning to advertise but if you are interested it will be a straightforward internal appointment.'

So a straightforward internal appointment it was and her working life was consigned to the horror of Pay as you Earn and Schedule D. Still, the scarf was something to show for the stultifying sentence that had been called her career.

She parked the car in the square at Yarmouth and walked around to the hotel. Joe appeared to be where she had left him the night before, sitting at a table in the large reception area. A tray with a cafetière, cup and jug were in front of him. He turned at the sound of the heavy door and waved in greeting.

'Come on in. Would you like coffee before we go?'

'No thanks.' She thought that after the initial shock of seeing his photograph at the barbecue he seemed to grow younger with each viewing. Dressed in cotton trousers and a short sleeved shirt, he looked fit and . . . the word that came to mind was virile. Cursing herself for the direction in which her thoughts were straying, she said, 'Did you have somewhere in mind or what?'

He stood up, picking up a jacket slung over the back of the seat.

'I do have somewhere in mind. Do you know a place called Bellcombe?'

'Yes. It's just a hamlet.'

'Can we go there?'

'If you like. It's a lovely ride along a

sweeping valley. As a matter of fact it is one of my favourite places.'

'Is it now?' Joe gave her a quizzical look. 'That might be significant.'

Equally curious and suspicious, Grace led the way to the car. The sun was making a valiant effort to drive off scudding clouds. The wind was coming from the east and had that damp patina that suggested an inevitable downpour sooner or later.

Their route from Yarmouth took them through Thorlea, and Grace wondered whether to point out to him where Duke Jamieson had lived and so recently died. She decided against it. Instead, she stuck to a neutral commentary on the villages and farms. When they reached Bellcombe she asked, 'Whereabouts are we going?'

'Place called Willow Vineyard—you know it?'

Grace's foot jerked on the brake stopping the car and she turned sharply to look at him. 'You're not thinking of buying a place here, are you?'

'Would it be such a terrible idea?'

She shrugged. Her shoulders felt as if they were in a vice. 'That's up to you.'

He said, 'It was pure coincidence. I picked up your local paper on the ferry and it was open at the property section. There staring at me was an advert for this place.' He in turn twisted round to look at her. 'It seemed like fate. You can't just ignore these things. Anyway, I rang them this morning and made an appointment.' Studying her thoughtfully, he added, 'I wondered what your reaction might be—and now I know.'

She shrugged again, lost for words. As they pulled through the gates she managed to say, 'I had no idea they grew grapes here. I would have thought the climate was too cold.'

'Obviously not.'

Their arrival was greeted by the yapping of a Jack Russell who, once it reached them, seemed to have forgotten what it had come for and promptly retreated again. A woman came from an outbuilding that looked like an office.

'G'day. Joe Weston.' Joe held out his hand as she approached, a healthy looking blonde, edging towards middle age, with powerful-looking arms, fine breasts and clear brown eyes.

'Annette Wilson,' she shook hands with both of them and addressed Joe as she started to explain about the vineyard.

Grace quickly stopped listening. This was all too much. Surely he wasn't really planning to sell up and move a few miles away? Oh God—she thought of Alex. What was she going to say to both of them?

They had a tour of the vineyard and Joe asked endless technical questions. Annette Wilson clearly enjoyed having a fellow enthusiast to talk to. It crossed Grace's mind that they would have a lot in common. She reminded herself to tell him that he must take time and look around before jumping into any sort of commitment.

'Would your wife like to see the house?' Annette Wilson asked when the tour of the land was over.

Before Grace could answer, Joe said, 'We'd both like to have a look around.' He gave her a look that said: Don't say anything, and she frowned at him but kept silent. They followed the owner round the rather delightful old stone house. Several times Annette glanced at Grace to gauge her opinion and she was carefully noncommital. At the end of the tour, Joe said, 'My son will be here next week. Perhaps we could both come back then.'

'Of course. We have had one or two enquiries but no serious offers.'

'Well then, perhaps next Tuesday we could come back?'

'Tuesday it is.'

They drove away in silence. The atmosphere was taut with recrimination. Driving with no particular direction in mind, Grace said, 'I can't believe you just did that.'

'Did what?'

'You know perfectly well. We don't know each other any more. We haven't met for forty years and you're pretending to that woman that I'm your wife. We can't just pick up from where we left off as if nothing has happened,

285

you know.'

'Hang on a minute. Have I asked you to pick up where we left off? Have I suggested anything except that we should spend a few hours together just to . . . catch up?'

Grace was too tense for words. Her knuckles were white with tension on the steering wheel. After a while Joe said, 'I've been a fool not to realize how angry you must still be with me.'

'I'm not angry.'

'Well, you're giving a very good imitation of an angry woman.'

She slowed the car and pulled in by the side of the road. Rolling cliffs stopped abruptly as they met the sea, chalk white, and further in the distance a seam of caramel sand. The view was stunning but both of them ignored it as they sought round for some bridge to reach each other.

'I'm not angry,' Grace repeated, 'but I feel you're bulldozing me into some course of action, and I don't know what it is.'

'I'm sorry. It was foolish to bring you to the vineyard. It just seemed like such a coincidence that I had to see it.'

'Well, what did you think of it?'

It was his turn to shrug. 'It bears little resemblance to our place back home. Everything is in miniature and I think you're probably right about the climate. Grapes need plenty of sun.'

'Will you go back?' she asked.

'I might. I'd like to see what Alex thinks. Who knows, he might like the idea of settling over here himself.'

There was nothing that she could say. This might be the very opening that Alex was looking for and here was his father making it possible for it to happen. The idea of Alex coming back into her life now seemed ridiculous. And the idea of Joe becoming part of her future? She had no idea. All she wanted was to be away from them all.

Their route took them past Carisbrooke Castle and, as she feared he would, Joe suggested that they should stop for a look around. There was no good reason to say no so Grace endured what felt like a repeat performance of a few weeks ago, this time with the father rather than the son. She managed to break the replay by going to another pub for lunch and gradually the earlier tensions eased off.

'Might you be serious about moving to France?' she asked to steer her thoughts away from the island.

'I've no idea. It would be a challenge, different ways of working and, of course, the language. I kid myself I'm not too old to start a new career.'

'You look very fit.'

He gave her a grateful smile. 'You're looking pretty good yourself. Do you remember . . . ?' And he started the reminiscences that had for far too long been the backdrop to so many of her daydreams. In spite of her fears, the years seemed to be rolling back and she was slipping into some distant role, a long-remembered, treasured performance made the sweeter with each sip of wine.

'Ah me, Grace.' He looked at her tenderly, regret and nostalgia etched on his features. 'What might have been.'

She looked away. 'It might have been a disaster,' she warned.

'It might, indeed. Will you have dinner with me tonight? Come to the hotel. They have a first class chef.'

As he saw her hesitate he added, 'I'll book a taxi in advance to get you home safely.'

She laughed and her treacherous insides lurched with undefined longing.

'I don't know if that is a good idea.'

'And why not?'

Why not? Without spilling the beans about Alex, she couldn't think of any other objection, and when she dropped him off at 5.00 it was with the promise to return two hours later. Two whole hours to regret the decision.

CHAPTER TWENTY-TWO

The hotel dining-room was nearly empty. A low-ceilinged, cavernous room, it nevertheless managed to give an impression of cosy intimacy. Tablecloths with a hint of pink picked up the deeper shade of rose candlelight and the rich burgundy of linen napkins added to the feeling of luxury. Grace thought that the tones were designed to flatter. Casting a rosy glow over the faces of diners, the management was determined that their female guests should be happy and their wellbeing would rub off on the men.

The dense pile of the carpet deadened most sound except for that of a white piano where a young woman looking like something out of an Agatha Christie mystery was playing 'Smoke Gets in your Eyes'.

As she sat down, Grace gave a fleeting thought to Holmes who must have sat in this same room, pondering his own thoughts of war and power. She would have liked to dwell on it but her own thoughts were altogether nearer to home, to where the journey this evening might take her. Had her namesake Grace Hooke, reputed mother of Mary Holmes, once been in this house and wondered the same thing? Well, at least she couldn't get pregnant!

Champagne arrived almost immediately.

Some bubbling imp deep inside Grace asked: what are you afraid of? After all this time, what can you possibly regret except for missed chances? She sat down, accepted a glass and savoured the dancing fizz on her tongue.

Joe was in good form. He told her stories of Australia, of near disasters, of crises averted. Many of the tales were against himself, underlining his own ineptitude and foolishness. Her laughter became increasingly tender. They ordered food, replaced the champagne with red wine chosen after some deliberation. The sommelier quickly recognized Joe's knowledge and took obvious pleasure in dealing with an expert.

Grace allowed the wine to explore her tongue. It seemed raw and belligerent, something not to be brushed aside without due recognition. With each mouthful it took control, softening, luring her into a sense of contentment.

Joe paid it his full attention and with a single nod of his head gave it the thumbs up. Grace realized that where wine was concerned, not to mention a thousand other subjects, she had a lot to learn.

The food came in tiny portions and there was no alternative but to give each mouthful due attention. The tastes were rich with subtle flavours. A sense of well-deserved indulgence wafted over her.

Replete, relaxed, Grace declined a pudding

but accepted a liqueur, settling for Benedictine. In the way of things, as the waiter poured second, tiny cups of rich coffee, the mood changed. For a while they sat silently, immersed in their own thoughts. Eventually, Joe said,

'I wish I didn't feel so guilty.'

'About what?' Grace returned from her own wanderings.

He shrugged, finding it hard to put his feelings into words. 'My wife is dead. I should feel sorrow, loss. I don't. I just feel . . . relief?'

Grace remained silent. His words echoed her own sense of failure.

'I was fond of her, you know?' he continued. 'We didn't have a bad marriage. Meg was loyal, committed to the business, a good mother.' His words dried up again.

'I felt something similar about my mother,' Grace offered. 'I feel bad because I didn't love her in the way that she probably deserved, or at least hoped for. I resented her, really; she was the barrier between me and the life I wanted to lead.'

'And what was that?'

Grace shook her head, not really knowing. 'If I'm honest, she was also a safeguard so that I didn't have to face all my daydreams and be found wanting.'

She knew that he understood. In a low voice, he said, 'I let her down. We went through the motions so that she could pretend that everything was all right, but it wasn't. I . . . I never really fancied her, you know? How sad that she should be stuck with a man who didn't want her. Oh, we went through the motions there too, but it was almost a duty rather than desire.'

Such a revelation, validating the daydreams that she had secretly clung to all these years but viewed as misguided. He hadn't moved on any more than she had.

'I have to ask,' he said. 'Is there someone in your life at present?'

'Not really.'

'Does that mean there is someone—sort of?'

'I don't know.' Now was the time to tell him about Alex, to clear the air, only she couldn't find any words that conveyed what had happened without it sounding like a terrible betrayal.

As if tuning in to her thoughts, he said, 'Alex doesn't know I'm here. I wanted him to go on to France and sort out whatever it is that interests him over there. I said I'd join him a few days later but the next day I caught a flight here. I . . . I'm not sure how he would view this . . . this indecent haste to see you. He was very attached to his mother, you know?'

Grace looked away. Seeing her expression, he said, 'Don't look so worried. He really likes you; he told me so. He just doesn't know what you meant to me. How could he, it was before he was born. Given time, let's just see how things pan out, shall we?'

She was sinking deeper into the mire. How on earth would he react if he knew what had happened between her and this son of his? There was nothing parallel in her life that she could imagine except that she suspected that she might still be jealous of any woman who came along and grabbed Joe's attention. If she was a mother, supposing it was her daughter? The enormity of the betrayal hit her again. A month ago and everything would have been marvellous. She would have been free, Joe would have come to claim her and she wouldn't have had a moment's doubt, but now . . .

Draining his coffee, Joe, now in confessional mood, said, 'It's a very long time since I made love—to anyone. Meg was ill and that side of our marriage quickly stopped. I didn't mind except that every now and then . . .' He gave her a quizzical grin. 'I was a faithful husband though. There were opportunities, but we live in a small town.' He left the rest unsaid.

Grace had a sudden sense of running a race, struggling for the finishing line before being crushed under foot by the other competitors. Putting her napkin aside, she excused herself and went to the toilets. Inside the cloakroom it was blessedly peaceful. There was a plethora of gold, door handles, taps, toilet roll holders.

293

Holmes would probably have approved. She studied herself in the mirror. As in the dining-room, the colour scheme and lighting were arranged to give her the most flattering view of herself. She wore the velvet trousers and top that she had worn on the night of Duke's party. She had been reluctant to do so but they were the smartest things in her wardrobe, and besides, that was another ghost she needed to lay. Well, she didn't look too bad. In the muted light and numbed by alcohol, Joe might not find the prospect of making love to her too abhorrent. But she choked back the thought even as it formed. Was she really contemplating this? When she got back to the table she would have to face the question—should she go home or should she stay? The only thing she knew for certain was that whichever choice she made, she would regret it.

* * *

Grace awoke to the familiar garden chorus. She kept her eyes resolutely shut, allowing the layers of sleep to peel away until she felt sufficiently in charge to face the world. She took small comfort from having done the right thing in coming home rather than complicating matters any more than they were already. But her puritanical self immediately began condemning her cowardice in not clearing the air. In a few hours Joe would be in France with Alex. What would Alex think when he learned where his father had been? How shameful was it that she should have left to Alex the task of telling his father. Would he tell him or would Joe guess? Had Alex really understood that she and his father had been lovers? She had never spelled it out. She had a bizarre image of them fighting a duel, pistols at dawn in true Gallic fashion. She could just imagine the headlines—*Father and Son in Deadly Duel over Ageing Mistress*. She slipped out of bed. Of course this was ridiculous, but nevertheless, people were going to be hurt, feel betrayed. And yet surely it wasn't her fault? How could she have known that within weeks of sleeping with Alex his father, now miraculously free, would turn up? God, it was like some foolish Penny Dreadful!

In the meantime, tomorrow she was going to London with Austin. Would this, could this be less complicated?

Once she was up, an innate desire for courage drove her into Newport where she scoured the shops looking for something 'suitable' to wear. Grace still favoured long skirts, her one concession to the hippie era she had never really been a part of. She found one she particularly liked and allowed the shop assistant to talk her into a top that really had too many flounces, but it was too late now. She packed it into her bag. Hung behind the bedroom door was a new tailored trouser suit that made her feel trim and slim, something she felt to be suitable for the memorial ceremony, although she had no real idea of what form it would take. These were the first clothes that she had bought in ages. Would they give her the elan she needed to get through the visit? Alone with Austin for a day and a night, how would their budding friendship unfold? She quickly closed off the possibilities. Only time would tell.

CHAPTER TWENTY-THREE

In spite of Duke's fame, both cathedrals and the abbey had declined the honour of holding his memorial service as a step too far. Instead, it took place in the huge Westminster Hall. Austin had obtained good seats near the front where the stage was almost within touching distance. As Grace glanced around she kept spotting famous faces looking the same and yet subtly different in the flesh. It was hard to believe that she was part of this familiar yet alien world. News cameras were panning across the crowd. What would Molly think if she happened to look in and see her here among the great and glorious? She hadn't even mentioned the journey to her friend.

The list of contributors made up a veritable

Who's Who of those who mattered. One after another, they stood centre-stage and evoked some aspect of Duke's personality. The Prime Minister stumbled through a praise that clearly sat at odds with his Calvinist beliefs. A junior royal tried to hide her very personal involvement with Duke, speaking of him as a 'dear friend'. Grace had a brief fantasy that the princess had secretly born him a love child.

Authority figures underlined his importance in contemporary society. Members of the band spilled the beans about some of their more outrageous, youthful pranks, causing indulgent laughter now. It seemed that death and the passage of time meant that they were finally forgiven.

Spokesmen for charities revealed another side of Duke, the one that Grace felt, had she had a chance to know him, would have drawn her closer to him. On a screen, film ran of various performances, his presence at an earthquake in North Africa, his self-conscious arrival in a suit at the Palace. Sitting in this exalted company, a wave of sadness suddenly claimed her. She tried very hard not to cry. Throughout the hall other eyes were dewy, noses were being surreptitiously wiped, sobs silenced.

The crowd emerged with that sense of having shared something momentous. As they stood on the steps, Grace recognized one of Duke's ex-wives talking to Quentin. Was she his mother? She still wasn't sure who was who.

They had come straight to the hall and now Austin hailed a taxi to take them to the hotel. He spoke briefly to a few people but it was clear that he was in a hurry to get away. In the taxi he was understandably quiet, facing again the loss of an old friend.

During the train journey they had both immersed themselves in newspapers, the *Guardian* for Austin and the *Independent* for Grace. Half way they had swapped over and then together struggled with the cryptic crosswords. It had been companionable, easy. Now the purpose of the day was over, the looming evening felt less assured.

The hotel was small but rather refined. Austin apologized that because of the late booking their rooms were actually on different floors. No adjoining door then. Grace chided herself for imagining something from a 1950s film. What would she have done anyway, kept her side securely locked?

'Shall we meet in the bar in half an hour and we can decide what to do this evening?' He said.

She nodded, looking forward to a period of solitude to think about the day, and the evening ahead.

Her room was clearly intended for two, containing a huge double bed, a desk and the inevitable trouser press. It also had a picture window looking across the Thames with Tower

Bridge in the distance, the iconic shape of the gherkin rising dark and phallic above the skyline. She felt a bittersweet affection for London, this unique city that was at the same time indifferent to the failings of its citizens and yet so very gracious.

She must speak to Austin about paying for her room. When she had raised it earlier he had brushed it aside, but that would not do at all.

Looking at the so familiar panorama seen in a hundred images from TV reports to calendars, she knew that she must come back soon and relive her all too brief time here. There was so much that she hadn't seen, so many treasures that had eluded her.

Realizing that the time was passing, she had a quick shower and changed rather self-consciously into the skirt and top. The girl in the shop had been right. They did go together and the shades of dusky pink, brown and gold were flattering. Appropriate for the autumn of her life perhaps? She did not want to be reminded of her age, so instead wondered what Austin might be wearing. For the service he had worn a dark suit and shirt but he did not look at home in them. His garish T-shirts betrayed a personality at odds with his slight, perhaps unexceptional appearance and Grace could only wonder at the deep waters that lurked beneath the shallows of his general demeanour. Austin Morris, archaeologist, bone man, grieving husband, friend of Duke Jamieson—she was sure there was more to him than he had so far revealed.

Grace went down to the bar thinking that this sort of meeting was becoming a habit. Austin was standing at the bar talking to the waiter. It looked as if they knew each other and Grace guessed that he must have stayed here before. When he saw her he waved and then ordered her a drink.

'Try something different. Georgio here has a great line in cocktails.'

She accepted the cold, sharp, bubbling glass, decorated with frosted salt and lime. It tasted exhilarating. On top of everything else, was Austin an expert in cocktails?

Leading her to a table, he said, 'What would you rather do this evening? We could go to see a play or a concert. On the other hand, you might be tired and we could simply dine here.'

'Oh no, it would be a shame to be in London and spend all the time in a hotel,' she said, wondering too late if he might be tired.

'Right. Tell me what you enjoy and I'll go and see if Reception can rustle up some tickets.'

What did she like? It didn't really matter, although she said, 'I'm not at all keen on musicals.'

'Good. Me neither.' He gave her his familiar twitchy smile. 'A play then, or music. Something classical perhaps? A farce? A mystery? Shakespeare?'

She raised her shoulders, which said it is up to you. Austin excused himself to go to Reception to see what they might be able to locate. He came back looking downcast. 'I'm afraid the choice seems to be *Phantom of the Opera* or something at the Whitehall Theatre.'

Grace could tell that neither appealed to him, or to her for that matter. She said, 'If you would like to see either that is fine by me, but if not perhaps we could just go out for a wander?'

He looked relieved, saying, 'In that case we could go up to Soho and eat. I know just the place, but again, I d better book a table. What time do you like to eat, early? Late?'

'Not too late.'

'Good. That suits me fine. I'll go and reserve a table then.'

While he was away Grace sipped her cocktail and let her mind drift. She could see Austin through the entranceway. He was at the desk chatting to a young woman who looked Eastern European. She was smiling. Grace had noticed that women seemed easy in his company, they liked him. She smiled too, taking in his violet shirt and dark waistcoat shimmering with some metallic thread. What was there not to like?

He returned moments later. 'Done. We eat at eight.' He glanced at his watch. 'I've ordered a taxi so we have half an hour before it comes.

Another drink?'

She nodded, happy to sit and enjoy more of the mysterious cocktail. She did not ask its name, already knowing that anywhere else it would not taste the same.

The restaurant was buzzing with activity. The staff worked like termites. At the same time they were polite and welcoming. It must take a lot of willpower . . . or perhaps desperation to act the part in a place like this. The menu was huge and, following Austin's advice, she ordered a dish rich with asparagus and exotic-sounding mushrooms. He ordered wine and they drank companionably as they waited. The background hubbub made conversation difficult so they sat mainly in silence.

The meal lived up to her expectations and somehow she managed a pudding light with whisked egg white and heavily laced with lemon and cream. Utterly replete, they stepped out into the street.

'Where now?' Austin asked. 'Are you too tired or could you manage a club? Nothing hectic, just a late drinking place with good music.'

'That would be wonderful.'

It was. As they went down the steep stone steps the underground cellar was transformed from the gloomy to the magical by the playing of a trio. The guitarist nodded to Austin as they were shown to a table. A bottle of wine arrived although Grace had not seen him order.

'Do you often come here?' she asked, carefully turning the words around so that it didn't sound too much of a cliché.

'Quite often when I'm in town. Before I moved to the island I was based at the British Museum. We . . . Percy and I loved this place. It took me a long time to work up the courage to come back after she died but I guess that she would be upset if I didn't continue to enjoy it.'

Grace absorbed the words along with the wine. What would Percy think of him bringing her here? She had no way of interpreting the significance of his choice of venue.

They stopped to listen to the music. She didn't recognize anything that they played and guessed that they were all their own compositions. They seemed to have an inexhaustible repertoire and each number felt appropriate for this late, dusky, after-midnight cavern.

'When was the last time you came to London?' Austin asked during a lull as the band took a break.

'A long time ago. My mother was ill for a long time so I didn't get away very much.'

He nodded to show that he understood. Part of her felt undermined by his easy transition from one role to another. Her world encompassed so little. She said, 'I'm afraid I'm

303

the typical, despised spinster daughter that stayed at home to look after her parents.' To her mortification tears formed in her eyes. I've drunk too much, she chided herself, trying hard to fight down the choking emotion.

'Hey, none of that now.' He reached over and placed his hand on her shoulder. 'You did what had to be done. No good regretting the past. What matters now is what's next? How long have your parents been dead?'

'My mother died three-four weeks ago.'

'Then no wonder you are feeling fragile. Would you like to go?'

She shook her head. It was easier to be here in the gloom surrounded by strangers than to be alone with him for then she might just have to pour her heart out, confess to weaknesses she had no desire for him to know about.

He said, 'If you'd let me, perhaps we could come up to London again when we aren't curtailed by other considerations. Today's ceremony isn't exactly the perfect background to being positive and happy.'

She nodded her agreement, although whether to his last statement or the invitation she wasn't sure.

They relaxed back into their seats, allowing the music to give them some space from each other. Grace wondered what he might be thinking. His manner was so gentle, almost respectful, and she knew that it was something that she could do with more of. How much more, she dare not contemplate.

They stayed very late. At about two a group of men in drag came in and sat at the next table. Austin seemed to know one of them, raising a hand in acknowledgement and smiling.

'Guy used to work in a bar near the Museum,' he said to her. 'He and his mates do turns in a gay club just down the road.'

Here she was, in a place she had never experienced and hardly realized existed. This must go on every day of the week, only definitely not in her quiet little village. Absorbed, she watched two of the men dance together. No one took any notice. She remembered that at the first mention of Percy she had assumed that Austin was gay. If he had been what would it have mattered? Looking at him, his intelligent grey eyes and generous mouth, she realized that she would have felt deprived.

Seeing her stifle a yawn, he said, 'Come on, time to go.'

They left the club and walked a short way along to the corner. Grace saw the road sign for Shaftesbury Avenue and exclaimed 'This is where I used to work, on the junction with Frith Street.'

'That's just down the road. Want to go and have a look?'

She wasn't sure that she did but he held her arm to prevent them being separated and

305

steered her down the road. Sure enough there was the long-remembered sign for Frith Street. Nothing else was familiar, though. By night, this area was buzzing in a way that it had never done in her time and certainly not during the day. She remembered none of the buildings and the prostitutes had long since been driven underground. They must still be there though, somewhere in the neighbourhood? Did she understand any more now than she had forty years ago? Certainly she had more compassion. She glanced at Austin, who had been a widower for three years, and thought of Joe whose marriage had been celibate for a long time. Was it men like them who visited prostitutes? In her ignorance, she realized that she didn't know. She could not believe that an impersonal exchange of money for sex would satisfy either of them, though. Besides, surely they would have more respect for women than to buy them—or was that a naïve concept when it came to exchanging cash for services rendered—no different perhaps than having a cleaning lady? She shook her head to drive out the thoughts to which she had no answers. The other things, the sharing and closeness, trust and affection, surely they would need that too?

She tried to imagine herself back then, standing on this very corner. Above all, it was a time when sadness had dogged her. The love of her life had been lost to someone else. How would it have all turned out if her dad had not been taken ill and she had stayed? Thinking of the love of her life, she remembered that he was suddenly, inexplicably back. That thought led to very dangerous ground.

Austin found them a taxi and they drove back to the hotel where he collected the keys from a very tired looking young man at Reception.

'I'll see you to your door,' he announced. She did not argue, wondering if that was all he meant. She was too tired to know what she would do if he expected to come in.

At her room, she stopped and fiddled with the key, one of those cards that had a habit of re-locking the door before she had time to open it. Austin took it from her, swiped it and pushed the door open. Holding it ajar he stepped back so that she could go in.

'Good night then, Grace. I hope you've had a good evening.'

'I have, it's been lovely.' He wasn't expecting to come in then. She didn't know if she was relieved or disappointed.

As he took a step back she turned awkwardly to him. 'Goodnight, Austin, thanks for such a terrific time.'

'It is I who should thank you. You've made a difficult day . . . memorable.'

On impulse she leaned forward and kissed him on the cheek. She felt the tension in his body. He was trembling. With sudden tenderness she wanted to hold him close but already he was pulling away.

Taking a few steps down the corridor he briefly turned and waved. 'Good night.' His movements were tense and she knew that he was struggling with his own feelings. As he stepped into the waiting lift, he left her with an alarming sense of loss.

CHAPTER TWENTY-FOUR

They arrived home late the following afternoon. At breakfast Austin seemed to be back to his old self and suggested that before catching a train they might visit the National Portrait Gallery to view some of the seventeenth-century people who were contemporaries of Holmes. They spent two entertaining hours while Austin, in his element, pointed out various personalities, recounting their quirks and the scandals that had underlined their lives.

Afterwards they stopped for a light lunch, still full from the hotel breakfast. Grace still hadn't managed to pay her way and at the restaurant she insisted.

'I tell you what,' said Austin, brushing away her money, 'Next time you can pay.'

So there was to be a next time?

At Yarmouth they collected his car from his friend's driveway and drove to the cottage.

The sharp, bright air of the island was cool on their faces and people were noticeable by their absence. She missed the hurly-burly of the London streets, the wealth of history surrounding every corner. The island had another kind of beauty, just as old, just as historic in its quiet way, but whereas London was created largely by man, the island had been forged by nature. There was no reason not to love both.

Outside her gate, she invited Austin in but he said, 'I must get up to the hall and collect Columbus,' adding, 'I shall miss being able to leave him there when I go away.'

'What's going to happen to the hall?' she asked.

'Well, eventually it will almost certainly have to be sold. It is left collectively to the kids but they won't have the wherewithal to maintain it. Besides, sooner of later their lives will take them in different directions.'

'What about the animals?'

'Duke's provided for them. They aren't in a position to make any decisions whereas the young ones are.'

'Did any of his wives have a claim on his estate?' She was curious now.

'Oh no. They were paid off years ago.'

She wanted to ask him if Duke had left him anything, not money but some memento of their long friendship. Instead, she said, 'If you have no one to look after Columbus I'd always be pleased to do so.'

He turned to her. 'That's very kind of you Grace and I may well take you up on it.' He hesitated before adding, 'But I hope there might be a time when you will come with me?'

Before she could say anything he continued, 'I've got a day off on Wednesday. Perhaps we could call in at my centre and have a look at the artefacts, including Paloma of course. Then maybe we could eat out in the evening?'

As she said yes, she realized that it would be her birthday. She was certain that he did not know, but when she thought about it she couldn't imagine a better way of spending it.

*   *   *

Indoors, she was greeted by the beep of the answerphone. She stopped to put the kettle on before pressing the button. You have three messages, the disembodied voice announced.

The machine clicked and the first filled the room.

Grace, it's Alex. I do hope you are OK. I had no idea my father would come and visit you. It must have been really difficult for you. Honestly, I don't know what's got into him. I think he might be getting senile or something. Anyway, he seemed to think you were pleased to see him.

In the circumstances, I didn't say

anything to him about . . . you and me. I thought it best not to for the moment. Anyway, I've shown him this vineyard and he seems quite impressed but he's got some bee in his bonnet that I wanted him to meet someone while he was here. Perhaps you know what's the matter with him? He also said he had something to show me when we get back to the island.

God, I miss you Grace. It will be good to see you again. The old man's booked us in at some posh hotel so perhaps I'd better stay there with him? Anyway, thinking of you. Much love.

As Grace grappled with the complications of this, the second message started.

Grace, it's me. I made it to this place in France. Seems nice enough but I wouldn't want to live here. Alex didn't say anything about any secret lover or anything so perhaps you were right and there isn't anyone.

He didn't seem too pleased when I told him where I had been. I guess he thinks I'm being disloyal to Meg. Anyway, give it time.

We'll be back in a couple of days. I've booked us both into that hotel. To be honest, I wish I was coming on my own but I'll take Alex to see that winery. If he really wants to leave Australia the island might be the place for him, and I could ask you to keep an eye on him. I hope it won't be too long though before you make a visit to see me in Oz?

God, it was good to see you, Grace! I feel like a kid. I can't stop thinking about you. I can't wait to get back. You take care now.

According to the time of the third message it was sent several hours after the first and it was from Joe.

Me again. I haven't forgotten that Wednesday is your birthday. We don't get back until late on Tuesday so although I wanted it to be a surprise I thought I'd better tell you that I've arranged a bit of a do at the hotel. We're going to have a meal and I'd like you to invite as many of your friends as you like. I know it's short notice but hopefully most of them will be able to come. The idea is to meet at the hotel at 6.30. Don't let me down now.
Miss you.

At some point she had sat down, and the complications threatened to smother her. Here was a father and son hiding their feelings about her from each other, but sooner or later it must all come out. Perhaps even worse, she had no idea how to unravel her feelings about them. Now there was a surprise party to disrupt her plans. It was certainly not what she wanted, but how to resolve it was another matter.

* * *

Having calmed down, Grace accepted that she could not avoid Joe and Alex indefinitely so the best thing would be to go along with the birthday plans and to invite lots of people. That way there should be safety in numbers. She started to draw up a list of friends and relatives but it turned out to be very short. There was her cousin Joan, and Joan's daughter Louisa. She remembered the animated way that Alex and Louisa had interacted at Carisbrooke Castle. Louisa was just the sort of girl to distract him, being pretty, interesting and, as far as Grace knew, available. That just about exhausted her relations so she added Molly and Reg to the list, wondering how Reg might cope in company. She then scanned other possible guests, neighbours, old work colleagues, but she really didn't have enough in common with any of them to wish to invite them. That, of course, left Austin. As a courtesy, she must ring and invite him and decline his offer of dinner that evening. She began to work her way through the very short list.

It was the first time that she had spoken to

Joan since the funeral and her cousin was apologetic for not having been in touch.

'Honestly, it doesn't matter. I've been pretty busy as it happens.' That, she thought to herself, is an understatement!

'Good.'

Grace went on to issue the invitation. 'I've some friends visiting from Australia, and they're arranging a bit of a do.'

'Not the boy you used to fancy all that time ago?'

Boy, that was a laugh. Aloud, she said, 'As a matter of fact it is, but don't get any ideas. He is visiting with his son.'

'What's his son like?'

Very good in bed, she thought. Aloud, she said, 'He's really nice.'

They talked for another couple of minutes, Grace extended the invitation to Louisa and then she rang off.

Molly was all for the party and had the clearly pleasing news that Reg was going into hospital on Tuesday for assessment so that he would be conveniently locked up for the night.

'What's all this about then?' Molly asked.

'My Australian friends will be here and they're arranging the party.'

'When you say friends, do you mean Lover Boy AND Lover Man?'

'It seems like it.'

'Good God, Grace, I wouldn't miss this for anything!'

Austin was out when she called so she left a message on his answerphone. 'I'm really sorry about dinner on Wednesday but some friends of mine have turned up from Australia and have organized a get together. They've asked me to invite some local friends, so I do hope you'll be able to come.' As an afterthought she added, 'I would still like to come and see your office during the day, though.'

Exhausted, she sat back and tried to imagine the evening. The scene grew more and more bizarre. Might Joe suddenly announce to everyone present how he had always loved her and now wanted to marry her? She saw him theatrically producing a ring box with a huge Australian sapphire blinding the guests. Would Alex then leap to his feet shouting, 'She's mine!' and punch his father? Perhaps the police would be called. Perhaps both men would be locked up for the night. Grace might never be able to show her face in Yarmouth again. For some inexplicable reason, she began to enjoy the farce so much she was actually looking forward to it. Whatever happens, she thought, this is going to be some party!

*   *   *

At about ten o'clock on Tuesday evening, her phone rang. It was Alex.

'We've just arrived,' he announced. 'Dad's

315

shattered so he's gone straight to bed. He hasn't got much stamina these days.' The observation wasn't wasted on her.

'Good journey?' she asked, for something to say.

'Well enough. Can I come round? There's a taxi here. I really need a chance to talk to you.'

She felt the slippery slope beneath her feet, the crevasse lurking dangerously near.

'I don't think—' she began.

'Please, Grace, I think we should talk before tomorrow. There have been some developments.'

'Alex—'

'I'm not daft, Grace. I didn't realize before but I do now that the old man has been carrying a torch for you all these years. What I don't know, is what you feel about him?'

She breathed out to relieve the tension. 'I don't know either, Alex. It's all happening too fast.' When he didn't respond, she added, 'I met your dad when I was seventeen. I fell in love with him but—well, he never came back.'

'But he's back now?'

'We're different people. It was you who said that you and Susie didn't know each other— well, nor do we. I mean, I don't really know either you or your father.'

He remained silent. 'Look,' she took the initiative. 'You must be exhausted too. Go to bed now. We can talk another time.' She felt that she was his mother talking.

He said, 'We've got to get back to the winery. We're leaving again on Thursday.' She recognized the urgency in his voice. When she didn't respond, he said, 'Dad wants to take me on some mystery tour tomorrow. Are you coming with us?'

'I can't. I'm doing something else.'

'Can't you put it off?'

'Afraid not.' Into the silence she announced, 'In a few hours I'll be sixty. Just think about it.'

'What's there to think about?'

'Everything.'

He blurted out, 'I think I should tell Dad what happened while I was here.'

'Why would you want to do that?'

'Are you ashamed?'

'No, of course I'm not ashamed but . . .'

When she couldn't think of anything else to say, he continued, 'What I want to know is what's happening between you and him. My mother is hardly cold. It just seems . . . indecent that he should rush over here like some rutting stag.'

'Alex please.' Taking control of herself, she said, 'Please don't confuse what happened between us with your feelings about your mother. You need to talk to Joe calmly about how he feels. I'm in no position to know what is going on in his head.' She didn't add that a few weeks ago her life was uncomplicated and neither he nor his father had featured at all.

To divert the conversation, she said, 'What

317

about Susie?'

'I know she wants to come back. Dad wants us to get back together.'

'You shouldn't even think of it to please someone else.'

Another long silence. She said, 'Look, I think we all need some space to sort everything out. You and I both lost our mothers recently and your dad lost his wife. We've all suffered bereavements and our feelings aren't really to be relied on at the moment. Let's just wait and see what happens, shall we?' She could imagine him sitting alone, fretting and hurt. As gently as she could, she said, 'Be patient. I'll see you tomorrow evening—let's try and get through it without any dramas?'

'All right, but I don't know what's going to happen.'

With those less than reassuring words he rang off.

She had hardly replaced the receiver when it jarred again. Her heart jolted in response and with a sudden surge of annoyance she picked it up. 'Look, just go to bed.'

'Grace?' Too late she realized that it was Joe.

'Oh, hello. I thought you were someone else.'

'It sounds like it. Are you all right? Is someone annoying you?' She had a vision of him rolling up his sleeves and coming round to sort them out. What would he think if he discovered that it was his son and heir?

'How are you, Joe?'

'I'm well. I don't know what's up with Alex but he's behaving like a rebellious kid these days. Listen, are you coming with us tomorrow to see that place?'

'I can't. I'm already doing something.'

'Can't you put it off?'

'No.' She bit back the urge to say, 'I don't want to.'

'Does that mean we won't see you until the evening? How many people have you invited, by the way?'

She did a quick count, 'Four.'

'Is that all?'

'Yes.'

'Right. Are you all right? You sound tense.'

'I'm fine, just tired. You must be tired,' she added.

'Too right. All this jetting around doesn't suit me. Well, if you can't make it during the day, we'll have to wait until the evening. Six thirty sharp, mind?'

'I'll be there. Goodnight, Joe.' For a terrible moment she nearly said Alex.

'Good night, then. I'll see you at the party, and Grace . . . ' She knew that he wanted to say more but before he could do so she put the phone down.

This party, she thought, is going to be something else!

CHAPTER TWENTY-FIVE

Grace woke from a troubled sleep and her first thought was that feeling as she did was not a good omen for the start of a new decade. Her head full of cotton wool, she thought, I'm sixty. That is old by anyone's calculation so how can I pretend otherwise? Someone had said that sixty was the new forty but she had not yet even come to terms with being forty. Now she was a pensioner, not just older but old. These gloomy thoughts forced her from bed and she went to shower remembering that Austin was calling for her at ten.

Given a choice, she would have liked to spend the day alone, away from anyone who might, by word or deed, add to her growing sense of disaster. She was just stepping out of the shower when someone knocked at the door. It was no use pretending not to be at home. Her car was outside and besides, they would only conclude that she was still in bed. Not wishing to appear ancient and bedridden, she opened the door. It was Molly.

'Happy birthday!' She came in clutching a huge bouquet of flowers and a package. 'They picked Reg up at eight o'clock so I've got the rest of the day free,' she announced. 'I thought we might go into town for lunch?'

'I'm sorry, Molly, but I can't.'

'Oh, what are you up to then?'

She explained about the skeleton and the archaeology department and how she intended to rebury the bones where they had found them.

'It gives me the creeps thinking of all those ghosts out there,' observed Molly. Her cottage was more recent, built on the other side of the church and away from the graveyard.

'Well, no one has come to haunt me yet.' Grace went through the routine of making a drink. 'Toast?'

Molly nodded.

'What are the lover men up to today, then?' her friend asked. 'I thought they'd be round here like a shot fighting over you.'

For once Molly's joke didn't seem funny. The attention of both men felt like a siege and she didn't want to think about it. Pouring the tea, she said, 'They're going somewhere else.'

'Couldn't you have gone with them?'

Grace did not explain that she had deliberately decided not to.

Molly asked, 'What about this archaeology bloke then, what's he like?'

'Very nice.'

'What does that mean?'

'What I say. He's very pleasant. You'll meet him tonight. He's coming to the party.'

'The party, yes. I wouldn't miss it for the world.'

Grace put the flowers in water and opened

the package Molly had placed on the table. Inside was a pair of gold earrings with tiny stones let into the floral centres. They glittered, although they could not, of course, be diamonds.

'Thanks Molly, they are really neat; I could wear them with anything.'

'That's what I thought.' Molly looked pleased.

Grace also opened a card with a resounding I Am Sixty blazoned across it. She smiled and placed it on the side.

They ate the toast and then Grace excused herself, saying that she had to get ready. Her friend was in no hurry to leave but finally took the hint and wandered off to spend her first day of freedom alone.

'I'll pick you up this evening,' Grace called after her. 'Six fifteen. Be ready.'

If everything else felt out of kilter at least the weather was anointing her birthday with a balmy splash of sunshine. She took a moment to look out at the garden, noticing the sudden blossoming of the Sweet Williams. She couldn't resist going out to smell them. The perfume was perfect. If there were a heaven then surely it would include smells like this.

Aware of the time, she hurried back indoors and dressed in her favourite long blue skirt with a light, soft cotton top that felt comfortable and clung just enough to her still-good figure. Tonight it would be the pink and brown and gold outfit.

As she was slipping her feet into her sandals she heard the gate click and looking out it was in time to see both Austin and the postman coming through the gate together. The postman, she noticed, was carrying quite a pile of mail with a sprinkling of envelopes in festive colours. Damn, now Austin would discover that it was her birthday and she hadn't wanted him to know, not until the evening, anyway.

She greeted them both and accepted the pile of letters, placing them on the hall table.

'What's this? Your birthday?' Austin nodded at the pile, adding, 'Aren't you going to open your fan mail?'

'I'll do that later, when I come back.'

'Right. Well.'

She looked at him and realized that there was something different about his demeanour. He seemed excited and his mouth twitched as if at some secret discovery. 'Is something wrong?' she asked.

'On the contrary. In fact, I think I might have a perfect birthday present for you, even though you kept the date a secret.'

She acknowledged her guilt. 'What is it?' she asked.

'I spent the last two days poking around the records and I've found something that might be quite astounding. I do hope that you will be pleased.' He looked suddenly uncertain.

'What sort of thing?'

323

'I'll show you when we get to the office. Oh, and would you mind bringing your house deeds with you? They might just confirm what I suspect.'

Sporting a racing green polo shirt and rust-coloured trousers, he led the way to his car. From the back she thought that he looked like a racehorse trainer or professional golfer. Perhaps all archaeologists had a penchant for colourful clothes? As they reached the car, from the back seat Columbus looked out at them, his face relaxing into what could only be a canine grin.

'Thank you for inviting me to this party.' Austin reversed the car out of the drive and set off in the direction of Newport.

'Not at all. It was all arranged before I knew about it.'

'Are you looking forward to it?'

She didn't say that it might turn into something resembling a Greek tragedy, just hoping that no one would dash out his own eyes or take hemlock. Aloud she said, 'You remember Alex who found the skeleton? Well, he and his father are both making a visit. I've known the family for years. They have organised this evening.'

'That is very nice of them.'

Very, thought Grace.

They arrived at Austin's place of work, a long-abandoned chapel with a great view across the valley. Columbus followed them down the path. Inside, two young women were bent over desks and studiously avoided looking at Grace. She had the distinct impression that they already knew something about her and were speculating as to who she might be and what, if any, connection she had with their boss. She nodded a greeting to their bent heads.

Austin led the way to what might once have been the vestry at the back of the building. A Victorian desk was littered with bones and artefacts, while dusty documents were piled high on windowsill and floor. Columbus went straight to a dog bed in the corner and curled up, promptly feigning sleep.

Grace placed the envelope with the deeds on the table and accepted the seat that Austin swept clean of more files.

Grace looked around, wondering where Paloma might be, and noticed a cardboard box on the floor near to the window. Sunlight played over it and she had the feeling that perhaps Austin had placed her there deliberately to warm her bones. She dismissed the idea as foolish.

'Right, now I want you to read through this.' He placed a file in front of her. Written on the cover were the words, Will of Robert Holmes. With prickling anticipation she opened it and took out the papers. They were not originals, for which she was grateful, and they had been typed some time ago on an ancient machine.

The important thing though was that they were legible.

Within seconds she was immersed in the contents of the will. Being of sound mind although frail in body, the ageing Holmes planned to leave his considerable estate to his nephew Henry. Lucky Henry, she thought, but was immediately diverted by the next lines. Henry would inherit with one proviso—that he married his cousin Mary, Robert's daughter. In the event that he declined to do so, then the estate would be offered to Henry's brother on the same conditions.

Grace sat back and contemplated the reality of what Mary might have felt. Did she even like her cousin Henry? Supposing she was in love with someone else? Supposing the love of her life was Henry's younger brother? Here was the stuff of romantic fiction. She dwelt on how it must feel to be auctioned off by your father. She couldn't imagine her own dad in such a role. The reality of those times hit home, how women were bargaining tools, chattels to be bought and sold. She wondered what would have become of Mary had she not been acknowledged by her father. Perhaps, just perhaps, she would have been better off—poorer yes, but free to live in a simpler world where it was sometimes possible for ordinary people, both men and women, to marry from choice.

As she was thinking this, Austin said, 'Mary

did marry her cousin Henry. They had sixteen children but tragically most of them died.'

'Poor Mary.'

Austin said, 'That is not the reason I wanted you to read the will, though. Look further on.' He leaned over her shoulder and shuffled several pages until he came to a section marked in pencil. 'Just look at this.'

Grace read it, then read it again.

That Parcel of lande, known as Palma Cottage shall pass into the hands of Rufus Stone, mason of this parish, to be held in his trust until his daughter Paloma shall many. Should she fail to do so, or if any said marriage shall be childless, then, there being no living descendants of the said Paloma, on the demise of the said Rufus Stone the land and tenement shall revert to the estate of my nephew Henry Holmes, my sole heir, and thereafter to his descendants.

Grace looked at Austin. 'Does that mean that Rufus Stone was Paloma's father?' she asked.

Austin was now so anxious to share his discoveries that he had a job to get the words out. 'No, not at all. I have checked through all the documents held here, at the Public Record Office and at Thorlea Hall and I have found an agreement that will surely please you.' He pulled it, like a rabbit from a hat, and set it before her, promptly spelling out the contents.

'This is an agreement between Lord Holmes's land agent and this man, Rufus Stone, who was in Holmes's employ. As you will see, Rufus Stone could not write so it is signed with a cross. In essence, in return for taking in the child Paloma and raising her as his own, Stone and his family would live in Palma Cottage.' As he saw her dawning awareness, he added, 'But, the property was then to be passed on to Paloma's descendants, and more than that, it was to go not to an eldest son but to her female descendants.'

'Really? Why would he do that?'

'Why indeed. I suspect that he was miffed because the local dignitaries slighted her mother and even refused her a burial in the churchyard. I guess it was meant as some sort of revenge, to give some independence to a black person and a woman.' He stopped to catch his breath. 'Did you know that when slaves were brought into England at this time they were regarded as free men but if you shifted the same people off to the Caribbean they were slaves again? I guess that Holmes felt a father's affection for his daughter, and giving her this sort of independence pleased him.'

Seeing that she was still trying to unravel the mystery, he said, 'I've spent the last two days ploughing through church records, baptisms, and if I may, might I look at the deeds of your house, because I think that it will be provide the missing link.'

Grace pushed the deeds over to him and he sat down beside her and began to filter through them. 'Yes,' he said, 'yes, it looks like it.' His eyes were now dazzled by discovery.

'What is it?'

Moving his chair closer, he said, 'Paloma did marry. I found the record in the church. Her husband was Bernard Gosden who was apprenticed to Rufus Stone. They had nine children.'

As Grace was absorbing this, he added, 'I next followed through the fate of her eldest daughter, whose name was Purity. In 1731, Purity married one William Godfrey and they too had children, two sons and a daughter. The daughter, Augusta, married an Amos Bush.' As he spoke, Grace picked up the list of owners of her cottage that she had drawn up earlier and stored with the deeds. With dawning disbelief she saw that the men that Austin named as the husbands of Paloma's descendants were the same as those on her list.

'Can this be possible?' she asked. 'Surely there must have been a time when there were no female descendants?'

'I've only found one, a Lionel Milmore, who was the only child of Hannah and Frederick Jolliffe. Hannah was Augusta and Amos Bush's daughter, by the way. Lionel Millmore seems to have kept the cottage but he had a

329

daughter and it was to her, not his sons, that the cottage next passed. Don't you see, there is a direct link with Paloma up until . . . ' he consulted his notes. 'The house was then in the hands of Eliza Galpine.'

'But that was my grandmother!' Grace said. 'Surely you're not saying—?'

'From her it went to her daughter—'

'Edna, my mother. No, it can't be true—can it?'

'It's all there.'

'But no one has ever said anything, not about it passing through the female line. My mother had brothers, why didn't they object?'

Austin shrugged. 'This would be after the First World War. I think you'll find your mother only had two brothers and they both died as a result of that tragedy, so they wouldn't have been round to object—and then your mother had you.'

Grace was silent for several seconds and gradually the enormity of the discovery hit her. 'Does that mean that I—'

He smiled. 'It looks very much like it. You, my dear, are a direct descendent of the young lady in your garden.'

'I can't be!' She was aware that her mouth had actually dropped open. Slowly, she shook her head in disbelief. 'But . . . ' she started.

Reading her thoughts, he said, 'Remember how many generations it is since Paloma became a mother. Her African blood has been

330

diluted over the centuries.'

'Does this really mean that Paloma is my ancestor?' she repeated.

'It would seem that you are descended from both Paloma and from Holmes.'

'I can't be—can I?'

Austin laughed and grabbed her hand. 'How do you feel about it? What is it like being the descendent of a Lord and a slave girl?'

'It's . . .' she had no words until the excitement bubbled up, when she said, 'It's wonderful!'

He hugged her, a joyous gesture of shared excitement. 'I'm so glad that you feel like that about it. I was worried in case you objected to having African slave ancestors.'

'How could I object? It's an honour to have such an unusual pedigree!'

His arms were still round her and she could not stop herself from kissing him. 'Thank you, Austin. Thank you for finding all this out. I would never have done so on my own.'

His eyes were suddenly misty with longing. She looked down, embarrassed by her excitement and his proximity. This was another complication, one that was warm and comforting, but just at that moment she couldn't even think of its significance. She drew back and turned again to scan the evidence before her. Austin drew his chair back and began to tidy up papers.

For the first time, the future of her house

seriously occupied her. She knew that she was remiss in not having already made a will. Indeed, since Edna died, it had crossed her mind several times but she had no firm plans as to who to leave it to. She had seriously thought of various charities, or to have it sold and the money divided between worthy causes. Now its history took on a whole new meaning.

'So what happens to the house next,' she asked, 'when I die? I don't have a daughter to leave it to.'

'Perhaps you should talk to your solicitor,' he said. 'I'm not sure that after all this time the original terms of the agreement could be enforced. For a start, I don't know if there are any of Holmes's descendants left who could make a claim on the cottage. It seems most unlikely. For that reason, you are no doubt free to do what you like with it.'

She nodded, still grappling with all the revelations of the morning. Standing up, Austin said, 'That leaves one other thing. What are you going to do with Paloma?'

As he spoke he went to the place beneath the window and brought the box over to the table, setting it before her. 'We've really finished with her now,' he said. 'You can take her home if you like. I've made a note in the file to the effect that she will be returned to where she was found. Is that right?'

Grace nodded, hardly daring to lift the lid of the box and look upon the mortal remains

332

of her eight times great-grandmother.

'Lift her out,' said Austin. 'Don't be afraid of her.' He grinned. 'I'm sure I can see a family likeness.'

'Not to me,' began Grace and then suddenly she thought of Joan's daughter Louisa with her lustrous brown eyes and dark crinkly hair. 'But I think I know who might have,' she added. 'You'll meet her this evening.'

*   *   *

They lunched at the local pub, took Columbus for a walk, and then Austin dropped Grace home. As she stepped out of the car she could see a great swathe of flowers by the front door. She was pretty certain that they would be from either Alex or Joe and she had no wish for Austin to see them.

He opened the boot of the car and retrieved the box that held Paloma's remains. 'Shall I bring these in for you?' he asked.

'No thanks, I can manage.' She took the box from him, anxious to get inside the house.

'Then I'll pick you up this evening?' he offered.

'No thanks. I've promised to bring my neighbour.'

She detected his disappointment, but he said, 'In that case, I'll see you there. Six thirty, isn't it?'

'Six thirty. I'll see you then.'

She struggled up the footpath with the box and put it down among the flowers while she searched for her key. A huge basket of roses and an even bigger bouquet of mixed flowers littered the doorstep. Having unlocked the door, she carried Paloma inside and put her on the draining board, then returned for the flowers.

The card on the roses simply said, 'Happy Birthday, love Joe.' The card accompanying the bouquet read, 'Happy Birthday, love Alex.' They were both in the same writing, no doubt that of the florist, and clearly someone's imagination had failed to come up with anything more original. The scent of Molly's flowers already wafted across to her and she wasn't sure that she had enough containers to put them all in. Fortunately, Edna had kept two wonderful old washstand sets with huge, floral jugs.

On the side was the post, but before she examined it she took the box that contained Paloma's remains through into Edna's bedroom. Whatever would Edna have thought, coming face to face with her African grannie? The prospect of such a reunion buoyed her up no end.

She opened the cards, touched by the number of people who had remembered. There were several she might have invited to the party tonight and now she wished that she had thought the list through more carefully. A few extra guests might have helped the evening along.

For ages she fiddled around, arranging the flowers, rereading the cards and arranging them on the dresser, then she glanced at the clock. She had about an hour to get ready. Time to go to work then—on this of all evenings she needed all the help she could get!

CHAPTER TWENTY-SIX

Grace collected Molly at 6.15 sharp. In spite of several cups of tea her mouth felt dry and the thought of food repelled her. Although she was tempted, she had deliberately kept away from alcohol and recognized that she had all the classic signs of anxiety. In the short journey between her own and Molly's house, she stopped the car twice, wondering whether to simply go home and phone to say that she could not make it. The thought of actually making the call, however, stopped her from doing so.

Molly had made an effort and was wearing a very elegant dress Grace hadn't seen before. Her thick grey hair was piled up in a style that suited her and she wore strappy sandals that Grace would never have dared to risk for fear of falling over. Bearing in mind that Molly was fifteen years her senior, she took heart. Age

335

alone did not determine one's beauty and dignity. She thought that released from the yoke of caring for Reg her friend looked suddenly younger and attractive. Above all, her irreverent wit drew people to her.

'Well, what's going to happen this evening, then?' Molly clasped her shiny black bag as they pulled into the hotel car park.

It was the question that continued to vex Grace. Not least, she felt that at some point she would need to say something to the guests but any sort of speech would be like crossing a minefield. Perhaps she could tell them about Paloma, but then it would be a bit of a shock to simply spring it on Joan and Louisa. She had no idea how they might react to hearing in public that they had slave ancestors. In any case, family reminiscences seemed inappropriate, as the majority of the party were not relatives. That left more impersonal subjects but to be honest she couldn't think of anything. A panicky part of her wondered whether she would feel compelled to confess to her affair with Alex, to admit to having secretly clung to the dream of Joe for decades—and to own up to feeling some complicated sense of affection for Austin. She could imagine the startled, embarrassed faces as she blurted it all out and stifled an hysterical desire to giggle.

Just as Molly thought she hadn't heard her question, Grace said, 'I don't know.'

As they walked into the hotel foyer, Alex was there to greet them. He was wearing a very crisp-looking linen shirt and cotton trousers and he looked enticingly wholesome. His face was strained, however. Seeing them, he came towards the door.

Grace said, 'Alex, you remember Molly? You saw her when you were staying.'

She remembered that morning with she and Alex fresh from bed, still unwashed but bathed in the afterglow. She looked at him now and for a moment couldn't imagine that this virile young man had actually lured her into his arms. She felt a surge of desire and her legs were suddenly weak.

Alex kissed her on the cheek and shook Molly's hand. 'Drinks over there, help yourself.' He indicated to Molly to go ahead and, taking Grace's arm, said in a low voice, 'Can I have a quick word with you?'

They moved a short distance away and he said, 'Dad's not well. I think I told you he has angina? Well, all this travelling around doesn't suit him.' Pointedly, he added, 'He's an old man, he needs a quiet life.'

Grace's concern was overlaid with a desire to laugh as the young bull attempted to dislodge the old one but her anxiety quickly surfaced.

'Where is he?' she asked.

'He's been lying down but he'd like to speak to you. He's in the Dutch Suite.' He indicated

337

the beautiful old staircase leading up to the hidden rooms above. Very quietly, he said, 'He knows. I've told him about us.'

'Why ever did you do that?' She was torn between wondering what Joe had said and insisting that there is no 'us'. Close to, Alex looked tired, as though exhausted by recent events. She said, 'I don't know what's going on. Your dad turning up like he did has—well . . . ' She didn't finish.

To distract him she asked, 'How did the visit to the vineyard go?'

'It was OK. Interesting, but . . . ' They were interrupted because at that moment her cousins Joan and Louisa were in the foyer.

Excusing herself, Grace went over to greet them. Her eyes were on Louisa, looking avidly for signs that something of Paloma might have surfaced after all this time. The girl's skin certainly had an attractive olive hue that could easily have come from anywhere in Southern Europe, or further south or even east. She thought that without fail, the entire population was a mixture of tribes and nations and races, only for most people the differences were so subtle that it barely showed. They only thought in terms of two or three generations. It was only the knowing about your distant past that made your roots recognizable.

'Happy Birthday!' They were both carrying presents and Grace hugged them before turning to Alex.

338

'Alex, this is my cousin Joan and her daughter Louisa.' She remembered that he and Louisa had met at the castle. Clearly he had not forgotten and he was already eyeing her with interest. She was torn between amusement and mild affront.

Joan shook hands and said, 'So you're the son?'

Grace wondered what he might make of the statement and how things might have turned out if his mother had not chosen to die recently. They moved towards the bar where trays of drinks were laid out. Alex was busy helping Louisa to a white wine.

Grace stood for a moment, wondering what she should do. She introduced Joan to Molly and the two women began to make polite conversation. Now would be an opportunity to slip away and see Joe. On top of everything else, she felt anxious about him. Little by little, the reality of mortality was creeping up on her. It struck her as a supreme irony that if after all these years Joe might return from the past only to promptly die. Alex had suggested that they had to hurry back home. In that case there would be no time to resolve anything. And what was Joe thinking now that Alex had confessed? Had he really come back hoping to pick up where they had left off? Quickly, she grabbed a glass and took a huge gulp.

Well, something had to be done. Quietly she slipped away, across the foyer, up the stairs in search of the Dutch Suite.

The hotel was really quite small and she found the suite immediately. Drawing sufficient breath to sustain her, she knocked at the door. She thought she heard someone speak, so carefully she turned the handle and stepped inside to be greeted by a plethora of yellow. Fleetingly she thought that the owners must know about Holmes and his passion for the colour. Her eyes went quickly to the bed and there was Joe laid out on the top cover, his head and shoulders propped up on a multitude of pillows. A guidebook to the island lay abandoned at his side.

'Joe?' She went over to him and he opened his eyes.

'Grace!' He struggled to sit up and she took in the blue tinge around his mouth, the dark shadows around his eyes that looked drained of colour.

'Oh dear, I'm really sorry you're not well.'

'Damned heart.' He leaned back looking exhausted. 'I'll be all right. I've taken the medication. I'll come down in a minute, but I wanted to see you first.'

He took her hand and the irreverent thought crossed her mind that she wouldn't dare risk making love with him in case the activity proved fatal. She could see the headlines: *Mystery guest found beneath dead resident at famous hotel. I was trapped, said the woman whose name has been withheld.* At the same moment the seriousness of the situation sobered her.

She sat on the edge of the bed still holding his hand. He smoothed her fingers and on impulse raised her hand to his lips then he shook his head and leaned back.

'I was a fool to come rushing over here,' he started. 'I had no idea what your situation might be. For all I knew you might have been engaged, living with someone, anything.'

She remained silent, studying the silk pattern on the bed cover. After a moment he went on. 'I realize now that if, and I know it is a very big if, if we were ever to embark on a new relationship it would need plenty of time for us to get to know each other again. I have no idea what you think of me, even if it is kindly.'

She nodded to show that she understood. Joe went on: 'As it is, I keep feeling crook so I really may not have too much time to find out.'

Seeing her alarm, he added, 'I guess I could drop dead at any moment, but then, couldn't any of us? I promise not to do so this evening. After all, this is your birthday.'

Blocking out the thought of his immediate demise, Grace remained silent. Joe took a few seconds to regain his strength before continuing. 'We've got to go back home tomorrow. We're needed there to sort out the business. I could, of course, send Alex back and stay on but I can see that that isn't what you would want—is it?'

She shook her head. 'I don't know, Joe. Everything has happened so suddenly, Edna dying, you losing your wife—and there are other things too.'

He said, 'Like my son? Alex told me, last night . . . about what happened between you. At first I felt, well, angry but then there are other things you don't know about. Alex is as confused as I am. You don't love him?'

'No, of course not. I like him but—it was just . . .'

He nodded to show that he understood, then he blurted out 'There is another complication, one I find it even harder to admit to.'

Squeezing her hand as if to draw courage from it, he said, 'You've got to know this, otherwise we'd be starting off with a lie. That is, if we are starting off at all. Anyway, I have to say this to someone. I haven't told Alex but, well, for a long time I've been growing increasingly fond of Susie.' He glanced at her and quickly looked away. 'Unforgivable, isn't it? How could a father feel like that about his son's wife? The fact is, though, that I do. I don't kid myself that it is mutual and I never gave any hint until she announced that she was leaving him and we had a long heart to heart. She is, well, fond of me and while she was there for the funeral she promised that if Alex would have her back she would come back—

342

and that she would look after me if ever I got ill. That sounds selfish, doesn't it, but now that Meg has gone . . . There, I've said it.' He glanced at her again and lowered his eyes, waiting for sentence to fall.

'I don't know what to say,' she admitted. 'We can't help how we feel. I suppose it is what we do about it that matters.'

Joe said, 'Alex is in two minds whether to take her back or not. She's a damned pretty woman. I think he's still got the hots for her but, of course, he's mad with her for leaving.' He shrugged. 'He put you on a pedestal, too, by the way, but I think he knows in his heart of hearts that that sort of romance doesn't last. So, I wanted to see you, to check out whether my memory of you and our time together was real or just fantasy.'

'And what did you decide?'

'I didn't decide anything. I knew this trip wasn't working out as I had hoped but that was because I had just rushed in without any thought as to your situation. It was selfish of me . . . crass really.'

She repeated, 'I really do need time, not just a day or two but weeks, perhaps months, to find out who I am and where I'm going.'

He nodded his understanding but said, 'At least I had to see you.'

She grabbed his other hand and squeezed it. 'Let's be fatalistic shall we and see what happens?'

'Would you consider coming to Australia?'

'One day perhaps, not immediately. I do have things to sort out here.'

'Of course. Well, I'd better tidy myself up and come down to host this special party.'

Before she got off the bed he kissed her. It felt partly fraternal but underneath, the desire of a still-living man began to surface. As he pulled her closer she pushed him away. 'Joe, not now.'

'Then later? Will you stay here tonight? For old time's sake?'

She shook her head. 'I can't. It wouldn't be fair on Alex.' As she said it she saw the flash of jealousy. Tread carefully, she reminded herself. Silently she also thought that it wouldn't be fair on Austin either, and above all she needed Austin's good opinion—or something like that. Whatever she wanted from him, this was not the moment to analyze it.

'I'll see you downstairs,' she said and before he could say more, she hurried from the room.

She made her way back and into the bar. Alex and Louisa were deep in conversation while Molly and Joan had found a table and were amiably chatting. She looked around for Austin but there was no sign of him. Glancing up at the clock, she saw that it was just after seven. A moment of alarm touched her. Supposing he had had an accident, been taken ill—or changed his mind? With increasing

344

certainty, she knew that she wanted him to be here. Within a few weeks he seemed to have become essential to her well-being. It was a revelatory thought.

She grabbed a drink from the bar and at that moment she saw him coming through the door. From habit, he wiped his feet on the mat and looked around as his eyes adjusted to the gloom. Seeing her, he smiled. She was not prepared for the wave of tender pleasure at the sight of him. Changing direction, she went across to meet him.

'Grace.' He kissed her on the cheek and pushed a small package at her. 'A token gift,' he said. 'But one that might bring you pleasure.' She took the book-shaped parcel and thanked him, leading the way over to the bar.

'I'm sorry I'm late,' he added. 'That rascal Columbus chose this evening to go walkabout. I'm sure he knows whenever I really want to do something and he sets out to prevent it.' With a smile, he added, 'The Lord my dog is a jealous dog.'

She laughed, comforted by the knowledge that he really wanted to be here, and slipped her arm through his. As they approached the bar, Alex turned away from Louisa and nodded at him.

'Alex, you remember Austin?'

'The skeleton man.' There was a hint of dismissal in his voice, the suggestion that he was surprised that she should invite this near stranger to something so intimate. Ignoring him, she offered Austin a drink and he took it, looking idly round the room. A few other hotel guests had wandered into the bar, thus increasing the numbers. Now, she realized, her evening felt complete.

Moments later, Joe came down the stairs, sprightly, upright, giving no hint of illness. He came straight across to the bar and ordered a brandy then turned and took Grace's arm. There was something possessive about the gesture and she stiffened. Quietly, Austin was watching.

Turning back, she said to Joe, 'This is Austin, a very good friend of mine.'

Joe nodded and held out his hand. Grace recognized the same alert look as to a potential rival that she had seen in Alex. Like father, like son, she realized with some surprise.

'Right, the meal is ready.' Joe took charge and ushered his small flock into an alcove set aside for their party. 'Grace must sit here next to me as guest of honour, me here, Alex, the young lady,' he then nodded to Austin to indicate that he was to be placed at the other side of the table between Joan and Molly. The seating arrangements seemed to spell out the scale of importance of the guests in Grace's life—only it was Joe's scale, not hers. She looked across at Austin and raised her eyebrows. In response, the quizzical smile greeted her.

There was, of course, champagne, and the food was exquisite. Gradually, the volume of conversation increased and Grace took rime to look around her nearest and dearest. She felt strangely detached. After pudding was served Joe stood up, gently banging a spoon on a china plate.

'Ladies and gentlemen, friends of Grace, allow me to welcome you. This is a very special occasion, being Grace's birthday. It is a special occasion for me too because I never expected to be here to celebrate it with her.' He raised his glass and nodded to her. 'Grace and I have known each other nearly all our lives. She has always been a most special person and I hope that, given time, we might be able to catch up on some lost years.'

Oh no. Grace looked away, not wanting any sort of public declaration of his feelings— although in fact it felt more like a claim of ownership. She stopped listening until she realized that Joe was proposing a toast and the gathered assembly rose to drink her health. This was the moment. This was when she must respond. Draining her glass she stood up, a little unsteadily, and addressed the gathering.

'Dear friends, it means such a lot to me to spend this evening with you all—with every one of you. In your own ways you are all important to me. Some of you I have known for a very long time (at this point she looked across at Joan) and some of you I haven't known for very long (her eyes rested on Austin and she felt tears unaccountably prickling beneath her eyelids). This is just to say that I value you all more than I can say and that I hope there will be many more gatherings like this.'

She realized that she was beginning to lose the plot so, to save face, she grabbed her glass rather unsteadily and said, 'To you all.' She thumped back into her chair amid the applause and cheers. As an afterthought she turned towards Joe and said, 'I forgot to say a special thank you to you for arranging this. I can't tell you how much I appreciate it.'

He looked directly at her and replied, 'I guess being your oldest friend doesn't make me the most important.' He glared across the table at Austin. 'Important is he—more than the rest of us?'

Grace felt increasingly out of control. 'You're all important,' she repeated, 'all of you,' but the very words shouted at her that some were more important than others.

Thereafter, Joe seemed to be drinking a lot. Alex was concentrating solely on Louisa while Joan and Molly looked on like two elder statesmen, enjoying the spectacle. Between them, Austin sat quietly, addressing remarks to one or the other but looking across at her.

Grace knew that she was in no state to drive

home. It must have been obvious because dredging up some vestiges of being the host, Joe suggested that he should book her a room. Her head now felt distinctly whoosy but she managed to say, 'I must take Molly home.'

'I can drop her off.' It was Austin, quietly taking in what was happening.

'No need. I'll get her a taxi.' Joe was not to be outdone in knightly gestures.

'In that case, the same taxi could take Grace as well—only I'd rather see that she gets home safely.'

Grace squinted. Were the two men squaring up to each other? Had the young buck gone off in search of pastures new, leaving the old bulls to lock horns? She began to giggle.

At this point, Molly took it upon herself to intervene. 'I'm quite capable of making my own arrangements, thank you very much,' she announced. 'I would be pleased to accept a lift home from this gentleman and I can perfectly well see that Grace gets home safely.'

There was nothing for it. Joe, poor old Joe, seemed to be outwitted. Grace's head had cleared enough to realize that in his quiet way, Austin was making some sort of claim to take responsibility for her. Just at the moment, somebody needed to. When this was all over, back in her cottage she would have time to take stock of her situation but for the moment, just for the moment, she was only too happy to give herself up to Austin.

*   *   *

At Grace's insistence, they dropped Molly off first. At first Molly demurred but then, taking in the situation, she agreed. Dear Molly, ever astute. She had come to her own conclusion that of all the men hovering around her friend, this was the one who was to be trusted.

As Grace and Austin pulled up outside her cottage, she said, 'Would you like to come in?'

Austin did not reply immediately then he said, 'I have to be getting back, for Columbus.'

'Of course.' She had no idea what he might really be thinking, whether that was a reason or an excuse. Did he want to take this friendship further, or was he still not ready to put his mourning aside? Was Persephone Morris in the car with them, willing him not to break free from his past?

Quietly, Austin said, 'I'm afraid of spoiling our friendship, Grace.' She was silent, not knowing how to respond, until he said, 'Am I right in thinking that both those guys at the hotel are after you?'

Even more quietly she said, 'Probably.'

'Well, I wouldn't want to complicate your life even further.' Just as she felt that he was slipping away from her, he said, 'On the other hand, you could simply come home with me.'

She looked at him in astonishment. 'I—'

Seeing her expression, he said, 'I apologize.

I never should have suggested such a thing.'

'But I want to,' she said too quickly. 'I . . . I don't know where I am going but—for the moment, I can't think of anyone I'd rather go home with.'

He suddenly smiled and she loved the gentle wisdom of his expression. Starting the car, he said, 'Then, my dear, for tonight, shall we simply go home together? Tomorrow, as you well know, is another day.'

CHAPTER TWENTY-SEVEN

Grace awoke from a very deep sleep, slowly emerging through a cocoon of soft cotton. Her eyes glided across the ceiling but it did not look familiar. The sound of Columbus scratching at the door brought back the events of the evening before. With alarm, she realized that she could remember nothing. Somehow she had got herself undressed and into bed, for here she was—in her underwear. She tried to remember taking off her clothes, wondering what delicacy had made her insist on keeping on her bra, panties and slip. Perhaps she had passed out and Austin had struggled unsuccessfully to part her from her garments. Had they made love? She didn't know.

Snuggled up in this old-fashioned bed with a deep soft mattress that enfolded her into its

351

heart made the prospect of leaving it very unattractive.

From outside the door she heard Austin shout, 'Columbus, shut up,' followed by the scrabble of the dog's paws on a wooden floor then the sound of a door latch being lifted and a woof of pleasure as Columbus had clearly bounded out into the garden.

Her brain seemed to be disengaged. No amount of revving it moved her thoughts forward. She needed to go to the loo, so gingerly she extricated herself from the bedding and sat on the side. Her head was doing crazy things and she thought that this was what it must feel like after a ride on a roller coaster. She looked around her for the rest of her clothes. They were neatly piled on a chair in the corner. There was also a silk bathrobe hung over the back of the chair and she grabbed it and felt her way to the door.

The bathroom was just across the corridor. Further down, she could hear the clatter of china in what was no doubt the kitchen. Thankfully she slipped inside the bathroom and bolted the door. As her head stopped pounding she took in its rather idiosyncratic décor, an old-fashioned painted loo with an overhead cistern and a huge, deep cast-iron bath with a complicated assortment of taps. She needed a bath but the depth looked intimidating. Suppose she got in and couldn't get out again? On the other hand, the shower

352

looked difficult to operate, and just at that moment she was in no state to grapple with anything complicated. Reluctantly, she decided to postpone both and meandered her way back in search of Austin.

He was indeed in the kitchen, quietly humming away to himself as he waited for a kettle to boil on an ancient Aga.

Seeing her, he asked, 'Did you sleep well?' He waved a hand and she noticed that the other was occupied with a frying pan in which eggs were spitting fiercely. Opening the bottom door of the Aga he took out a plate and transferred the eggs then proceeded to make toast on a wire tray on the top of the cooker.

'I hope you're hungry,' he said. 'Personally, I'm starving.' He looked across at her and smiled. 'Bit of a rough night?'

Was it? Again she tried to recall what had happened after they had left the hotel. Had they slept together? Surely she wouldn't have put her clothes on again? Surely she would remember?

Austin poured tea into chunky deep-blue mugs, probably from some small private pottery. The glaze was less than perfect, adding to their charm.

'Thanks.' She accepted one and sat in a chair sipping it. Her dry mouth welcomed it like a shower in the desert. It tasted strong but not bitter, just the way she liked her tea to be.

The door flew open and Columbus bustled in wagging his tail and greeting her with a wet snuffle. She patted his head and thought how comforting it was to wake up to company, especially the four-legged kind. The door stood open and at the end of the passage, like some Dutch interior, a rectangle of light framed a positive kaleidoscope of flowers in the garden beyond. She squinted at it, her eyes hurting from the glare of the early sun.

'Your garden is lovely.'

'I've tried to keep it up, a sort of memorial to Percy. It was her domain.'

She felt a jolt of discomfort. There was definitely a worm in the apple, the memory of a woman who still held sway here. With shock she realized that she was probably wearing her bathrobe. She couldn't think of anything to say.

While Austin was juggling an assortment of food on to a plate she remembered the present he had given to her the evening before. She hadn't had a chance to open it and it was in her handbag lying on the sideboard. Carefully she got up and fetched it. Inside the wrapping was a slim volume of verse. The cover was beautifully illustrated with sinuous fronds of fern and the collection was entitled *A Thousand Selves*. Inside he had written a simple inscription *To Grace, a modest token of my friendship, Austin.* It was dated yesterday. She realized that the verses were his. Quickly

354

she glanced through the entries. She stopped at one called Loss and she knew that it must be a tribute to Persephone. The pain of emptiness brought tears to her eyes. This man had loved his wife very much and its very intensity broke through to her own vulnerability. Seeing what she was doing, Austin came around the table and nodded at the book. 'I didn't realize it was so bad that it would make you cry,' he said.

'Sorry. On the contrary, it's lovely.' Her words sounded so inadequate.

'Well, put that aside and come and eat.' He placed plates with tomatoes, mushrooms and eggs on the table.

Her first reaction was to refuse but, as she reluctantly began to eat, the food soothed the nausea.

He asked, 'How are you feeling?'

'I've felt better.'

'How's your head?'

A wisp of memory curled its way past her, of her making some type of convoluted speech, feeling suddenly dizzy then waking up here.

'I'm sorry,' she said, 'but I don't remember too much about last night.'

He smiled. 'I guessed as much. I brought you home because—well, to be honest, you weren't really in a state to drive.'

She was about to wonder why he hadn't taken her to her own place when another tendril of fog parted and she had the distinct impression that they had had some discussion about whether she should come home with him . . . *We could go back to my place*? Had he really said something like that, and if so . . .

He saved her from having to think further by saying, 'You fell asleep as soon as we got here.'

'Oh God—I'm so sorry!'

'You were rather drunk,' he conceded. 'There was a bit of tension between you and your Australian visitors.'

'Was there? Oh dear.'

All the while, she had been eating the food and drinking more tea.

'Perhaps I should ring and apologize?' she suggested.

'The phone is there.' He nodded towards a table. 'I'll just go and check on the garden.'

She found the directory, looked up the number of the hotel and asked for Mr Weston. The clerk searched for a moment then said, 'I'm sorry madam, but both Mr Westons checked out this morning.'

'Really?' Before she could hang up, he said, 'Are you by any chance Miss Harrison?'

'Yes?'

'Well, Mr Weston asked me to give you a message. He said: *It's always a mistake to go back.* He said that you would understand.'

'Yes, I do. Thank you very much.' She replaced the receiver and a sense of drifting from the shore came over her. With sudden anguish she thought, Joe, have you gone? If he had, then a lifetime of unfulfilled dreams had gone with him.

Apart from the ticking of an old-fashioned mantle clock and Columbus's gentle snores, the house was silent. It would be easy to sit in this quiet room and be caught up in regrets, in nostalgia that painted the past in glowing colours and swamped her with thoughts of *if only*, but it was too late for all that now.

She looked around the room. On a shelf were several photographs, one of Columbus wearing a funny hat, two or three of Austin with other people one of whom she recognized as Duke, and what was clearly a very personal and intimate portrait of a woman who must be Persephone. Grace studied her closely. She looked small, with a gentle doe-eyed face surrounded by thick wavy hair. Her eyes gazed with love at the photographer, an endless communication between them reaching to eternity.

Austin came back into the room. Seeing what she was doing, he came over. 'That was Percy's birthday,' he said. 'The year before she died. We were in Wales. It was a special day.'

Suddenly Grace wanted to cry, for him and his loss, for her failings as a daughter and a friend and a lover, for all the missed opportunities.

'Hey, don't get upset.' Austin bent close, cupped her face between his hands.

'I'm so sorry. I don't know what has come over me. I'm being stupid.'

'No you aren't.' He took her hand. He said, 'I think I let you down last night. I wanted to make love to you but, to be honest, I was afraid. When I realized that you were falling asleep I felt . . . well, relief.' He shook his head at some memory. 'When Percy died, I couldn't accept it. It's been three years and still I sometimes wake in the night and reach for her . . . in my darker moments I still can't accept that she's gone. That's why—'

She stopped him. 'You don't have to explain. You don't have to feel guilty either for still being alive, and I can't think that Persephone would want you to be unhappy.'

He squeezed her hand in gratitude. 'It has been a very long time since I was last a lover.'

Grace thought of the passion of her response to Alex, out of the blue, unexpected. There was no explaining such things. Aloud, she said, 'Might I use your shower—if you could show me how it works.'

'Of course.' He led the way to the bathroom and fiddled with an assortment of taps. 'A bit Heath Robinson,' he said, 'but I'm rather fond of it.'

As he turned round he almost bumped into her. 'Whoops, sorry.' She could not stop herself from reaching out and touching his arm.

She saw him swallow, saw his eyes drift to

his wife's robe. She heard herself say, 'Austin, if you want to, we could still make love.'

'Grace.' Reaching out, he ran his hand down the side of her face then over her shoulders. She moved closer to him, wanting to give him comfort. He began to undo the knot at her waist and she let the garment drop to the ground then peeled the slip over her head and unfastened her bra. Pulling her to him, he pressed his body along the length of hers. She in turn helped him out of his shirt and jeans, closed her arms about him, reached down to caress his erection.

He picked her up. She was momentarily surprised by his strength as he carried her across the corridor and into the bedroom. Placing her on the bed, he lay across her and found his way inside her. It did not last for very long but she could feel the tension easing away from him.

'I'm so sorry, it's been too long, I couldn't wait,' he apologized.

She kissed the crown of his head nestled against her shoulder. 'Don't apologize. There can be other times—if you want there to be?'

She thought, this isn't young, virile Alex. This isn't long dreamed of Joe. Instead, here is someone thoughtful and clever, someone sensitive and gentle who has already demonstrated the depth of his loyalty. This might not last but while it does it will be priceless.

Lying close beside him she registered his sudden grin as he grasped her hand. 'Lady,' he said, 'never say that I don't try to be a perfect host.'

*   *   *

They made love again, then slept. It was after lunchtime when Grace surfaced and savoured the delight of moulding herself to Austin's body. He in turn gave a little grunt of pleasure.

She tried to remember what day it was and whether she should be somewhere else but just at the moment there was nowhere she would rather be. The unfamiliar scent of the house reminded her that this was still another woman's sanctuary and that Persephone had not yet quite let go of Austin. More properly, Austin had not yet quite let go of her. That was something he would have to do in his own time—if ever—as she would have to finally abandon the dream of Joe. She reminded herself that this might only be a diversion, a temporary escape for both of them, but even if it were, it would be worth it.

She felt again a surge of sadness that Alex and Joe had departed under such circumstances but, given their joint history, perhaps there could have been no other way. Too much water under the bridge, too many events that couldn't be undone, perhaps this was the best way to end it all, cleanly.

Austin stretched and heaved himself out of bed. He was naked and she looked at his body, feeling only affection for it and just a hint of still unsatisfied desire, but she admonished herself and in turn got up and began to dress.

The sun was shining brightly and their first priority was to take the long-suffering Columbus for a walk. As they strolled down the lane to the nearest field, Austin said, 'The last time I saw Duke, on the night of the party, he told me that he had found me a woman. I thought he was joking, for he was always teasing me about my fidelity, but this time he was serious. He said that she was the sort of woman to take life as seriously as I did.'

Grace shivered. The memory of that evening, of Duke very much alive and the surprise of discovering that he was Austin's friend, all flooded back to her.

Austin said, 'Duke was a very good judge of character.'

'You think he might have been right, then?'

'I'm prepared to give it a try.' Taking her hand he asked, 'What are you planning to do next?'

'You mean now?'

'No, about your life, I suppose.'

She thought for a moment and then said, 'Well, first of all, I want to bury Paloma—only I'd be pleased if you would come and do it with me. I think she deserves some sort of ceremony.'

'Of course.'

'Then, I need to collect my mother's ashes and scatter them over my father's grave.'

She did not suggest that he should be part of that ceremony too. This was personal, about people he didn't know. She thought that she could invite Joan and Louisa, as her only relatives, to come to lunch and help her. She had plenty to tell them, too.

'Thirdly,' she said, 'I need to make a will.'

'Have you decided what you are going to do with your earthly goods?'

'Oh yes. Did you see my young cousin Louisa last night? Do you think she might bear some resemblance to Paloma?'

'The pretty dark girl? She might do indeed.'

'She's going away to university to study history. Perhaps when she comes back and when I'm gone she might like to set up home in Paloma's cottage and rear a family, perhaps even have a daughter to pass it on to.'

'Perhaps she will.'

'If not, well, nothing lasts forever, does it?'

He shook his head and took her hand. 'We like to think that good things will last,' he said, 'but like the bad, at some point they have to change. I don't know about you but I feel I might have reached a point where the bad is about to let me go. Thanks to you I feel alive again.'

As they walked, Columbus edged his way between them and pushed his nose against

Grace's hand, asking to be stroked.

'That dog likes you,' Austin observed. Suddenly quiet he said, 'I told you that he belonged to Percy. When she died he pined for her. He wouldn't eat. It has taken until now for him to really settle down. Somehow I get the feeling that he approves of you coming into our lives. Perhaps he knows that Percy would understand too. I guess we have both missed having a woman around.'

Grace was quiet, humbled by the thought that both Duke and Columbus approved of her.

Putting his arm around her, Austin said, 'Right then, Grace Harrison, what shall we do for the rest of the day?'

Her thoughts turned to burying Paloma. The tree, Alex's tree, would have to be dug up again. She had already decided not to replant it in the same place but find somewhere else in the garden where it could go.

Taking Austin's hand, she said, 'There's only one thing to do this afternoon.'

'And what might that be?'

'Let's go to the garden centre and buy a tree.'

Chivers Large Print Direct

If you have enjoyed this Large Print book and would like to build up your own collection of Large Print books and have them delivered direct to your door, please contact **Chivers Large Print Direct**.

Chivers Large Print Direct offers you a full service:

✧ **Created to support your local library**

✧ **Delivery direct to your door**

✧ **Easy-to-read type and attractively bound**

✧ **The very best authors**

✧ **Special low prices**

For further details either call Customer Services on 01225 443400 or write to us at

Chivers Large Print Direct
FREEPOST (BA 1686/1)
Bath
BA1 3QZ